KINCADE'S FEAR

⋆═ Michael Chandler & Loahna Chandler ═⋆

**WAGONMASTER
BOOKS**

2009

**WAGONMASTER
BOOKS**

The word "Wagonmaster Books" and the depiction of the Branding Iron logo are trademarks of Wagonmaster Books, a division of TCMC Inc, and are registered with the Colorado Secretary of State.

Library of Congress Control Number: 2009908090

ISBN: 978-0-9841651-0-0

Printed in the United States of America

Published by Wagonmaster Books
A division of TCMC Inc.
826 1/2 Grand Avenue
Suites 10, 11, & 12
Glenwood Springs, Colorado 81601
wagonmasterbooks@sopris.net

TO MY DARLING MICHELE

...whose reflection in the mirror of these
pages looks remarkably like Josephine

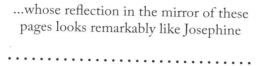

ACKNOWLEDGMENT

We wish to acknowledge our appreciation for the help with the Lakota Sioux language given us by Laura Redish, a linguist with Native Languages of the Americas. This is a nonprofit organization dedicated to preserving and promoting indigenous American languages, located in Saint Paul, Minnesota. Also to Pinny Lavalier who is a bilingual Lakota speaker with this organization.

. . . .

SPECIAL THANKS TO A VERY SPECIAL MAN

His name is Hiram Richardson.

Born amidst the rigors of real working cattle ranches spanning ten thousand acres, raised as a working cowboy skilled at team roping, bareback and bull riding. Hiram is a 21st century man carved from the wonder and folklore of the 1880's. The skills shown with his hands extended far beyond handling the rough stock on those wild Colorado lands. He began to draw and paint the life he knew so well, creating action filled paintings of the vitality and spirit of the Old West. Hi won a full scholarship to the American Academy of Art in Chicago and the Art Center College of Design in California, becoming so skilled that as of today, his stunning paintings grace the covers of over 650 western books, including the covers of *Kincade's Fear* and *Kincade's Blood*.

Like Michael Chandler, Hi loves the Old West. Visit with Hiram, and he'll recall one particular moment at one of Chandler's gunfight reenactments of the OK Corral battle. "It was a great thrill seeing Michael fire his pistols from the back of a spinning unbroken horse. As wild as it was, when the dust settled he was still in the saddle, reins in hand and calmly dropping six more shells in his revolver. Michael is the real deal. He puts on a great show and his stories capture the life of a cowboy. I highly recommend this terrific western novel."

More books by Michael Chandler
Dreamweaving, The Secret To Overwhelming Your Business Competition
The Littlest Cowboy's Christmas with John Denver
Kincade's Blood
Available globally through amazon.com

Coming soon from Wagonmaster Books
Kincade's Early Years
Kincade's Death

KINCADE'S FEAR

1

Kincade tipped back in the swivel chair and stared at his size twelve boots crossed atop the roll-top oak desk. Never in his life, never in his wildest imaginings, had he pictured himself sitting here.

Wyatt Earp's roll-top cradled over thirty drawers festooned with tarnished brass handles and pulls. A 12-guage shotgun belonging to dentist turned gunfighter, John "Doc" Holliday, perched on top, held upright by a wooden stand. Before leaving for Colorado, Doc told Kincade that since the death of the McLaury brothers, he no longer had any use for it. Assortments of little Indian fetishes gathered by Kincade over many years were arranged on the roll-top's crest. The desk's writing surface was covered by a thick slab of tooled saddle-leather, hiding the dents and gouges chipped into the oak over time. At the hide's top center, five words were burned into the latigo: US MARSHALS OFFICE TOMBSTONE ARIZONA.

He opened one of the thirty small drawers of the desk and took out, for the umpteenth time, the embossed letter from the Territorial Capital:

"Greetings. Having discussed the following matter with the former Marshal of Tombstone, Wyatt Earp, and after receiving the wholehearted endorsement of Tombstone Mayor, John Clum, I hereby officially appoint the man known as Kincade as U.S. Marshal in the town of Tombstone, Arizona Territory. This is done in recognition of his courageous efforts in the disbanding of the Wil Logan gang which had long been a menace, not only to Arizona, but to other western communities. His position as Marshal commences upon receipt of this letter. Details of duties and salary will follow. Refusal will not be considered. Good luck, Kincade. John Jay Gosper, Governor of the Arizona Territory"

Kincade ran his rough fingers across the wax seal near the Governor's signature. Regardless if he wanted it or even knew how to do it, Kincade was now charged with filling the shoes of a United States Marshal, and was fully expected to be damn good at a job he'd never even dreamed of, let alone tried.

From the letter he'd received from the Governor, to the new outfit that Josephine had picked out for him to wear, Kincade's life had taken an enormous about face. "A Marshal you are, and a Marshal you shall look like!" Josephine smiled as she brushed the dust from Kincade's black hat, nodding her head with so much pride that Kincade had to laugh. She kissed him anyway. The two loved one another beyond words.

Whiskey Pete might not have recognized him without his cattle drive gear. Yes, Whiskey Pete would have chuckled over this new Kincade slicked out in black pants, white shirt, black string tie, and vest adorned with a pocket watch and fob. But inwardly Whiskey Pete would have been proud, very proud, of his old pard's appointment and appearance.

Kincade missed Whiskey Pete, and the big man's loveable cowdog Little Blue. He ran his left index finger across his chin, thinking of the months the three had spent together laughing, enjoying one another's great company. The bottomless hollow in Kincade's heart for them both would always be there. The loss of true friends did that to a fella. It happens, when people care.

It all seemed so long ago.

Kincade swung his feet onto the floor and smoothed the letter onto the desk top, carefully folding out the creases with his fingertips. He looked around the small room. He could feel it. The office walls held the formidable ghosts of the Earp brothers. Kincade could feel the wrath of Ike and Billy Clanton who'd been jailed behind bars not fifteen feet from where Kincade sat. He could sense the rage of the McLaury brothers who swore vengeance within this very room. He could hear Doc Holliday as he'd argued about the right and wrong of the gun battle that eventually broke lose in a vacant lot behind the OK corral, not two blocks from where Kincade sat.

The weight of this office, of all those who had made or lost their lives after walking its floor, bore down on Kincade in a way he had never before experienced. He looked again at the Governor's letter of appointment, moving his fingers through his hair, wondering where all this would go.

"The answers will come," he thought to himself. "I know the difference between what's right and what's wrong. That's gotten me this far. It brought me Josephine. It'll get me the rest of the way." He returned the Governor's letter to one of the thirty rolltop drawers, softly sliding it closed.

Suddenly, the front door of the office burst open.

"You the Marshal?" A young Indian boy, no more than seventeen, stared wild-eyed at Kincade, gasping for breath. "You him?"

Kincade paused, but only for a second. He looked into his soul. He believed in the law. He hated those who broke it. He made a silent promise to himself – he would be everything possible to uphold the position and integrity of a United States Marshal. This single promise would guide him, console, inspire, and eventually come back to haunt him in ways beyond his comprehension. He looked directly into the eyes of the boy.

"I am."

"Marshal, they took my dog!" The boy screamed with fear. "They're gonna kill my dog!!" He ran out the door and disappeared to the right.

Kincade strode to the entrance of the office, took the latch in his left hand as he removed his black frock coat and hat from the rack. He stepped out to the boardwalk and into his new life as a duly appointed United States Marshal.

He turned to see the Indian boy halfway down Allen Street where it intersected Toughnut. The youngster was charging headlong into a knot of two-dozen onlookers watching three ragtag men tighten a rope around the neck of an animal that looked like a wolf.

2

Kincade quickened his stride. He could hear the shouts, laughter, and cheers of brutish men ahead as the boy's animal howled and yelped. Reaching the edge of the crowd, Kincade placed his outstretched hand on the shoulders of the onlookers who would turn, see Kincade's U.S. Marshal badge, and yield, allowing him entrance into the center of the commotion.

Three men were torturing the boy's dog, who was indeed a direct kin to a wolf. The Indian boy was far beyond frightened, charging the men, only to be thrown to the ground by one of the three, only to stand up, charge and be thrown back to the ground. The other two men had lassoed the wolf's shaggy gray head and were jerking the creature back and forth by its neck, up onto its feet, down to its knees, sometimes to its belly. One of these two dropped his rope, reached to his belt and removed a bull whip.

"That's enough," said Kincade.

The man with the whip uncoiled the braided leather, preparing to snap it back, then forward into the animal's flank. Kincade moved, grabbing the man's wrist.

"I said that's enough." Kincade held the man who tried to wriggle his arm free. Kincade increased the pressure on the wrist bones, making the man wince.

Seeing his friend in pain, the second of the two men began to approach Kincade.

The pressure on the wrist increased to such a degree that the man dropped the whip, which Kincade caught in midair. Maintaining the vice-like pressure on the wrist with his right hand, Kincade brought the bullwhip back with his left fist and suddenly forward to nearly its full length, yanking it back once again in a blurred motion, causing the latigo at its very end to detonate with a thundering crack.

One man approaching Kincade stopped, and the other quickly ceased his thrashing of the Indian boy. The crowd fell silent as the explosion of the bullwhip finished in an echo off the brick exterior of the two-story building just across the street. The only sound remaining came from the whimpering dog, now being comforted by the Indian boy.

Kincade increased, ever so slightly, the force on the man's wrist. Another pound or two of pressure and the bones would snap. Kincade looked into the man's eyes, holding his attention for a full ten seconds before uttering three words: "Hurts, doesn't it."

The other two men began to advance towards Kincade. The third shouted, "No! Stay there! He'll break it!" They stopped. Kincade kept his eyes squarely on the man whose wrist was moments away from shattering.

"Do you have something to say to the boy?" Kincade said to the man who dropped to his knees from the tremendous stress on his right hand.

"What…?"

"Say it."

"I...."

Kincade increased his grip. The man could feel one of the fragile bones start to give way.

"All right! I'm sorry kid. We didn't mean your dog no harm!"

"Mean it," said Kincade.

"We're sorry, ain't we boys!"

"Now tell the dog." The man knew that if he didn't do as he was told, and do it immediately, he would no longer have the use of his right hand. Ever.

"We're sorry!" Tears began to fill the man's eyes as the pain in his wrist became unbearable.

Kincade turned to the other two men, his deep blue eyes locking onto them both. "Anything you want to add?"

Without moving, they both shook their heads. Kincade released his grip. He slowly coiled the bullwhip into four loops, brushed it against the back of the kneeling man to remove the dust, and handed it to him.

"I believe this belongs to you."

The man slowly reached up with his left hand and took the whip.

"Gentlemen," said Kincade. "I don't believe this young boy and his dog would appreciate seeing you again. Perhaps you have business outside of Tombstone?"

The three quickly nodded their heads. The two helped the third to his feet. "Yes sir, Marshal."

"Good day then." And Kincade turned his back to the three, walked a few paces to kneel at the side of the Indian boy who sat with the collapsed animal's head on his lap, softly sobbing as he stroked the bloody fur.

"He's not dead yet," the boy whispered.

"Of course not," soothed Kincade. "He's a wolf, isn't he? They're survivors - and so are you. Come on. I'll carry him back to my office and we'll see what he needs most."

"Probably a drink of water."

"I could use some of that myself." Kincade heaved the limp animal into his strong arms and motioned with his head for the boy to follow.

3

Kincade and the Indian boy bathed the blood from the wolf's fur. As the clean water ran red, the wolf kept his eyes locked onto Kincade's. Not one blink, not one twitch, just a penetrating stare - beast to man.

"You gonna arrest those bullies for what they did?"

"Unfortunately, I don't believe they broke any laws," said Kincade. "They're probably drovers who've had to deal with packs of hungry wolves that follow cattle drives."

"No sir, Marshal! Those men were being cruel just for the fun of doing it!" The boy stroked the wolf's shaggy, gray head. "There ought to be laws protecting animals as much as people."

Kincade's mind flashed back to the horrible death of cowdog Little Blue, roasted on a spit over a campfire near the town of Gypsy. How he wished he could have been there for both Blue and Whiskey Pete when his twin brother, Wil Logan, ran a red hot poker thru his pard's eye and into his brain. Torture of man or beast filled Kincade with rage. "You're right, men like that should be punished!"

He looked at the young boy, about the same age he had been

when the old Indian left Kincade to fend for himself in a strange place. Kincade remembered how frightened he'd been that day so long ago. So alone. "My name's Kincade," he said, smiling. "What's yours?"

"Mahpiyasa."

"That's quite a name. You Apache?"

"No, Sir. I'm Lakota. My name means Red Sky."

"And your battered friend on the floor?" The wolf's eyes remained on Kincade.

"He is Shotahoda. It means Gray Smoke."

"Have you had him long?"

"Since I was a young boy." Red Sky hesitated. Should he trust this man with his story? Well, why not? He had saved Gray Smoke, hadn't he?

"Not far from my village, three wolves made their home. We boys would watch them play and hunt. The male was very strong. We named him Runs With The Wind. The mother and her pup would romp with one another as Runs With The Wind proudly watched over them as they spun and played in the dirt. We named her Swirls In Dust and her pup Gray Smoke."

Kincade nodded. He knew how very important names were to the Indian way of life.

"The three became more comfortable with us, and would follow our hunting parties. We began leaving them scraps of buffalo meat after a kill. During one of the hunts, the three did not follow. Winter winds were coming. We thought they have moved on. But we were wrong.

"One night, as our village slept, I was awakened by the distant cry of a wolf. I knew it came from Gray Smoke. I took my pony and rode as fast as I could, following the howl.

"When I found Gray Smoke he was caught in a trap – a big iron jaw thing used by white trappers. It held his right front paw." Red Sky's brow furrowed as he remembered that day. "His parents, Swirls in Dust and Runs With The Wind, must have tried to pull him loose. Most of his skin had been torn away. When they couldn't free him, they left him to die. Gray Smoke started to chew his leg off. Another day or two and he would have succeeded and probably died from loss of blood. But I found him."

Kincade was fascinated. "And you freed him?"

"Yes, with great difficulty for it was a strong trap. Then he fought me when I tried to pick him up. But he was weak from hunger and struggling to free himself."

"You nursed him back to health?"

"It took many months. But we needed time to get to know one another." Red Sky stroked the wolf's head with great affection. "We have been Spirit Brothers ever since."

Kincade nodded at the boy. "No wonder you were riled when those bullies were almost killing him."

"If you hadn't come, they would have killed him. I know it." The wolf's eyes remained on Kincade.

"What brings you to Tombstone?"

"My people have always been in motion."

"The Lakota Sioux are a Black Hills tribe," said Kincade. "You've come a long way."

The boy nodded. "From the center of the world. The Black Hills are the heart of everything that is... everything spiritual, everything material."

Kincade understood. The old Indian who'd raised Kincade had told him about the Lakota Wars with the Mandam, Pawnee, Arapahoe, Blackfeet, Crow and Shawnee. Kincade knew the Sioux warrior society had driven the Cheyenne from the Black Hills.

"Whoever didn't fear us," said the boy, "hated us."

The wolf continued to stare at Kincade. "Your dog listens."

Kincade's remark surprised the boy. This white man knew Indian ways. "Gray Smoke's wisdom comes from a time when dogs could talk."

The Marshal nodded. The old Indian had told him about time long past when dogs could indeed, talk. "Now the white man does most of the talking," smiled Kincade. "Maybe we were better off back then."

The boy didn't respond. The little Indian fetishes on Kincade's desktop had caught his attention. Red Sky walked to Kincade's desk, looking at the fetishes carefully arranged across the wood. There were the six directions: the Eagle, the Wolf, the Bear, the Mountain Lion, Badger and Mole. There was a small Dream Catcher hoop with a web of sweet grass strung side to side. Beautiful feathers of small birds hung from the edge and a tiny turquoise nugget was lodged in the center. Kincade had fashioned this miniature of the one that the old Indian had lulled him to sleep with as a boy.

Red Sky spent long moments holding each fetish, showing deep respect and reverence for the life force and invisible power of their spirits. Carefully replacing them, the boy slowly turned to Kincade with eyes as penetrating as the wolf at their feet. "You are not of the white man's world," said the boy.

Kincade didn't move.

"No white man would have these," continued the Lakota, waiting for the Marshal to respond. He did not.

After a few moments, the boy spoke again. "You have Guardian Spirits." The boy looked back to the fetish sculptures that Indian legend held were once real animals turned to stone by the sons of the Sun Father. Red Sky could feel their power. "You are strong in your heart as well as within your flesh."

Kincade said, "You too have great power, Red Sky. But your Guardian Spirit lives and breathes. Gray Smoke gives you love and friendship, and he will be with you through all time."

Silence returned. Red Sky now knew that this tall white man was more, much more than just a U.S. Marshal. He nodded to Kincade. The wolf still had not blinked. It listened to them both. The three were walking a path that lead to a new appreciation of one another. Red Sky extended his hand to Kincade, who took it in friendship.

Sensing their newfound trust of one another, Gray Smoke was satisfied Kincade was not like the three white men in the street. The wolf yawned, put his shaggy head between his paws, and closed his eyes.

Kincade spoke. "Well, Red Sky, if a Sioux boy and his Gray Smoke are as hungry as a Tombstone Marshal, we'd better do something about it. There is a lady named Josephine who I believe would like to meet you both. She's just down the street." Kincade moved towards the door.

The boy looked questioningly at Gray Smoke. "We won't leave

him for long," said Kincade.

"No, you go ahead," said the boy. "I'd better stay close in case he wakes up." He paused, and then asked in a much softer voice, "Would it be all right if I slept on the floor next to him?"

Kincade admired this kind of loyalty. "Only if you pull a mattress off a bunk back in the jail and lay it on the floor alongside your wolf. That'll be just fine with me." He smiled again. "I'll bring us something to eat. Any requests?"

The boy shook his head. "Thank you."

Shortly, Kincade was back with a bag full of meat scraps that he'd picked up at the butcher shop. The young Indian sniffed and wrinkled up his nose. "I'm not very hungry, Marshal."

Kincade burst out laughing. "These are for your furry friend on the floor when he wakes up - not for us. Miss Josephine, herself, will bring along beef stew as soon as the corn bread is finished baking. That be okay with you?"

"Just fine, thank you. We had stew and corn bread sometimes at the Mission School. I liked it a lot." The boy gently shook the wolf who looked up at him. Reaching into the bag of scraps, he began to hand feed the animal.

"So you went to a mission school. Is that how you're able to speak English so well?"

The boy suddenly seemed shy to reveal more about himself. Perhaps he had said too much already. "Yes," was all he said. Silence fell between them.

Kincade understood the boy's hesitation. He let the question rest. "When you rushed in here yelling, 'They're gonna kill my dog,' I thought you meant a dog-dog. Nothing as handsome as your friend Gray Smoke."

The boy finally smiled. "Would you have come so fast if I'd yelled, 'They're gonna kill my wolf'?"

Kincade smiled. "True enough! That would have slowed me down a bit. I was a cattle drover myself long before I became a Marshal."

"But never a cruel one, I bet."

"You know, I tried to tell those heifers what a nice fellow I was, but they just wouldn't listen!" Red Sky smiled in return.

The ice between the two had melted. They now felt comfortable with one another.

"My name hasn't always been Red Sky," offered the boy. "I named myself that. My childhood name was Little Owl - Popotkala - because I could always learn things very quickly like the baby bird. When I was still quite young, a man named Mahpiyasa - Red Sky - came to our village to talk with the elders.

"He said the white men crossing the plains in their wagons had an endless supply of people. They would never stop coming, and coming, and coming, until the Indians would have nothing left of our own lands.

He said our only hope was to have some among us learn the white man's language and their customs so we could deal with them without need of a translator."

Kincade nodded his head. "He was right. I know that some white men don't always translate correctly, especially if there's money to be made by adding a lie or two."

The boy nodded back. "This man, Red Sky, formed a Mission

School for Indian of many tribes."

"You were taught by missionaries?"

"No. The name Mission meant the school had a mission - a purpose - to help Indians survive. My father was the wisest of the elders - the otancan - and he convinced the others of our tribe, including my mother, that I should be the one to go to the Mission School and acquire this learning for my people."

"So you left with the man named Red Sky?"

"No, Sir," replied the boy. "He had other villages to go to, including those of our enemies - the Kiowa, Pawnee, and the Crow. He said all Indians must learn to band together against the invading whites."

"When did you go to the Mission School?"

"Right after the first snow of that year. My father took me and we had to ride many days. When he left me at the school he took my horse away with him. He was afraid I would become homesick and try to ride back to my village."

"And you stayed at the school from then on?"

"Only 'til the snows ended. My father said when the spring grasses began to grow he would come for me. I would then return to my village to renew my friendships, to hunt and fish, and talk with the elders about what I had learned at the Mission School. I wondered if Gray Smoke would remember me when I came home for the summer months. But he always did and we were together day and night. Even when I would sit in the council circle he would be at my feet, apparently listening."

"So you've never lost your identity as an Indian?" Kincade asked.

"I am proud to be Lakota Sioux. It was my responsibility to sit with both the men and women and read the notes I had taken in the classes. Then we would discuss the differences and problems with the whites."

"So you learned to read and write."

"The language was the first thing I had to learn. But that was easy for me. My mother said I could talk like a magpie while I was still in the cradleboard. To read and write was the second thing I learned, for there was always too much to just remember. The elders could not understand the white man's marks. The Sioux have no written language - only picture symbols."

"Red Sky was one of your teachers?"

"Yes, after he returned from seeing other tribes. He was very smart. He had been to the white man's eastern college and returned to the west to help his people. I admired him. I would have liked to help my own people like he helped me. So I took his name – Mahpiyasa."

"Why aren't you with your tribe now - helping?"

At Kincade's question, sadness filled Red Sky's face. "One year when the snows ended I waited for my father. But an old trapper who sometimes visited our village came instead. He brought Gray Smoke with him. My wolf was so happy to see me that he almost knocked me down. I loved him back, of course, but I didn't understand why he was with the trapper. Then the old man explained my village was no more. A disease called smallpox had killed nearly everyone including all my family. Those who survived had scattered to other Sioux tribes. He remembered how Gray Smoke and I were Spirit Brothers so he brought him to the Mission School. He said I should go to my father's people. He was Cheyenne.

"When Gray Smoke and I got there, whiskey had destroyed the Cheyenne more than the smallpox had destroyed my village. They were lazy and quarrelsome. For one summer I tried to help them but they wouldn't accept me. When they tried to kill Gray Smoke, saying he was an evil spirit, we fled back to the Mission School. I begged Red Sky to let me stay, but he refused. He said I knew all they could teach me. They needed room for other boys who could fulfill the mission of the school."

"But what are you doing here in the Arizona Territory?" asked Kincade. "Sioux lands are far north."

Red Sky smiled and then laughed. "It's warm here."

Kincade joined in the laughter just as Josephine opened the door to the Marshal's office. She swept into the room followed by two of her servants who carried baskets and a steaming pot of beef stew. She gave the boy a dazzling smile as she overheard his comment to Kincade.

"If you're referring to my stew, young man, you'll find it piping hot." The delicious odor was enough to make Red Sky's mouth water. It had been a long time since he'd eaten well.

"Kincade," said Josephine, "Please do me the honor of introducing your new friends. Then you two can get down to the serious business of eating."

"Josephine this is ... how do you say it?"

"Mahpiyasa. It means Red Sky."

Josephine smiled at the boy, her eyes sparkling. "May I call you Sky? I like special names for special people."

Kincade grinned, "She calls me Darling."

"You can call me anything you like, Mam - except darling."

Josephine smiled. "That name is already taken." She blew Kincade a kiss. "And who is the fellow on the floor wearing the fur coat?"

"That's Shotahoda." The wolf opened one eye upon hearing his name mentioned. "It means Gray Smoke."

"May I just call him Smoke?"

"Just a minute. I'll ask him." The boy got down on his knees and whispered in the wolf's ear. There were a few grunts and then the animal closed his eyes again.

"He says you can call him anything you like, Mam, because you're so beautiful." He had never before seen hair the color of a golden palomino.

Kincade and Josephine smiled at one another, as Kincade asked, "Did the Mission School teach you how to flirt?"

"That's what Gray Smoke said, Sir – not me."

The wolf looked at Kincade, as if to verify that was what he said. "All right, Josephine. It's settled. The names are Sky and Smoke from now on."

The boy added, "And Darling!"

Josephine and Kincade burst out laughing. They realized that their lives were taking on a new measure of fun. And it felt good.

4

Sky watched Josephine prepare the office table for the meal. Her hands moved with the grace of gentle winds over prairie grass as she softly hummed to herself. The boy looked at Kincade. It was clear that this man was deeply in love with this woman who fluttered and fussed around the Marshal's office. His eyes never left her.

Josephine's full black and white checkered skirt made swishing noises. A tight fitting, black velvet top was fastened with ivory hooks that allowed a bit of snowy lace to peek through the openings. Her golden curls were clustered atop her head, held in place with black and white satin ribbons that trailed down her back.

Sky whispered to Kincade. "How'd her hair get that color? It's so different."

Kincade paused and suddenly smiled. "You've never seen hair that color?"

"No, Sir," said Sky. "The women in my tribe all had hair and eyes the color of night. And she has eyes like yours – the color of turquoise."

Kincade nodded and smiled. "Her heart is far more beautiful than her hair or her eyes, Sky. Wait until you know her. She has a beautiful soul."

"That is a word which is hard for me to understand."

"Given time, she will show you its meaning, not by what she says but by what she does."

The wide table, which had been piled with wanted posters, train schedules, and gun advertisements, had been cleared and then covered with a white linen cloth. Dinner for two was set with folded napkins resting by china plates and silver flatware. Kincade held out a chair for her next to the boy who was agog in her presence. Sky took note of the great respect Kincade gave to Josephine. Only after Josephine was comfortably settled did Kincade seat himself.

Josephine looked at Sky, paused, and said, "Sky, Kincade and I are happy to meet you, and welcome you to Tombstone. Please… eat before your stew gets cold."

"Will you eat with us, Josie?" Kincade asked.

"I would love to," she replied, withdrawing a small checkered bundle from one of her baskets. She opened the cloth which held apple slices and fresh blue berries. She picked out two and put them to her lips as she smiled at Sky.

Her servants ladled the steaming stew onto the plates and placed big squares of corn bread alongside. Sky inhaled deeply, wondering if he'd died and gone to a happy hunting ground. The boy ate without talking, too engrossed in what lay before him to utter another word.

Kincade and Josephine watched in amusement. As Sky ate, they discussed the business of The Josephine Saloon, which she now owned, and the Cosmopolitan Hotel which she managed.

"There's a whole fresh apple pie, if you're still hungry," she said when Sky had wiped what was left of the stew with the last of the corn bread.

"Yes, Mam." He nodded eagerly. "I wouldn't refuse that even if I were belly full."

The servants cleared the table and placed a quarter of a pie on each plate before Kincade and Sky. Josephine still toyed with her fresh fruit as the men finished in silence.

"Everything to your satisfaction, Sky?" asked Josephine as the boy savored the pie.

Over many years, Sky had seen people ask questions without really caring to hear an answer. But not this woman.

"I am fine," responded Sky.

Josephine nodded, looked over Sky's shoulder at the sleeping wolf. "And your friend, what might I do for him?

"He is very fine," smiled the Indian boy, pleased that Josephine showed interest in the wolf that meant so much to him. "And I thank you for asking us." This must be what Kincade meant by saying Josephine had "a beautiful soul." He began to understand.

She looked at the boy. "Did Kincade tell you he was raised by an old Indian?"

So that was the reason for Kincade's knowledge of the fetishes and Indian history. "No, Mam. We haven't talked about much except Gray Smoke – uh, Smoke." He turned to Kincade. "What tribe was he, Marshal?"

"Seems strange, but I don't know. We always lived by ourselves."

"Just like Smoke and me."

"When I was about your age, Sky, the old Indian brought me to a town and left me there. I had nothing. I had to fend for myself without knowing anyone, or even the language."

"Just like me. I have nothing except Smoke and must fend for both of us." He picked up the last crumb of pie crust and popped it in his mouth. "At least I know the language, and now I know you and Miss Josephine."

"Show him your medicine bag, Kincade," Josephine said. Then, once again turned her attention to the boy. "It's all that the old Indian gave him. It took Kincade many years to find out its full meaning."

Kincade undid the top button of his shirt and pulled the leather pouch from around his neck.

Sky took it. "That's the Circle Of Life."

"You've seen it before?"

"Of course. For everything there is an opposite that brings balance and meaning to living. Fire and water, sky and earth, light and dark, strong and weak, full and hungry, even good and evil. The Indians believe it is the right balance of opposites that is important."

"Then this is a Sioux symbol," said Kincade. "I never knew that."

"No, it's not just Lakota. At the Mission School there were boys from many tribes. We had to learn each other's ways as well as the white man's. Several boys had medicine bags with the Circle Of Life." Sky returned the pouch to Kincade who slipped it over his head. The medicine bag's Indian symbols on the outside had taught Kincade much more than about opposites that balance.

The beaded leather patch kept inside had taught him that he had a twin brother who was everything Kincade despised and strove never to become. But no longer. Wil Logan's rotting remains were on Tombstone's Boot Hill.

Sky left the table and went to check on Smoke. It was obvious that the animal meant everything to the boy.

"He's so sweet to him," Josephine said to Kincade. "May I come near him, Sky?"

"Yes, but don't pet him until he knows you better. Then he can be very affectionate."

Kincade pushed back from the table, moved to where Josephine sat, and gently pulled her chair back as she stood. She quietly approached the bed and looked down with sympathy at the many bruises on all sides of his body. "Oh dear, I think his front leg is broken! Did you notice how bent it is, Kincade?"

"No, Mam. It's been like that for a long time. It healed crooked after he was caught in a trap. He limps some, but it's nothing new."

Smoke chose this moment to lift his head and search for Sky in the strange room. The boy whispered some Indian words in the wolf's big ear. Smoke licked his face and then collapsed again onto the saddle blanket. Sky continued stroking the rough, gray fur. The animal's eyes looked fondly at the boy. Those eyes said everything any friend needs to be told.

"Well, it's time for me to dress for tonight's guests at The Josephine." Her servants gathered the remains of the meal. "I'll check on your patient tomorrow."

She turned to face Kincade. His two arms reached out to encircle her waist. She placed her hands on Kincade's arms. They looked into one another's eyes. Though no words were spoken, Sky knew much was being said.

After a few moments, Josephine removed her hands and turned to the Indian boy. "Next dinner we eat together, Sky, must be at The Josephine." She gave him one of her winning smiles. "Marshal Kincade's office is really not adequate to show you my role as a charming hostess."

"You mean you'd let an Indian come into your saloon?"

"With great pleasure.   And I'll put your charges on Kincade's tab." She winked.

"I don't drink whiskey." The boy remembered what had happened to the Cheyenne.

"I also serve sarsaparilla, lemonade, and branch water," Josephine said warmly. "Will any of those do?"

Sky paused to stroke his chin thoughtfully. "If I may come three times, I'll try one of each."

All three laughed together at Sky's clever response. Josephine held out her hand to the boy who took it in his, bowing slightly. The Mission had taught him more than just language.   Kincade watched from the doorway until her shadow disappeared.

"That's what I mean about her beautiful soul."   He closed the door. "Josephine sees a person for what they are - not the color of their skin, or the job they do, or the amount of money they have. She judges both the good and the bad by honesty. She loves the good in everyone and will not tolerate the evil she finds in a few."

Sky thought about that. "I think she's beautiful, even if her hair isn't black."

Kincade stood. "Will you be all right on the floor next to Smoke if I leave for the night? I have my rounds to do. Seeing that the streets of Tombstone are safe for one and all…and that includes that handsome wolf of yours…is not only my job but my pleasure."

"Sure. Go." But the boy was holding back something. Kincade could tell there was something Sky wanted to say but didn't know how to start.

"It's okay, Sky. Speak up. Whatever it is, I'll understand."

Sky thought about Kincade being raised by an Indian. He thought about Kincade's collection of fetishes and his understanding and belief in the Circle Of Life. The boy realized he was beginning to trust the Marshal as a friend. He took a deep breath.

"I haven't told this to anyone before."

Kincade waited silently.

Sky did not look at Kincade as he continued. "It is the Sioux custom to make a relative by choice. It is called Hunkayapi. Blood relatives make a person's body. But Hunkayapi recognizes a man's true spirit in his chosen relative. Hunkayapi is an appreciation of yourself because you see it in your chosen relative. Do you understand?"

"I do," Kincade said, opening up to the boy as Sky had to him. "I once had a friend who was my chosen blood brother. He helped me see and understand myself." Jesse Keller had done that for Kincade. In fact, Jess had given his very life for Kincade.

The boy continued, looking at the wolf. "I have chosen Shotahoda, Gray Smoke, for the true relative of my spirit – Hunkayapi. This is the most enduring pledge a man ever takes. We have survived because we have understood and depended on one another. We have never, and will never fail one another." Sky gently stroked the wolf's side.

Kincade knelt on the floor between the saddle blanket where the wolf slept and the mattress where Sky sat. He put his hand on Sky's shoulder. "I will always respect your bond and do everything I can to protect it."

The two of them looked at each other. The two of them understood.

"Thank you, Marshal. Thank you for listening. Go secure the town." Then Sky added, "Oh…I believe Miss Josephine is expecting you to drop by." The boy smiled brightly, and with respect for them both.

"Goodnight, Sky."

As Kincade made that night's rounds of Tombstone, he made a silent vow. "I must keep this boy and his wolf with me. I don't know how, but I must. He is a balance for my losing Jesse. I need him. My spirit needs him."

Little did Kincade know then just how much the town of Tombstone would soon need this Indian boy and his shaggy, gray wolf.

5

When Kincade arrived at his office the following morning he found Smoke gnawing on a bone which he'd stripped clean of any meat. Sky had put the saddle blanket and cot mattress in one of the jail cells and was sweeping where they had been.

"Good morning, Marshal," beamed Sky. "Look at him! Just like new!"

Kincade felt good, seeing how happy the Indian boy was. "You and Smoke are definitely survivors. I'm proud of you both." Kincade hung his frock coat and buckaroo hat on the stand by the door.

Kincade motioned the boy over to stand by his desk. "Sky, I need your advice, and I'm counting on you to help me out, just as you helped Smoke last night."

The boy eagerly nodded his head, ready to assist his new friend.

"Smoke knows he's a wolf, right?" More eager nods from Sky.

"And you know he's a wolf.   I know he's a wolf, and Josephine is very impressed that he's a wolf."

"A good one too."

"I'm trying to figure out what would be best for Smoke when it comes to the rest of the good folks here in Tombstone." Kincade cleared his throat and continued. "Do you suppose that it might be better if the other townsfolk think he's just part wolf - maybe his father was a wolf and his mother was a nice gentle cow-dog who strayed a bit. Do you suppose that the people around town might be a bit friendlier to our friend Smoke if they thought he had a strain of waggin' cowdog in him?"

Sky laughed. "Fine with me, but you'd better ask Smoke. He's a right proud animal."

"I see," said Kincade, thoughtfully nodding his head at the boy's suggestion. He turned to look at the wolf whose piercing eyes were boring into Kincade.

"Sky, would you mind explaining it to him in a convincing manner? I think he'd take it better from you than me."

Sky got on his hands and knees and put his lips to Smoke's ear. There was much whispering and a few grunts. Then the boy stood up. "He said, okay, but don't ever call him a mutt."

Kincade smiled inwardly. He liked this boy. "Wouldn't think of it!"

Kincade paced around the room, straightening things which didn't need fixing, looking for things which were right in front of him. Finally he said to Sky, "Sit down. We need to talk business."

The boy sat at the table. "Did I do something wrong in sweeping?"

"No, no. Place looks much better." Sky was pleased that he'd helped his friend.

Kincade cleared his throat. "Were you headed any place in particular when you landed in Tombstone?"

"Sure, some place warm. It's cold in the north and I have no buffalo robe."

"Do you like it here in Tombstone?"

"I like you and Miss Josephine. I liked the stew, and corn bread, and pie. I don't like the men who attacked Smoke. That's all I know about Tombstone."

"Well supposing I could find work for you here. Would you stay?" asked Kincade.

"Smoke too?"

The boy was strong - strong-willed, strong-hearted. Kincade liked that. "Well...I meant work for you both."

"What is this work?" asked Sky. "You may tell me whatever you wish. I've been trained to examine your offer without a translator."

Kincade laughed. "Good, Sky. That will help all three of us. I just want to know how you'd feel about staying in Tombstone."

The boy paused, carefully weighing Kincade's question. "We could give it some thought." He turned to the wolf. "Couldn't we, Smoke?"

The wolf was busy with another bone and left such serious matters up to his Indian brother.

"Before you say yes or no," Kincade added, "you have to pass one more test."

"I've been tested? Like in the Mission School?"

Another smile from Kincade. "By Josephine and by me. And we agree that you pass with flying colors. But there's one more test, and it's perhaps the most important." Kincade paused for several moments, and then asked, "How are you with horses?"

"You're right Marshal. That is the most important test."

Kincade waited, knowing that Indians held horses in the very highest regard.

"I rode horses before I learned how to walk," said Sky.

"But do you like them? Do they like you?"

"Those horses which have been treated with respect by their owners like me. Those who've been mistreated by their owners do not, but they change their minds after we come to know one another. It is not the horse's fault, but rather the owner's." Kincade appreciated the boy's honesty.

"There's a horse I want you to meet," said Kincade. "His name is Gold Digger. While he doesn't take easily to strangers, he is a good judge of character."

"What breed of horse?"

"Think of the color of Miss Josephine's hair…"

"A palomino!" said Sky.

"Not just any palomino. But you'll see…" replied Kincade.

"Where is he?"

"There's a stable at the back of the house where I live. Shall we go meet him?"

"Smoke too?"

Kincade smiled again, at the boy's allegiance to the wolf. "Come along, Smoke. You have to take the test too." The newly christened "dog" put down his bone and followed as if he'd understood every word.

Kincade made his home in a small, brown frame house at the far end of the lot where the marshal's office and jail stood. The adjoining stable was bigger than the living quarters. In an emergency Kincade could leave the office on a dead run, throw open the stable doors, and be on Gold Digger and down the street in less than a minute. It was perfect lodging and had been used by lawmen before him.

When the trio entered, Gold Digger whinnied and pawed the straw in his stall. "I know, old friend. I've missed you too. But a Marshal must think of his work." Kincade's excuse carried no weight with Digger.

Kincade checked the water bucket and supply of oats. The hay was clean and fresh. "Chuff," said Digger.

"Now don't complain about the job old Teddy is doing," Kincade said to the stallion. "He's caring for you just fine."

Sky stood in awe of the big golden palomino stallion. Its long tail and mane were indeed almost the same color as Miss Josephine's hair. Its coat had been groomed until it glistened. Its big eyes missed nothing and soon were fixed on the boy and his four legged friend.

Gold Digger nickered. Kincade rubbed his nose and between his ears.

"We have new friends, Digger. I want you to meet Sky - he's the boy - and Smoke - he's the wol... He's the dog."

Digger gave the strangers an inspection worthy of an army drill-master. Then he pushed Kincade aside and walked out of the stall towards them. Sky stayed back, standing comfortably. Smoke seemed just as comfortable, but stepped forward as though he knew exactly what to do. The wolf walked slowly but confidently and with natural grace toward the big horse as it approached him. He tipped his head up to look into the eyes with their long lash-es. Then he raised himself up just enough to have his nose meet the horse's. They tested one another's moisture, sniffed, and both snorted satisfaction. Then Smoke turned and left the stable. Gold Digger remained still, his attention now directed toward Sky.

"That takes care of one test." Kincade was pleased. "You're next, Red Sky." The boy smiled at Kincade's use of his full name.

Rather than move forward, Sky stood where he was, about a dozen feet away from Gold Digger and looked directly into the eyes of the palomino. He kept his hands lose at his sides, his body relaxed. Once he was sure that he had Gold Digger's full atten-tion, Sky knelt down, all the while keeping his eyes locked onto the stallion's.

Digger watched.

For the next five minutes the boy knelt before the horse with-out moving. Though no words were spoken, it seemed as though Sky was talking to Gold Digger through his eyes. Kincade stood back, duly impressed, for he too knew that all real communication comes through the eyes.

The boy gradually stood, keeping his eyes on Gold Digger. Then he slowly turned to face the stable's entrance with his back to the stallion, slightly lowering his chin as though he were looking to-ward the ground. Continuing to relax his body, Sky stayed in that position without moving.

Gold Digger pricked his ears and blinked. Within the next

minute, as the boy remained where and how he was, the stallion snorted and raised his head up, then down, snorting once again.

Sky didn't move.

In another moment, the stallion gradually moved forward towards the boy. Upon reaching Sky's back, Gold Digger paused, and then moved his muzzle to nudge the boy. Just after the first touch, Sky moved away from the stallion, slowly, two feet to his left, stopped, and again lowered his head to face the ground. He held his body still.

Gold Digger watched. A few moments later the stallion once again moved forward, nudging the boy a second time. Sky didn't move. Another nudge from the horse. Sky gradually turned on his heels to face the horse. They were now inches away from one another. The boy looked deeply into the palomino's large, dark eyes, and for the first time spoke in a soft voice. "Hau, kola."

Gold Digger blinked. Sky slowly raised his hand to touch the horse's nose, which the stallion gratefully received, welcoming Sky.

"Nice to meet you, Gold Digger. Let's take a ride together real soon." The boy continued to stroke the horse's nose. Kincade smiled broadly, realizing that the boy had considerable skills with horses.

"What did you say to him?" Kincade asked as he joined the boy and horse.

"That's between the horse and me." And the boy smiled. "Did I pass your test?"

"With flying colors."

"How long did it take for the horse to come to you the first time?"

Kincade shook his head, remembering that it must have been a good week or more. But he'd keep that bit of information to himself. "Sky, shall we eat some breakfast at The Josephine?"

"Do you think there's any stew left over?"

"I doubt it, but Josie will have some bread that's freshly made."

"Smoke too?" Again Kincade admired the boy's bond with the wolf.

"Miss Josephine used to let Whiskey Pete's dog, Little Blue, come in her saloon at Benson, so I'm sure it will be all right. In fact, Blue loved a bowl of beer - made him sneeze."

Sky laughed. "No liquor for Smoke - doesn't set well with Indians, you know. You can pretend he's half wolf - half dog, but he's all Indian to me."

The three left the stable and went back into the office. "Who were Whiskey Pete and Little Blue?" Sky asked.

Kincade paused, remembering the impact the two had made on his life, forever. "A good man. A good dog."

That was all Kincade said.

6

As the three left the stable, Kincade looked down Allen Street and the townsfolk going about their business. "Let's walk down the street shoulder to shoulder. I'll be on the right, you on the left, with Smoke between us."

"Sounds like the gunfight behind the OK corral to me," said Sky.

"You know about that?"

"Everybody knows about that," replied the boy.

"A fight is exactly what we're trying to avoid," said Kincade, remembering the jeering he had received so long ago when the old Indian had left him in a white man's town. "No sense attracting trouble with an Indian and a wolf."

The boy stopped and looked at Kincade. "Are you ashamed of me?"

Sky's question slammed into Kincade's gut. He took the boy's shoulders in both hands. "You don't ever have to ask me that question. Not ever."

The boy never did again. Not ever.

"Marshal Kincade?"

"Yes...?"

"You're supposed to call him a dog – not a wolf."

Kincade laughed out loud at the boy's quick sense of humor. He liked Sky a great deal. "You'll make sure Smoke stays between us, all right? We don't want him sniffing around the men sitting in front of the barber shop."

Sky shook his head.

"...or chasing small children, or frightening old ladies."

Sky gave another reassuring shake of his head. "He's a very well behaved wo...dog. I'm the one you should worry about! I can be very unpredictable." Sky laughed, thoroughly enjoying the Marshal's concerns.

Kincade stopped, and then said, "I don't like to admit this..." He placed his hand on the boy's shoulder. "But you and I both know there are folks who don't like Indians. We've both felt their ridicule. The Apache are not Tombstone's friendliest neighbors and ranchers are always losing cattle to wolves.

"I just think its better, for now, to take our time, get used to things." Kincade affectionately tousled the boy's hair. "If anyone stops to talk to me, just wait and say nothing."

"Smoke too?"

Kincade could see the gleam of friendly mischief in the boy's eyes, sighed in exasperation, and then looked at Smoke. "Same goes for you." The animal wagged his tail in perfect understanding. They returned to Kincade's office and hung out a sign that read: Out for breakfast. Back at 9.

"The Josephine doesn't open for breakfast, but the lady of the house always invites her favorite customers to join her in the morning."

"Favorite, meaning you?"

"And one or two others – like you." The walk to The Josephine went without incident. "We'll use the side door." They entered and immediately the smell of fresh roasted coffee and bread in the oven greeted them.

"I'm liking Tombstone more and more, the longer I'm here," Sky said as they pulled out chairs at a round table. Smoke made himself comfortable at Sky's feet and appeared to go to sleep.

"Good morning, gentlemen." Josephine came down the stairs at the rear of the saloon, looking fresh as a spring day in a flowing dressing gown of gray silk. Her golden hair hung over her shoulders in a long cascade.

"You'll have your usual, my darling?" she said to Kincade.

"The usual."

"How about you, Sky?"

"I'll have the same as the Marshal." Sky leaned over to Kincade and whispered, "There's that 'darling' again..." Kincade laughed out loud.

"Two of the usual," Josephine called toward the door behind the bar. "So..." she continued as Kincade pulled back her chair. "Kincade told me he'd like you to stay in Tombstone. Is that going to suit you?"

"Suits me fine, Miss Josephine, and Smoke is ready to settle down for awhile too."

"Give us your advice, Josie," asked Kincade. "Sky needs a job - they both need a job. Any ideas?"

She tapped the fingers of her right hand on the table and twisted a lock of curls with her left. "Hum, let me think. We can always use help here at the saloon or at the Cosmopolitan Hotel next door. Hardly jobs that Smoke could do, however. I've heard that Big Red at the smithy was thinking of training an apprentice. You might ask him."

"I doubt that Smoke would be much good at shoeing horses," Kincade responded.

Breakfast arrived. Sky had never seen such a platter of food served to only one person. Each of them had a steak the size of a shovel, a mound of scrambled eggs that must have required six shells to be cracked, a hunk of sourdough that was still warm, and a mug of black coffee.

"This serving could have fed five boys at the Mission School," Sky said in awe. "Would it be all right if I gave Smoke the steak, Miss Josephine? He's always hungry."

"Then he should have one of his own." She called toward the kitchen. "A steak for Smoke, please Sam – very, very rare - and that's a regular."

In just a few moments Sam brought the meat and Sky dropped it in front of Smoke's nose and he immediately woke up, devouring it before the boy could lift a fork to his mouth. "His under-the-table manners are terrible," Sky told Josephine apologetically.

"I forgive him," said Josephine, and with a wink added, "It took me forever to break Kincade of exactly the same habit."

Sky dropped his fork, laughing at her joke. Kincade's eyes sparkled at Josephine's efforts to see the boy comfortable and at home.

"You're not eating with us, Josie?"

"Yes, my usual."

Sky looked at the little French roll and cup of tea placed before her. "That's all?" he whispered to the Marshal.

Kincade gave Sky a sly grin. "Keeps her girlish figure that way."

"Now what were we discussing?"

"A job for Sky – and Smoke," Kincade said between bites.

Seeing how hungry Sky was, and how quickly the breakfast was disappearing, Josephine immediately added, "Maybe the boy could work at the butcher shop and the wo… dog could dispose of the scraps."

Sky was having fun listening to the banter between his new friends. Happy couples always joke with one another – even in his village.

The Marshal continued with a twinkle in his eye. "Or maybe I could run a theater. Josie, you play the part of Little Red Riding Hood. I'll be the brave hunter, and Smoke, you could be the wolf."

"I don't know the story," Sky said. "But I bet the wolf gets killed in the end. So Smoke refuses the part."

Now they all laughed and Smoke came out from under the table to sit next to Sky and smile his big-teeth grin.

"Are you sure he doesn't speak English?" Josephine asked, looking at the wolf.

"Maybe he does. He learns very quickly at whatever he puts his mind to."

At that very moment there was a terrified shout of a man from the street outside. "Help! Somebody get the Marshal! I've been robbed! That man! He's getting away with all my money!"

Kincade, Sky, Josephine, and Smoke ran to the door and threw it open to see a man leap onto a horse, yank it roughly to the left, and spur it to head south. Kincade started to bolt out the door in pursuit.

"Takpe ape," Sky shouted to Smoke, slapping his rump, and the dog took off like he'd been shot out of a gun. The thief had not yet turned on Toughnut to head out of town before the canine was right behind him. A crowd watched as the dog bit the horse's heals until finally the animal stumbled and fell. Its rider sprawled, face down, onto the dirt street. He tried to scramble to his feet, but Smoke put his front paws on the shoulder blades of the culprit and pushed him flat. The huge wolf bared his teeth at the back of the man's neck and growled menacingly. Then the animal raised back his head and gave a bone-chilling howl.

"Get him off me!" the prone man shouted. "He'll tear me apart!"

By that time Kincade and Sky arrived. The boy said, "Ayustan-yo," and the dog released his victim. Then he patted Smoke's head. "Wasteste mihunka." Kincade put handcuffs on the thief and pulled him erect.

Stout Mister Perkins who owned the General Store arrived out of breath and very excited. "My money! There's my bag of money! Oh, thank you, thank you! It was my entire week's receipts and I was headed for the bank when this scoundrel came in with a gun and took it!" Kincade handed him the heavy bag. "How can I ever - ever- thank you, Marshal?"

"Thank the dog. He's the hero of the day." Smoke came to Kincade to be patted, wagging his tail. It was the first time that the wolf had allowed Kincade to touch him.

A man in a tight plaid suit rushed up to Kincade with note pad and pencil in hand. "Marshal Kincade, I'm a new reporter with the Tombstone Epitaph. May I interview you about this spectacular arrest?"

Inwardly, Kincade had to admit that Sky and Smoke's apprehension of the thief may have been exactly that - spectacular. Kincade thought about directing the reporter to the Indian boy. Looking at Sky, Kincade saw the boy looking squarely into his eyes, almost imperceptibly shaking his head.

Kincade understood immediately. The two of them had agreed that, for now, Sky and Smoke's interaction with the citizens of Tombstone would be done gradually and in good time. The boy was letting Kincade know that the Marshal's wishes were to be respected and followed. Kincade smiled, ever so slightly at the boy, acknowledging what they both knew what was best for now.

Kincade addressed the reporter. "Walk with me, Mr.....?"

"Cook," said the newspaper man. "David Cook."

"Walk with me, Mr. Cook," continued Kincade. "You and I will escort this rogue to the jail and you may ask me whatever you like." The reporter grinned as if it were going to be his first big story.

"Sky, will you and Smoke please take the horse to the livery and tell them its owner may be awhile in claiming it."

"Of course, Marshal." And then he whispered, "Where's the livery?"

"On your right as you go back to The Josephine. You can't miss it."

Sky added in a low voice meant only for Kincade, "Can I go finish my eggs afterwards?"

Kincade smiled again. "Yes, and ask Josephine to give Smoke another steak and put it on my tab." The Marshal was discovering that, when it came to Sky and his wolf, he was smiling a great deal.

When the thief had been put behind bars, Kincade waited for Sky's return. As soon as the boy entered the office he told him to sit.

"What did you say to Smoke that made him do that?" There were many languages across the Indian nations. Kincade did not recognize the one used by the boy.

"I told him to attack and wait."

"And he obeyed, just like that?"

"For him it's not much different than chasing a deer and then holding it until I come with my knife to kill it. He howled to show me where he was in case the chase had taken him out of my sight."

"If Smoke is used to chasing an animal, why didn't he go for the horse instead of the man?"

"The horse was just lying there and the man was still trying to get away."

The boy was very direct and clear in answering Kincade's questions. "What did you tell him when he let the thief go?"

"I said, 'Quit it!' and then 'Very good, my chosen brother.'"

Kincade was very, very impressed, looking at Smoke and his young master with increasing respect and admiration. "What else can he do?"

"What do you have in mind?" asked the boy.

"I don't know, but I'm thinking."

In a moment, Sky spoke. "He's very smart. He learns very fast." Sky shuffled his feet under the chair. He waited as Kincade looked at him without speaking.

After a few minutes passed, Sky said, "When I told Miss Josephine what happened with the thief she said she had thought of a job for Smoke and me."

"And what was that?"

"She said you'd already know."

Kincade smiled. He wasn't surprised. He and Josephine frequently thought alike.

Kincade moved to within a foot of the boy, towering above Sky. "How'd you like to be my Deputy?"

Kincade expected the boy to show considerable surprise at his offer. But the surprise was his when Sky simply responded with his own question. "Smoke too?"

"Yes."

Sky paused, as if he were carefully considering the offer, because actually, he was. In a moment, another question. "How much do we get paid?"

Kincade burst out laughing. "Is that one of the questions the Mission School taught you to ask a white man?"

Sky grinned too. "How much, Marshal Kincade?"

"I have a budget that includes a Deputy's salary, but only if I get you two for the price of one."

Sky put on a serious look. "My father told me that the white man's government agents always promise one thing and mean another. But Smoke and I like you, Kincade." He extended his hand. "It's a deal."

The next morning, the three law enforcement officers sat at Josephine's table eating the usual. Kincade read the headlines from the Tombstone Epitaph.

MARSHAL KINCADE HIRES LAW DOG

"Where's my name?" Sky asked. "I was hired too."

"It's coming. Be patient."

Kincade began to read David Cook's news story out loud:

"Yesterday Tombstone had a demonstration of outstanding law enforcement when Marshal Kincade's two new Deputies went into action to save the entire week's receipts of the General Store. Mr. Perkins was ready to take his bag of cash to the bank when a lone gunman held him up and fled. A large dog named Gray Smoke, that strangely resembles a wolf, charged out of The Josephine in hot pursuit. After pestering the horse until it tripped and fell, throwing the thief into the street, the Law Dog held the man in check until the Marshal and the dog's handler, a young lad named Red Sky, arrived to make the arrest."

Kincade handed the paper to the Indian boy, who smiled broadly as he saw his name. Sky continued to read aloud.

"Marshal Kincade said he had read about this unusual team of dog and handler in a telegraph bulletin from the Dakota Territory where they have been effective for some time. Canines were first recruited for police work in Germany and only recently have been introduced in this country. Marshal Kincade told this reporter that Red Sky has been attending a Law Enforcement Academy for almost five years…" Sky put the paper down.

"You told the reporter that?"

"No, I thought you did."

"I did not! You did all the talking. I was taking the horse to the livery."

Kincade winked at the boy. "Makes a good story though, doesn't it?"

Josephine smirked. "Give me the paper. Where were we? Oh yes:

"Gray Smoke was whelped by a Wyoming cattle-dog with fine blood lines. His sire was a timber wolf. This has made for an admirable blend of high breeding and natural instinct."

"Hey, you lazy bones," Sky said to the dog under his feet. "Get up and look admirable." Smoke yawned.

Kincade continued reading: "Tombstone is fortunate that the two heroes of the day had arrived in time to save Mr. Perkins a sizable loss. We must extend our thanks to the Marshal for his foresight in bringing to Tombstone the latest in law enforcement technique, and we look forward to seeing other ways in which Red Sky and his dog Gray Smoke can make Tombstone a safer place to live."

All of them smiled in utter satisfaction, with the exception of Smoke who'd closed his eyes for a mid-morning nap.

"Another thing they taught me at the Mission School has just been proved correct," Sky said. "Just because you read it in the paper doesn't necessarily mean it's true."

Kincade and Josephine nodded their heads in amused agreement. "Sky, your words of wisdom is what every Law Enforcement Academy graduate needs to know."

Josephine reached toward the two men and retrieved their plates. "More breakfast, gentlemen?"

Sky looked at Josie and asked, "Smoke too?"

7

Since Tombstone had no sitting judge and the circuit judge was not due for several months, Kincade decided to take his prisoner to Bisbee where there was a municipal court. From the moment the court bailiff finished saying "All rise!" everything went wrong. It only took the judge three minutes.

"Lowdown wolf in sheep's clothing…" muttered Kincade as he left the Bisbee courthouse and headed back home.

Hours later as he reached the edge of Tombstone, Kincade stopped Gold Digger at the weather-beaten gate of Boot Hill to sit at his friend's grave and talk to the ghost of Jesse Keller.

A chill crawled down Kincade's spine as he looked at the grave's tombstone, barely visible in the fading twilight. He and Jesse had been blood brothers from their youth, sharing the problems and secrets which no one else would have understood. "Listen to me now, Jesse," he whispered to the wind. "This very morning a municipal judge decided to release the bandit who held up the General Store owner, Mr. Perkins. With one pound of his wood gavel, the damn judge cut him loose without a trial whatsoever. The guilty thief crowed like a proud rooster. The judge even admonished me about not having 'probable cause' to chase the outlaw, let alone sic a vicious dog on him in the process."

Kincade punched his fist into his palm over and over. "I know that somehow that bastard got to His Honor with a mouth full of bribes, sweetened with a pocket of gold. Damn it to hell Jess. It just isn't right..."

Then Kincade took a deep breath, already feeling better as if Jesse actually had heard him.

A gust of wind blew a tumbleweed past Jesse's grave and into the tombstone of another dead man: Kincade's twin brother Wil Logan. The two had killed one another that night in The Josephine... Logan trying to murder Kincade, Jesse trying to save Kincade. In the end, both died while Kincade lived. Jesse's death pained Kincade beyond words. Logan rotted in hell, which was where he belonged.

Kincade glared at Logan's tombstone, hating him for what he'd done, hating the Bisbee judge for what he had done, hating the injustice rained down on the lives of law-abiding people across the frontier. "Blaggard!..."

Kincade stared at his twin brother's name carved into the stone slab, his jawbone clenching again and again. The Marshal slowly shook his head, took a deep breath, and tried to let it go. While his mouth may have begun to relax, something else took its place. There, at Kincade's right temple, a dull ache appeared, unlike any Kincade had ever experienced. It was deep, as though the pain came from the center of Kincade's brain, radiating out towards his right temple, slamming into skull and flesh, trapped there unable to break free, but trying with all its might to punch through bone and flesh.

Kincade raised his right hand and massaged the area in front of his ear, trying to lessen the sudden flash of pain. "Damn justice! Hell, the Court tried to convict Wyatt Earp for murder! If he and Doc hadn't headed to Colorado, they probably would have done it. The Clantons woulda' paid to see them hang."

For a moment Kincade thought, "I should have taught Perkins' bandit a lesson myself. Should have handed out justice on the high plains, not in some crooked courtroom."

Strangely, he heard an Other Voice - a breathy whisper - answer him, "YOU SHOULD HAVE KILLED HIM."

Kincade turned back to face Jesse's grave. The dull ache diminished and within another two minutes disappeared altogether. The Marshal felt ashamed. "Whispers in the wind... What am I thinking?..."

As night enveloped Boot Hill, covering over the graves of Wil Logan and Jesse Keller, the door of an even deeper darkness cracked open and first entered the heart of a good man named Kincade.

8

The next morning, David Cook insisted on Kincade, Sky, and Smoke posing for a photograph to be printed on the front page of the next issue of the Tombstone Epitaph. Everyone would soon recognize the boy and dog as official members of Marshal Kincade's staff. Kincade decided not to tell Cook what had happened before the Bisbee judge. "That cocky bandit will be back," Kincade told himself. "And when he shows up, the two of us will have a little visit."

That afternoon Sky and Smoke sat outside on the wide veranda of the Cosmopolitan Hotel alongside Josephine who was enjoying the sunshine that filtered through her lace parasol. "The former Marshal of Tombstone, a gentleman named Wyatt Earp, made me promise that I would see that Kincade's wardrobe befit the responsibilities and demeanor of his office," Josie said to the boy. "Black frock coat, trousers, and vest, white shirt and string tie.

"Now, my young Sky, I know that Wyatt would want me to take whatever steps necessary to see that you, too, dress in the manner of a Tombstone Marshal."

"Miss Josie?"

"Yes…"

"I'm just a Deputy," and Sky smiled at her.

"Very well, Deputies too," said Josie, thinking to herself how very refreshing and bright this Indian boy was. "We're going to buy you some clothes."

"Smoke too?"

"You love him dearly, don't you…"

"Yes, I do," admitted Sky. "But Miss Josephine, Smoke has a problem."

"What is it?"

"I walk on two legs, he walks on four. I don't think they make black trousers like that."

"Oh, Sky!" She laughed. "I wish all white men had your sense of humor."

"Have you ever heard an Indian's sense of humor before now? Are we that different?"

"Let's just say that I like yours," she replied. "Come along, Deputy."

Josephine stood, brushed smooth her skirt, adjusted her parasol, and the three headed for the General Store.

The counters had piles of dungarees, flannel shirts, belts, and drop-seat underwear. There were hats and boots on the shelves. Coats and jackets hung on a rack. Josephine collected an armful as Sky followed with Smoke at his heels.

"Miss Josie, I'd sure like a black suit like Marshal Kincade," Sky said as she held dungarees up to his waist to check for size.

"And I suppose you'd like a white shirt and black string tie like his also."

"Yes, Mam. I'm his Deputy."

"That's what I hear," Josephine said, smiling at him.

"So what are you picking out that looks like him?"

"I think this black leather vest and that wide-brimmed buckaroo crease hat will do nicely. Kincade used to wear clothing like this before he was Marshal." Sky brightened considerably. "And we'll have to see if any of these boots fit you. If not, we'll order some."

The boy looked at Josie, grateful for her kindness. With each day, Sky began to truly understand what Kincade had meant by the beauty of her soul. "Miss Josephine, you're very nice to me. I'll pay you back when I get my salary at the end of the month."

"You're sweet, Sky, but the uniform goes with the job. Kincade can repay me from the Marshal's budget."

"Can I wear them now?"

"I believe there's a room in the back for changing purposes."

In a few moments Sky appeared with a questioning look on his face. "There's no mirror back there. Do I look like Marshal Kincade's Deputy?"

Josephine carefully walked around Sky, adjusting here, smoothing there, squaring the buckaroo hat, and stepping back to observe her work. "I never saw anyone look more like the Marshal himself."

Sky's face broke into a wide grin. "Come along," coaxed Josephine. "We're not through yet."

"Where we going?"

"To the barber shop."

Sky's eyes grew wide. "I don't shave, Miss Josie."

Josephine smiled. "A Deputy Marshal of our fair city needs the grooming of a true man of the law, don't you think?" Josephine could see fear growing in the eyes of the boy. Concerned, she stopped and added, "I'll make sure your hair looks just like Marshal Kincade's."

Sky swallowed, reluctant to speak. "What is it?" asked Josephine.

"Miss Josie," Sky began hesitantly as he removed his hat in respect. "If I have to cut my braid, then I can't be a Deputy." Josie could see sadness begin to fill the boy's eyes.

"Sky, its only hair." She pushed several black strands away from his face and brought them behind his ears with soothing hands.

"Not to a Sioux. Our hair is the symbol of the man-spirit's determination to stay alive on earth. When a Sioux takes a scalp it is to show victory over his enemy's spirit as well as his body."

"The barber isn't going to scalp you, Sky." But it was apparent to her that Sky was frightened by the very thought of losing his spirit and his chance to live on earth.

She looked at him with her kind eyes, full of compassion for the boy. "Thank you for explaining, Sky. I had no idea. You've taught me something today, and I am better for it." She leaned forward and gently kissed Sky on the forehead.

The boy beamed, greatly relieved at Josephine's understanding and acknowledgment of a sacred Sioux tradition. Smoke took all this in and whimpered.

Sky looked at the wolf, cocked his head as though listening, and said to Josephine, "Smoke wants to make sure he's not going to the barber either."

Josephine laughed, ruffled the fur on the wolf's head, and laughed again. "Let's go show Marshal Kincade how grand you look."

As the boy stood smartly before Kincade's office desk, the Marshal nodded his approval. Sky did look good, and both Josephine and Kincade sensed the pride the boy felt about himself and his new position of responsibility.

"Sky, as U.S. Marshal of Arizona Territory, I declare you my first Deputy, and in accordance with that appointment, I now invest…" Kincade opened his desk drawer, fumbled for a second, and brought out a metal star. "I now invest you with this badge so that all who see it will recognize you as a Deputy of my office."

Kincade pinned the star on the new leather vest. Then he turned to Josephine. "Looks very official, doesn't he."

"You both look very official wearing those badges. I'm so proud of the two stars in front of me."

"Thank you, Miss Josephine. I'll try very hard to do a good job. Marshal Kincade, do I need to take an oath or something?"

"Of course, I almost forgot. Raise your right hand and repeat after me: I, Red Sky of the Sioux Nation, declare that I will uphold the laws of the Territory of Arizona and assist my superior law enforcement officer, Marshal Kincade, in the performance of his duties whenever called upon."

Sky repeated. Then he polished the Deputy star with his shirt sleeve. "I like it. I'll try to be worthy."

Josephine and Kincade looked at one another. No Marshal or

Sheriff could ever have made a better choice than Kincade had this morning.

Josephine put her hand on Kincade's shoulder. "Darling, we need to find Sky and Smoke a place to live. Sleeping on the floor of the Marshal's office is neither fitting nor healthy."

At Josephine's use of the word 'Darling', Sky looked at Kincade with a twinkle in his eye. Kincade winked back and whispered "She loves me. She simply can't help herself," – which immediately caused them both to chuckle. With each passing day, the Marshal's fondness for the boy continued to grow.

Kincade agreed with Josephine's concern. "I suppose we could clear out the tack room in the stable for him. I slept in a shed behind a livery when I was a boy. I got along just fine."

"Good. I'll bring a bed from the storage room at the Cosmopolitan Hotel," she added.

"Miss Josie…?" interrupted Sky.

"Hmmm?"

"I thank you, but I've never slept on a bed. Smoke and I are fine on the floors. We really are."

"All right, I understand," Josie said, continuing to learn about this remarkable boy. "I'll find a dresser for your new clothes."

"The tack room has nails on the walls. They'll do."

"A mirror?"

"I have no whiskers."

"A chair?"

"The floor is fine, Miss Josie. If Smoke and I want to sit in a chair we'll come into Marshal Kincade's office."

Kincade tried to imagine the wolf and his long legs fitting into one of his chairs.

"Would you like a wash basin and some towels?"

Kincade laughed. "Josie, I think these two will have matters well in hand."

"Miss Josie, a blanket would be nice," said Sky.

"I'll bring several, just in case Smoke needs some of his own. Is there anything else I can do to please the three of you?"

"It pleases us just to have you around, Josie." He kissed the palm of her left hand, staring into her incredible blue eyes.

Josephine kissed the tip of her right finger and playfully touched the end of Kincade's nose. She winked at Sky and waved goodbye as she left for the Cosmopolitan Hotel.

The Marshal turned to his Deputy. "Josie has taken care of your living accommodations. Now I need to do my part. It's only fitting that you have your own horse."

"My own horse?! Haho, haho, haho!" Then he looked earnestly at Kincade. "Is another horse in your budget?"

"No, but it's in my best interests. Shall we go to the livery and see what's available?"

"Yes Sir, Marshal!" Sky squared his hat and his shoulders.

The corral at the livery had many horses that were either for sale, trade, or being boarded. Sky walked among them and Smoke made an independent survey. Kincade watched but didn't make suggestions. The horse was an Indian's most important possession, and said much about the man who owned him. The old Indian had instilled in Kincade a great respect for horses. Finding and eventually owning Gold Digger had been one of the most significant events in Kincade's life.

After a half hour Sky approached Kincade. "I just can't tell, Marshal. They all seem like fine mounts, but something's missing. You know what I mean?"

"I do. Shall we try next week? The stock is always changing."

At that moment Smoke bounded up with his tail swishing like a dust devil. He bumped and pushed Sky toward the rear of the lot where a paint horse hugged the rail. The boy hadn't noticed this horse before and it was a beauty.

"Marshal Kincade, will you ask about this fellow please. Smoke likes him."

Kincade went into the livery office and Curley Smith, the owner, came back to the corral with him. "That's an Apache pony I took in awhile back. Stubborn little devil. Haven't been able to get a saddle on him."

"May I ride him?" Sky asked.

Curley chortled. "Son, no one's been able to ride him. But you're the Deputy, so be my guest. It's your backside." He pointed to the tack shed. "Saddles, blankets, and tack are hung over the rails. Take your pick."

"No thank you. This is an Indian pony." Quick as the wind he grabbed the horse's mane with his hands and swung onto his back. The horse was startled and took off around the enclosure, snorting loudly with each long stride. Sky only laughed softly and stroked his neck with one free hand. This sent the horse to bucking, but not with great conviction - more like bursts than bucks. The boy leaned over his neck and spoke to him in a tone the horse understood even though the words were strange.

Then, with only the pressure of Sky's knees, the animal walked toward Kincade and Curley Smith with perfect calm and obedience. Smith was amazed at what he'd seen.

"You've found another brother-of-choice, Sky," Kincade said.

"If he's all right with you - in your budget, I mean."

"How much for this one?" the Marshal asked.

"Consider it a gift," said Curley, who then turned to Sky and said, "But I want your dog to save my butt next time I'm getting robbed." He held out his hand to the boy. "Is it a deal?"

"Deal!" Sky said.

Curley Smith gave Sky a rope halter and he led the horse from the corral.

"I've been thinking," Kincade said as they walked slowly down Allen Street. "We'll put this horse in the third stall closest to your new room. We'll move the tack to the middle stall, and keep Gold Digger where he is. That okay with you?"

"Uh-huh."

"You must ride him every day and curry him yourself so he'll get to know you. You won't mind that will you?"

"Huh-uh."

"Old Teddy who takes care of Gold Digger can clean out his

stall and give him water and food because he needs the job, but..." Kincade's voice trailed off as it became clear to the Marshal that Sky was no longer listening. "Sky?..."

"Yes, Marshal Kincade."

"What are you thinking?"

"About a name for him."

The old Indian who had raised Kincade taught that choosing a name was another enormously important matter. Great respect must be given the decision. Kincade silently walked alongside the boy, his wolf, and his new and unbelievably precious horse. Eventually they arrived and stood outside the stable behind the Marshal's office.

"So....?" Kincade asked.

Sky nodded, his decision made. "My father was called Huste. He was an honorable man and I loved him. In this short time you have been like a father to me, Marshal Kincade. May I call the horse Kinhuste because I have admiration for you both?"

Kincade wondered if he'd heard the boy correctly. Sky's decision touched him deeply. "Like a father..." the boy's choice echoed within Kincade's soul. Never in his life had anyone ever said or suggested such a thing to him. "Like a father..." This boy was truly remarkable. His sensitivity, insight, and ability to care went far beyond his years.

"Kinhuste is an excellent name. And I shall try to be worthy of the memory you have of your father." He placed his large hand on Sky's shoulder. The boy felt much more than just Kincade's touch. It was a rare moment for them both.

"Now let's see if Gold Digger likes his new stall mate."

9

When the sun set behind Arizona Territory's mighty Dragoon Mountains, the line between Upper and Lower Tombstone became as clear as the cut-glass chandelier in the high-vaulted ceiling of the Cosmopolitan Hotel. Every human being who ventured out had best be aware of which side of the line he walked. Life, or death, hung in the balance. The Cosmo and The Josephine Saloon were the cornerstones of the Upper. The seedy Silver Dollar and other unsavory establishments clustered around Boot Hill were the Lower.

The darkened streets and garbage strewn alleys of Lower Tombstone twisted like snakes writhing in a bottomless pit. Here were dirt-floor saloons dispensing Indian whiskey distilled on back lots, Chinese opium dens, and cheap whore houses. There were fights in bars, shootouts in the streets, waylaying of strangers, burglary of stores and warehouses, destruction of property, and just disturbing the peace by shooting into the air. The Marshal and his two Deputies began making their regular rounds of the more troublesome spots after the sun had set.

In contrast, the gas lights of Upper Tombstone brightened Allen Street where The Josephine was located. Gayety flowed from the doorway – a magic realm of music and laughter. And the Queen of Graciousness was Josephine herself, dressed to perfection, winning the rapt attention and admiration of all who entered.

Josephine welcomed everyone to her establishment who could enjoy themselves without interfering with the enjoyment others were having. This made for a strange mix of clientele. Tombstone's upper crust mingled with travelers staying at the hotel. Dirty drovers just arrived from a long cattle drive were never turned away. She gave each person her smile and a few minutes of her time. This endeared her to the hearts of all who swung open the batwing doors.

Josephine held a strict policy of honesty at the casino tables and private card games. Little trouble occurred at The Josephine that wouldn't be handled by her admirers themselves. Kincade was rarely needed there, but that didn't keep him from checking in nightly just to admire the perfect hostess that she was. Sky and Smoke usually waited outside, ostensibly to guard the street, but also to keep Smoke from intimidating any new comers who didn't know his role in Tombstone.

Venturing into Lower Tombstone was another matter. The Marshal and his Deputies would walk each street, three abreast, and enter each saloon. Kincade moved among the tables and along the bar while Sky and Smoke stood just inside the entrance performing what Kincade called The Intimidation.

When Sky first heard what he was supposed to do he said, "This is a word I don't understand. What does Intimidation mean?"

"It means scaring troublemakers spitless just by looking at them."

Smoke quickly caught on and played his role to perfection. As though squinting into a blazing sun, he made his eyes into mean, little slits and developed a wolf-fang sneer which took the starch out of the toughest hombres. Seeing these three, the con-artists, sharks, and crooked gamblers of Lower Tombstone quickly folded their game and put their cards in their pockets. Those at the bar leaned over their drinks, trying to look innocent of any wrong do-ing.

With his Deputies in place, Intimidating, Kincade would slowly and deliberately pass each table, looking squarely into the eyes of each secretive face, making sure they knew who he was and what he expected. Moving to the bar, Kincade would touch the brim of his hat to the saloonkeeper. He knew them all by name, and by reputation. "Hello, Jake. Everything quiet tonight?"

The man would nod and say, "Evenin', Marshal."

"Those boys at the back giving you any trouble?"

"We're peaceful here, Marshal, but thanks for droppin' by."

Kincade would answer by jerking his thumb over his right shoul-der to the saloon's entrance where Sky and Smoke waited. "My Deputy Law Dog will be glad to hear that." Then, the Marshal would slowly pivot on the heels of his mule-eared boots to face the entire saloon. In a raised and firm voice, he would say "Goodnight boys." Moving deliberately, Kincade would make The Intimida-tion crystal clear by walking back to the entrance with the jingle-bobs on his spurs stilling any conversations. Joining his Deputies, the Marshal would face the room once more, tip his hat, and the three would move on to the next establishment.

Occasionally when strangers arrived in Tombstone and didn't know about the new law enforcement team, Smoke had to attack-and-wait. Then he would throw back his head and howl so that Sky and the Marshal could find him. When the townsfolk in Up-per Tombstone heard this call, they'd laugh and say, "Law Dog's caught another one."

As the culprit was being hauled to jail, he might declare that he had been unjustly mauled by a wild beast. Kincade always an-swered, "I shouted a warning for you to stop. Are you deaf or did you think I was vocalizing?   If you come to Tombstone you only stay by obeying the laws." The news of such actions spread like a grass fire across the Arizona Territory, and as the weeks passed there were fewer and fewer occupants in the jail.

Kincade added a new and dangerous dimension to The Intimidation. The first time was shortly after the judge in Bisbee cut Perkins' thief lose. A green horn stranger had wandered into one of Lower Tombstone's toughest saloons and was sitting at a table with men that Kincade knew had no honor among themselves, let alone with a gullible cowpoke who more than likely would end up beaten and robbed in a dark alley.   Kincade began taking pleasure in stirring this very volatile pot by walking up to, and then towering over the shoulder of that table's most dangerous gambler.

As the players fell silent, Kincade called to Sky and Smoke, "Come over here. I want you to meet an old acquaintance of mine. This is Frank Sullivan. Frank, these are my Deputies, Sky and Smoke." The wolf responded with a low growl that put shivers up the spine of everyone seated.

Kincade continued. "I was happy to hear you've stopped that practice of putting aces up your right sleeve, Frank. These three gentlemen at your table appreciate it too."

Then the Marshal waited, looking directly into the eyes of that piece of gutter trash, Frank Sullivan, as Smoke sniffed the legs of every man at the table.

The other gamblers froze, wide-eyed at Kincade as the cheat's face burned red with anger. But each of them had learned from gamblers who had come to Tombstone, and left, you kept your mouth shut when Marshal Kincade singled you out.

"Frank..." Kincade said, "... you got a problem with what I just said?"

Frank shook his head. "No."

Kincade responded by saying "I didn't think so." Then he looked hard at the remaining players. "Anybody else have a problem with what I just said to Frank?"

More heads, no.

"That's good, that's very good. And what about you, stranger? Would you like to continue playing with these boys or would you rather leave when my Deputies and I do?"

The stranger stood, gathered up his money, and ran out the door as the other players at the table glared at the card cheat Frank Sullivan. Kincade, Sky, and Smoke backed up and left through the doors which were still swinging.

Sky took a deep breath as the three headed down the dusty street. "Marshal, I suppose you know what you're doing, but isn't it dangerous talking to them like that?"

"Oh, I probably could outdraw any one of them." Kincade walked on in silence as the two Deputies followed. The most curious thing happened. The same ache Kincade first felt the night he visited the graves of Jesse Keller and Wil Logan began to pulsate in his right temple. Again he heard the Other Voice – a raspy whisper, "IN FACT... YOU KNOW YOU COULD." But rather than massage the pain as he had when kneeling on Boot Hill, Kincade's hands moved to his deadly Colt revolvers. The Marshal's voice became an echo, and Sky could swear that he heard Kincade say, "In fact...I know I could."

"Marshal, you okay?" Sky asked.

But Kincade didn't answer. He was too consumed with trying to shake clear the ache near his right temple, and avoid the return of the whisper.

10

Sky always rose at the first hint of pre-dawn light. He put on his Indian clothes. He quietly led Kinhuste from the stable. Smoke had taken to sleeping with the horse and he always joined them. The three roamed the prairie and hills around Tombstone - sometimes galloping, sometimes just walking. All three would drink from a stream if they came upon one, or they'd roll in the grass if it was fresh with the morning dew. Those hours were devoted to all three becoming acquainted. Smoke seemed to feel a responsibility for pointing out his choice in horse flesh to Sky, and would guide Kinhuste with short yelps and running in front of the paint.

This early hour was a precious, private time for the Indian boy - no one even knew what he did. This was just for himself, his wolf, and his horse.

When the eastern sky turned rosy with sunrise, the three would return to Tombstone. Kinhuste and Smoke would stand side by side, drinking water from the trough and then willingly return to their stall.

Sky loved caring for Kinhuste. "Mitasunke," he would say, "My horse," rubbing him down with complete attention. The boy knew old Teddy could have used the job and the coins it would pay, but he wanted to do it himself. The relationship between Kinhuste and Sky was precious.

After tending to the paint, Sky would wash himself at the pump outside Kincade's house and put on the Deputy clothes Josephine had bought him. Kincade would arrive and they would both head up the street to The Josephine for breakfast.

Whenever the Marshal could get away in the afternoon, the two of them would mount up and ride to the hills outside of town, Smoke following stride for stride. Kincade wanted to learn and be able to give the commands that Sky used for directing Smoke.

The first time, Sky reminded Kincade as they jogged along, "Remember that Smoke doesn't speak a language. He just responds to commands that he's familiar with."

"Perhaps the legend is true, Sky," said Kincade. "Smoke is an old soul... from the time when dogs could talk. Just look at him now. He seems to know exactly what I'm saying - and even what I'm thinking. It can be a bit unsettling."

"He pulls that with me too."

The horses walked up a rise through sweet grass as Sky began the lessons. "We can do this one of two ways. You can learn my Indian commands or Smoke can learn the same thing spoken by you in English. Which do you want to try?"

"Since I don't have your Sioux language skills, let's see if Smoke can learn some English."

Sky nodded. "Good. I'll tell you what my Sioux command means. Then I'll shout it to him. Just as he takes off, you shout the same order in your English."

"Let's give it a try."

"The command means 'Come on, let's go!' Ho iyaya yo!" yelled the boy.

Immediately Kincade repeated, equally loud, "Let's go!" Smoke pricked up his ears and preceded the horses down the hill they had been standing on. Kincade felt good about the wolf's reaction and response. "I think, given enough practice, this is going to work."

"He's a very smart wolf, Marshal." Sky had a mischievous grin. "It will work provided you are an equally smart man." Kincade shook his head, smiling to himself. Sky's sense of humor reminded him of his dearest friend, Jesse Keller.

Before long Kincade could be the first to shout to Smoke without Sky prompting, and the animal recognized the command.

As the weeks passed, Kincade and the boy discussed other ways that Smoke could be useful in enforcing the law in Tombstone, and together they devised ways to teach the wolf. They would work on these ideas far out of town where any curious townsfolk would not detect that they invented enforcement techniques on a day-by-day basis or that Sky had never learned them at a Law Enforcement Academy.

Besides attack-and-wait, which Smoke executed perfectly, they contrived ways to teach him to find lost people, or recover stolen articles, to detect odors which could identify a suspect, and even locate decomposed bodies.

The wolf thought it was all a wonderful game. He didn't seem to care that he was chasing an antelope and not a robber, or digging up a bag of rotting carcasses from the slaughter house instead of a decomposed body. His favorite game was playing hide-and-seek – inahmekiciyapi - with Josephine, never thinking he was rehearsing for finding a lost child.

"Smoke's already a great tracker," Sky boasted when Kincade

suggested they teach the wolf those skills. "The command is 'akita maniyan yo'."

"So what do I tell him?"

"Look for it as you walk."

"I'll try to shorten my command to 'Look for it!'," smiled Kincade.

At the conclusion of this day's training, as the two rode towards Tombstone, Sky shared a story with Kincade. "Once when we were nearly starving to death we came upon a campsite that had been cold for several days. But we knew that whoever had been there had food because coffee had been spilled onto the ground and meat bones thrown into the bushes. Smoke sniffed all over the place and soon he set off at a trot.

"I followed, and about a day later, in the evening, we came upon four tough looking men, getting liquored up with a bottle of whiskey. By midnight they were passed out cold without having finished a pot of beans and bacon."

Kincade listened attentively to Sky's story about tough men, wondering if they had been outlaws on the run. The dangerous notion troubled him, and he began to wonder what would have happened to the boy and his pet if the men had awakened. They could have been like his brother Wil Logan, who would have enjoyed torturing and killing anyone who came upon his camp. The Marshal rubbed his right forefinger into and around the soft depression to the side of his right eye, as he thought about all those who had suffered at the hand of Wil Logan. Trying to override the memories and the pain they caused made him wince slightly. "I must just listen – not remember," Kincade told himself.

"So you had yourself a good meal?" asked Kincade, deliberately blinking several times.

"We ate as fast as we could. Then we stole all the food they had in their saddle bags - jerky, hard tack, coffee, flour, uncooked beans - as much as I could carry."

"Did you take their money?"

"Marshal, what are an Indian and a wolf going to do with money? I couldn't walk into a store in some little town with a bag of gold and say, 'Give me this, and that, and these other things I need.' I'd be shot or jailed. No, Smoke and I survived more than once by tracking, not by having any money."

His story now ended, Sky waited for Kincade's response. But it didn't come. The Marshal rode silently forward. His gloved hand rubbing the right temple. Wil Logan would have stripped them of every possession.

"Marshal?"

Nothing.

"Marshal Kincade, are you all right?"

Kincade deliberately blinked and shook his head slightly, "Yes, sure, Sky. Sorry. Just a headache."

Kincade could see the boy's concern. "Kind of like the headache you gave those four men when you stole their beans." Kincade laughed, which relieved Sky.

But the headache remained until they arrive in Tombstone and put their horses away for the night. Alone in his office, Kincade took a seat, tried to relax, and eventually shook it off.

11

Two weeks later during one of their afternoon learning sessions, Kincade said, "You've been teaching me things. Maybe it's time I taught you to shoot a gun."

"No, thank you Sir."

"A rifle then."

"Neither one, Marshal Kincade."

"Smoke would try to save you, Sky, but there are men – very bad men – that not even a wolf can stop."

"It isn't a matter of being saved. It's a matter of my being brave."

Kincade didn't speak, preferring to listen.

"The gun has a long, safe reach, but the arm has a short, daring one. Indians praise the one who will touch his enemy. We call it 'counting coup'. Do you remember when the bullies were torturing Smoke and you came to rescue him?"

"The day you and I first met."

The boy nodded. "You could have shot those men but you didn't.

You touched one in such a way that he was made helpless, and his companions backed down because of your grip."

"And for the Indian this shows more bravery than shooting them?"

"Let me tell you about a ceremony which makes the Indian prove his bravery. A Sioux warrior plants a stake in the ground. He will stand by it with a knife, or spear, or just his hands and he will kill any enemy who comes at him. One of his fellow tribesmen must ride up to rescue him and pull up the stake. They will gallop away together on the tribesman's horse. They are brave – the man who stands and the man who rescues. They do not shoot the enemy – only defy him."

Kincade was silent. Then he said, "And you think that's what I did when I saved Smoke from those three men?"

"Well, no guns were fired. I saw you touch the enemy and then lift a helpless wolf into your arms. I have honored you ever since."

Kincade thought back to that day. He remembered the agony suffered by the wolf through the cruelty of three men. He recalled the terror that gripped the very soul of the boy. He could clearly see the faces of the scum who had brought such terrible pain into the innocent lives of a boy and his pet.

The moment after Sky finished, Kincade swore he heard the Other Voice. But it was not a whisper. It spoke clearly and distinctly, as if the Other Voice were beside him.

"YOU SHOULD HAVE KILLED THEM"

A second later the Voice disappeared and in its place rose the headache beneath the soft depression to the side of Kincade's right eye. The same headache that was becoming more and more throbbing.

12

Until put to use, the skills Kincade and Sky had taught the wolf could only be called "tricks". But that was about to change.

One Wednesday morning as the Marshal and the boy shared breakfast with Josephine, there was a loud knocking at the front door, still locked until time to open for business. Josephine left the table to see who was there.

"Well, Curley Smith!" smiled Josephine. "Good morning. Will you come in for coffee?"

"Thank you, Miss Josie, but I'm looking for Marshal Kincade. Is he here?"

"Yes, Curley, he is. Please, come in."

"Thank you, Miss Josie," Curley said as he removed his hat.

Kincade stood and offered his hand to the owner of the livery stable. "Hello, Curley. What brings you here so early?"

"Marshal I need your help." It was clear that Curley was deeply troubled. "Some of my best horses were stolen last night."

"Sit down, my friend." Kincade offered him a chair as Josie headed for the kitchen to get Curley some coffee.

"Thanks, Marshal." Curley sat, took a breath, and began. "Howard Philips of the Bar-Circle-Bar paid me a goodly sum to locate and buy five prize brood mares for his ranch. I found them in Texas. He paid me half the cost for getting them here to Tombstone. The final payment was to be on delivery."

Sky and Smoke listened intently. This sounded like work for them.

"The horses arrived three days ago after being packed into a train boxcar for nearly a week. I wanted them to be in top health, so I brought them over to the livery and put them in a separate corral to keep the stallions away from them."

Josephine returned, setting the steaming mug of black coffee in front of Curley who gratefully took a big gulp. "Thanks, Miss Josephine." He put the coffee down and wiped his mustache. "I went to check on them this morning and they were gone – stolen! Gate was down. Tracks everywhere.

"I've got to get those mares back, Marshal, or I'll lose a heap of money as well as my reputation."

Kincade stood and placed a reassuring hand on the big man's shoulder. "We'll find them, Curley."

Sky nodded, stood and said, "Yeah. We'll find them, Mr. Smith."

Josephine walked over to Kincade and pulled his arms around her waist. "Please be careful. Horse rustlers can be...."

Kincade leaned down and looked into her concerned eyes. "Don't worry." He gestured toward Sky. "I have my Deputy with me."

"Smoke too," added the boy.

As the four left The Josephine, Kincade spoke to Curley. "Let's start at the corral where the mares were kept."

When they got there, Sky commanded Smoke, "akita maniyan yo."

"Look for it as you walk – right?" Kincade asked and Sky nodded.

The wolf went round and round, sniffing every hoof print and pile of dung. He put his nose along the railings and his paws up on the gate. Then he came back to Sky and woofed.

"He's ready, Marshal Kincade," said the boy. "We can go." Curley wanted to join them which Kincade agreed to, knowing that Curley would be needed to identify the mares should they be found. As Curley saddled his own horse, Kincade and Sky returned to the Marshal's office to saddle Gold Digger and Kinhuste.

Soon the three were galloping out of town with Smoke in the lead. There were no tracks in the dust for them to follow. Countless horses had churned the earth since the previous rain. But Smoke seemed sure of himself and kept up a good pace.

It wasn't long before the wolf's nose went to the ground and he prowled back and forth over stubby growth at the side of the trail.

"Do you see any hoof prints there?" Curley asked Kincade.

"No, I don't. But trust me, if Smoke knows something, we'll know it soon." The dog stopped sniffing and went back to trotting down the road, his nose smelling the air as well as the dirt.

Sky offered his opinion. "My guess is that the horses stopped there to munch some grass and then went on."

Smoke's next investigation was of a rocky outcropping just to the side of an arroyo. The wolf became very excited and bounded up the embankment, yipping for them to follow. Kincade nodded to Curley, and gave Smoke a command. "Come on, let's go!"…which was immediately repeated by the boy, "Ho iyaya yo!"

The three rode on for several miles. No sign of rustlers or the mares. Smoke kept his nose to the ground, occasionally back-tracking for a yard or two, but never faltering.

After riding nearly two hours, the wolf suddenly stopped and dropped to his belly. He turned, making sure Sky and Kincade were close, and stealthily inched ahead towards an amphitheater of rocks. The two men and boy silently slid from their horses. Kincade withdrew his Winchester from the saddle scabbard, put his fingers to his lips and mouthed the word, 'Listen'.

Sure enough, there were voices talking and laughing among the rocks. They overheard one saying, "Bet old Howard Philip's got a big headache this mornin'."

"Not as bad as the one Curley Smith's got," said another. "That's all he'd talk about for weeks – him getting these mares."

A third voice. "Serves Philips right for lettin' you go, Charlie."

"I don't care no more," said the second voice. "I'll get more for sellin' them horses than he ever would a'paid me."

Kincade mouthed the word "three" and held up three fingers. The other two nodded. Kincade motioned for Curley to go to the right as the Marshal went left. Unarmed, and preferring it that way, Sky stayed back to secure the horses, Smoke at his side.

The Marshal and liveryman cautiously crept around the rocks. Kincade verified the presence of three rustlers, and only three, looked over at Curley who nodded his head. Kincade moved forward and boldly stepped into their circle.

"I'm U.S. Marshal Kincade. Put up your hands. You're under arrest for horse rustling."

Two of the three gasped, dropping their tin cups to raise their arms. The third made the mistake of reaching for his gun. Kincade was fully prepared, raising the muzzle of the Winchester.

To the left of Kincade, and at a blur, Smoke appeared, leaping onto the chest of the third rustler, knocking him over, and flattening him into the dirt. The outlaw's pistol flew from the man's fist, up, and into the rocks behind. The wolf bore down with his full weight on the rustler's chest, pinning him to the earth. He raised his shaggy head and gave a victory howl. The other two rustlers stood frozen as they watched the wolf's fangs flash in the sun.

None of the bandits was going anywhere. Sky could see that. Curley Smith could see that. The boy turned to Kincade, eager to share his pride in what Smoke had done. But the look he saw stopped him cold.

There was a fury on Kincade's face, his eyes full of rage. Sky was certain of it. Kincade heard the Other Voice again. It was a sharp command: "SHOOT THEM!" Kincade slowly turned the Winchester towards the chests of the two rustlers with hands held high, and racked a cartridge into the chamber. The Marshal's finger extended to the trigger as though preparing to fire.

Sky immediately reached out to touch Kincade's arm. "Marshal!" he said. "They're giving up!" The boy could see Kincade's finger begin to tighten on the Winchester's trigger.

Startled, Sky ran between Kincade and the two outlaws. "You two! Get on your knees!" he ordered. He turned back to Kincade. "Marshal, help me. We need handcuffs on these men."

Kincade blinked. He blinked a second time. The headache was stronger than previous bouts. Kincade shook his head, trying to escape the throbbing - throbbing.

"Marshal Kincade!" repeated the boy.

It was as if Kincade had stepped into the circle of rocks for the first time. He looked at the boy, looked at his rifle, and realized that with any more pressure, the Winchester would have fired a round squarely into the chest of the second of the three bandits.

Curley stepped up to Kincade as the Marshal lowered his rifle. "Are you all right, Kincade?"

Kincade nodded. "Yes, Curley. Sorry. Got distracted for a second there." The headache throbbed as Kincade rubbed the temple by his right eye. The Other Voice did not speak again.

Kincade handed his Winchester to Curley. He walked back to Gold Digger and got three sets of handcuffs from the saddle bags. He handed two of them to the boy as Curley covered the kneeling men with the rifle and Sky cuffed them. Smoke hadn't moved from the third man's chest. Marshal Kincade knelt to cuff the third. He then reached out his hand and gently stroked Smoke's back. "Very good, my chosen brother." Smoke released and walked back to Sky.

Watching Kincade gently interact with the wolf, Sky thought that he must have been mistaken. Kincade couldn't have been about to shoot these three. He was just trying to scare them, like The Intimidation. He was just doing his job as Marshal. The rustlers were caught. No one had been hurt.

Sky repeated, "Wasteste, mihunka." Smoke jumped up to lick the boy's face and then walked back through the rocks.

Kincade roughly shoved the three rustlers forward. He ordered them to mount their own horses facing backwards. Then he tied them to their saddles and secured the rope between the horses. They weren't going anywhere except to jail.

"You seen any sign of the mares?" Curley asked.

Just then Smoke came bounding back, panting hard, with his tail wagging. "No, but I think Smoke has," Sky shouted, following the excited wolf.

There they were – all five mares – hobbled but unharmed, feeding on a patch of grass. Unbuckling the leather hoof straps and letting them fall to the ground, the boy took their lead ropes and brought them back to Curley Smith.

"Is my horse paid for now?" he asked the livery owner with a smile.

"In full," beamed Curley. "And if you want a saddle for him just come around any time and that'll be yours too."

"Thanks, Mr. Smith," said Sky. "But this is my job. Marshal Kincade pays me well." The Indian boy turned to look at Kincade. The Marshal was looking with great intensity into the very frightened eyes of the rustlers, left hand fingering the grip of his pearl-handled Colt revolver, as his other hand massaged the soft indentation just by his right eye, slowly and deliberately.

Two of the bandits cowered at Kincade's glare, afraid if they moved so much as an inch, Kincade would jerk his pistol and go to work.

The third bandit wouldn't look at the Marshal. He'd seen the look of a killer before, and had no wish to see it again.

13

David Cook, the reporter from the Tombstone Epitaph, arrived in his tight plaid suit just as Kincade was locking the three thieves in the jail.

"Spectacular!" Cook gushed, waving his pencil and pad of paper in the air. "Congratulations, Marshal! And you also, Deputy Sky."

"Thank you," said the boy, and he walked over to stand proudly alongside Kincade who put his arm around the boy's shoulders as a father would embrace his son.

"Smoke too," Sky said, pointing to the wolf who was making his way out the rear door to curl up in the stable.

"Everyone will be talking of this after they read my story tomorrow morning," claimed Cook. "Now, Marshal, where would you like to start?"

Kincade, feeling better now that the headache had disappeared, looked at Sky, letting the boy know with his eyes that it was okay if the boy took his turn at being interviewed by the zealous David Cook. But Sky shook his head, waved, and followed Smoke out the back door of the Marshal's office.

The Indian boy gave Kinhuste fresh water and a bucket of oats. Then a good brushing, combing out the mane and tail with his fingers as he'd seen Kincade do with Gold Digger.

"Pilamaya yelo," Sky said to the paint. "Thank you." The boy brought his forehead to the horse's nose and rubbed it up and down with great affection.

After the Tombstone Epitaph ran the story, everyone who had ever had anything stolen – from a lollipop at school to long-handles off a wash line – all hoped Kincade would take their case. The line to file a report in the Marshal's office sometimes grew to five or six people. Soon a stack of cases covered the top of his desk.

"You want to help me look over these?" the Marshal asked his Deputy.

"Not at the salary you're paying me," came the reply. "I'm just joking, Marshal. What do you want me to do?"

Kincade leafed through the various crimes. "Looks like most of them happened too long ago to be solved. Our success with Curley was largely dependent on our acting quickly."

"And on Smoke's nose," Sky said with pride.

The Marshal smiled. "Sorry, Law Dog. I didn't intend to take the credit." Kincade leaned over and patted the big, gray back of the wolf stretched out alongside his chair.

Returning to the stack of cases, Kincade pulled out one in particular. "Here's one for you to look at." He handed Sky a page written in shaky penmanship.

Sky read aloud:

"Dear Marshal Kincade. My name is Ruth Wappler. I am 78

years old. My husband, Fred, was a miner in the hills outside Tombstone. Two years ago he was killed when there was a cave-in at his mine. Some of the men here said they'd go find his body. But when they got to the mine there were three tunnels all filled with rocks. They said they didn't know which tunnel my Fred was working in, and it would be too hard to dig out all three. So my Fred lies buried somewhere in the mine. I would like to give him a decent, Christian burial before I die. Do you think your Law Dog could find my Fred? I'm begging you. Your faithful servant, Mrs. Ruth Wappler."

Neither Kincade nor Sky said a word. The Marshal took the letter, folded it, and put it in his shirt pocket. "I think we should consider this one. Let's go talk to the Widow Wappler."

They found her to be a short and plump, white haired lady with piercing gray eyes in a wrinkled, leathery face. When they said they would try to help her, she burst into tears and had to bury her face in her apron.

"Thank you, thank you," she sobbed. "I know finding my Fred is not like tracking horse rustlers, but I had to take a chance that you'd know a way." She grabbed the Marshal's hands. "Thank you, thank you, Marshal." Kincade was deeply touched. He had known the grief of loss when Jesse Keller was killed.

"Mrs. Wappler, may I introduce you to my best Deputies." The boy removed his hat and the wolf wagged his tail. "This is Red Sky, and this four-legged fellow is named Gray Smoke."

"I read about you in the paper. Pleased to meet you, I'm sure. Won't you please come in for some coffee?"

"Smoke doesn't drink coffee, Mam," answered Sky politely. "But he's very fond of water."

"I'll get him a pan full!" She shuffled off, eager to do anything to please them.

By the end of their hour-long visit in her tidy parlor, Kincade and Sky knew where the mine was located and most of the pertinent facts about its operation. At one time the dig yielded good silver. The Wapplers had lived well. But in the last years Fred had to go further into the hillside for pay ore. The timbered shafts went deeper and deeper underground where the damp air became rare and toxic.

"Mrs. Wappler, do you still have a piece of Fred's clothing that we could take with us?" asked Sky. "Smoke needs to get the scent of the person he's looking for."

Rising from her chair with great effort, she shuffled to a closet and pulled a battered black hat from the shelf. "Fred wore this constantly when he wasn't at the mine. It was almost like his wig." She laughed nervously.

"Thanks, it will do just fine. " Kincade accepted the hat. "We'll go to the mine in the next day or two, Mrs. Wappler. Then we'll get back to you with a report and Fred's hat."

"Oh, can't I go with you? I won't get in your way, I promise." The widow was so hopeful.

"Why don't you let us check first," soothed Kincade. "I'm sure your husband would want to keep you safe." The widow understood, remembering how Fred had doted on her personal safety the entire fifty-eight years they'd been together.

"Wish us luck, Mrs. Wappler." Kincade waved goodbye.

"Thank you for Smoke's water," added Sky.

"I'll pray for your success." She waved until they rode out of sight.

"Nice lady," Sky said. "My mother was fat with lots of wrinkles."

"As you will be one day, my friend," Kincade smiled.

"And you!" the boy retorted.

"I don't want Smoke to think he can retire after one success," said Kincade. "Let's put him to work tomorrow."

The mine was an hour's easy ride from town. It was the only dig in the area and they had no trouble finding it. They inspected all three tunnels as best they could for the debris was considerable. Smoke had been shown the old hat and took to carrying it around in his mouth. The three probed into the depths as far as anyone could, walking carefully over the compacted stones.

"My guess is that the stream we crossed originates up above," observed Kincade. "There could have been a cloud burst. The waters swelled, weakening the banks, and like a thunderous avalanche careened down into the mine tunnels. Poor old Fred probably didn't know what was happening until all hell broke loose."

The boy imagined the chaos of that day. "I hate to picture him trying to run ahead of it."

Smoke made his inspection of the site and returned to lie down at the main entrance of what was left of the mine, dropping the hat between his paws.

"Doesn't look very encouraging, does it," Sky said.

"Afraid not," Kincade replied. He took off his wide-brimmed hat, wiped his brow with his sleeve, and replaced it. "We'll just have to tell Ruth Wappler that it either happened too long ago or Fred's body is too deep in the mine for Smoke to catch a scent."

"Poor, lady," said Sky, shaking his head. "I'm sorry for her." They returned to their horses and started down the trail next to the stream which was running bank full. "Come on Smoke. We're going home."

The dog stopped to get a drink from the rushing water, when suddenly his head pulled up and he woofed as he often did when tracking. Then he ducked his whole head under the water and came up yelping. Back and forth, the wolf ran for a full twelve feet along the stream bank.

"What's he doing?" Kincade asked.

Sky suddenly smiled. "Marshal, I think our luck is about to change."

Both men leaped from their horses and followed the dog in his frantic pacing. Without warning, the wolf jumped into the water, paddling furiously as he kept his nose under the current.

Sky saw it first. "Marshal Kincade, come quick! Under those willow branches, stuck between the boulders. See it?"

"My God!" Kincade declared. "There's a body – at least what used to be a body."

The way the wolf reacted to the human remains, the Marshal and Deputy were certain that Smoke had found Fred Wappler.

"He wasn't in the mine at all – he was panning for ore by the river and got swept away!" Sky pulled Smoke into his arms, and the two men praised and patted the wolf for his discovery of the missing miner.

Kincade stood and spoke to the boy. "Deputy Red Sky, would you please get my lasso and rain slicker from Gold digger. Let's pull old Fred from his watery grave."

"Yes Sir, Marshal Kincade!" replied Sky smartly. "Mrs. Wappler can now plan a long overdue funeral."

Tombstone Epitaph reporter, David Cook, used the word 'spectacular' again in his page one story, and even Kincade didn't think it was an exaggeration.

"You're strutting, my darling," Josephine chided him, showing her obvious pride in the man she loved so dearly.

"I'm embarrassed to say, you might be right," said Kincade. "You know, Josie, Smoke finding Fred Wappler was a miracle."

"I don't see Smoke strutting," she smiled.

"Oh, he's strutting all right. When I strut, it's a swagger. When the wolf struts, it's a waddle."

Thanks to the lavish praises of David Cook, the requests from the Tombstone citizens flooded Kincade's office daily. The Marshal and his Deputy read each plea for help, separating the requests into two piles. One pile was for those considered to be potentially solvable. The other stack, sadly, was used for fueling the potbelly stove that stood in the corner of the office. The Marshal responded to these refusals, expressing condolences that there was nothing that could be done considering the lack of concrete evidence. The incident had happened too long ago.

The men knew that for each of the cases and each of the victims there had been true loss and that the issues on the desk were serious in their own unique way. The end of each day found them both exhausted. But one particular request stopped Kincade midway through a wide yawn. He laughed out loud, which was a welcome relief.

"Sky," said Kincade, "here's one we have to handle. No way to put it off and certainly no time to waste. Seems that Pastor Elsea wants us to help him perform a shotgun wedding."

"A what?"

"Never mind," said Kincade, walking over to the stand near the door to retrieve his hat. "Let's just go over to the church."

"Smoke too?"

"If this case involves what I think it does," Kincade said with a twinkle in his eye, "I think there is already a wolf involved."

Patting Smoke on the head, the two left the office, giving the law dog permission to call it a day. Kincade felt good. His relationship with the boy, his good luck with Smoke, the cases solved, the praise of the townsfolk and the continued admiration and adoration of Josephine – yes, all was well.

Kincade's headaches had disappeared. "I'm glad they're over," Kincade smiled to himself as he saddled Gold Digger, "Whatever it was, it's gone."

14

Pastor Jedadiah Elsea was waiting for them in the church yard. He was a short man with a bald head and thick neck. He wore little horn-rimmed glasses that slid down his long nose. He shook their hands like they were members of his congregation. "Thank you for coming so promptly and at this discrete hour." He paused, looked around the immediate area in which the three stood, lowering his voice and asked, "I hope you've not told anyone about my letter."

"No," said Marshal Kincade. "But there wasn't much to tell. What is the problem, Pastor?"

"Come to my office where we won't be overheard, please." The Pastor turned and began to quickly walk up the steps to the church. Kincade looked at Sky and winked as a slight smile crossed his face.

Sky was at a total loss.

The three ended up in the cramped church office. After the Pastor brought in two chairs, the space was smaller still. The Pastor lit a kerosene lamp, sat behind his desk, and cleared his throat.

"I have a small congregation, as you probably know. We are a close knit group and little happens to a member that all the other members don't eventually know about." The Pastor inserted a white finger behind a very tight collar and wiggled it around in the hopes of increasing the amount of air he felt he needed to proceed with his story. "Would you like some coffee?"

"No, thank you, Pastor."

He cleared his throat again. "The lovely matron of our most prominent church family came to me, quite in confidence, without even her husband knowing of her visit." The Pastor gulped and Kincade could see a slight drop of perspiration form just above the man's upper lip. "She confessed that their only daughter has been frolicking with another member of our congregation."

"Frolicking?" asked Kincade.

"Yes," replied Pastor Elsea.

"I hope they're having a good time," offered Sky, which made the Pastor's upper lip twitch and glisten.

"Yes...uh,no! Uh, I really wouldn't know...but I suppose they are...uh, were...I...oh, dearie me!" and the Pastor ran out of breath.

Kincade decided to help the man regain the use of his lungs. "Oh, I see, Pastor Elsea. You mean that the other member with whom the young lady is frolicking is of the opposite sex."

Sky's eyebrows lifted in anticipation of what was sure to come next in the story.

The Pastor nodded enthusiastically, relieved at Kincade's understanding. "Yes, Marshal Kincade. She is now, unfortunately, in a family way."

Sky leaned over to Kincade and whispered, "Does that mean

she's pregnant?"

"Yes."

The boy's whisper became almost inaudible. "Well, why didn't he just say so?" Kincade had to check himself in order to keep a straight face.

"Excuse my Deputy for interrupting, Pastor. You were saying?"

"The girl will not say who the young fellow is because she knows her father will shoot him. She declares she will either kill herself or run away to join the circus in Saint Louis."

Kincade bit his lip, hoping that the brief pain would stifle the laugh he knew was brewing deep in his gut. The boy tapped Kincade on the shoulder, voice still as a whisper. "What would a pregnant girl do in a circus in Saint Louis?"

The Pastor continued. "The mother and I feel that a wedding would be much better than either of the alternatives...if only we knew who the groom should be."

Kincade couldn't help himself. "It's not me, I assure you, Pastor."

Sky vigorously shook his head as he pointed to Kincade. "I've been with him. Everyday. Nights too."

The Pastor turned crimson and cleared his throat once again. "Gentlemen, it never occurred to me that either of you were involved."

The boy quickly added. "Smoke too!" which nearly caused Kincade to fall off his chair.

"Go on," encouraged Kincade as he gently kicked Sky's foot.

"Marshal," Elsea continued, "I have requested your assistance in finding the girl's lover because I read that your Law Dog has talents that could prove useful – to everyone concerned."

"That's Smoke!" echoed Sky proudly.

"I must warn you, Pastor," said Kincade with a deliberately serious face, "the boy's dog has not had experience in this line of detective work."

"But he's very smart at anything he puts his mind to," Sky assured the man.

"Will you please do your best? For the sake of the family?"

"And for all the members of the congregation. When we solve the case, I'm sure they will all want to know what happened," added Sky, causing the Pastor to moan slightly.

Both the law officers frowned and rubbed their chins in a thoughtful gesture. "We'll need to have Smoke - that's our Law Dog - meet the girl to catch her scent. Then I should talk to the mother and get details as to where this frolicking probably took place. We'll need to inspect the spot."

"I understand." The Pastor cleared his throat nervously. "The matron and I were certain these steps would need to be taken. She has asked me to intervene in her behalf."

"What does that mean?" Sky asked Kincade.

"Means the Pastor's got all the answers right here and now."

"The mother has entrusted me with an article of the daughter's intimate apparel which should be sufficient for your dog's identification purposes." He pulled a bag from a drawer and handed it to Kincade.

The Marshal removed some unwashed bloomers with lace ruffles and pink ribbons. Snapping the two leggings to attention, Kincade and Sky inspected the fabric. "Perfect. And the location of these clandestine frolickings?"

"The mother is sure that they occurred in the barn at the rear of their property."

"And where might this property be?"

Pastor Elsea coughed and blushed. "You are familiar with the home of the Mayor?"

"John Clum's place?"

"It's the Mayor's daughter!" yelped Sky. Then seeing the Pastor's saucer-size eyeballs, the young Deputy dramatically reduced the volume of his voice and asked with professional calm, "Our young lady is the Mayor's child?"

"Yes," whimpered the Pastor.

"Mayor Clum has an extensive piece of property," said Kincade.

"At the far corner there is an old barn not easily seen from the road. A stairway leads to the loft. The matron found a rumpled saddle blanket on scattered hay. The lad's scent should be prominent."

"Looks like the mother had done some detective work herself," Sky whispered to Kincade.

The Marshal nodded seriously. "I can understand your desire for secrecy, Pastor."

"Thank you. Any plan is strictly between you two, the matron, and myself."

"Smoke too," reminded Sky.

"Yes, and your Law Dog too," said Pastor Elsea. "Not even the girl must know there is a ploy. She must believe any proposal of marriage from the young man is his idea without coercion."

Kincade looked at Sky. The boy thought for a minute and shrugged his shoulders. "I guess we could try, Marshal Kincade."

The Pastor nearly clapped his pudgy hands with eager relief at hearing the two men's decision to help. "Speed is of the essence," Pastor Elsea continued, "considering the girl's advancing condition."

"You mean she's starting to get fatter?" asked Sky. More twitching and perspiration on the Pastor's lip.

"What do you suggest for a time table?" Kincade tactfully continued.

"If you can do your investigation before day after tomorrow, we are having an ice cream social on the church grounds at three o'clock. My entire congregation will be there - undoubtedly including the boy we are trying to identify. Can you come?"

"Smoke too," Sky reminded him.

"Of course."

"We'll be here Friday," Kincade confirmed. "About three you say?"

"Yes, about three," nodded the Pastor. "Goodbye, and thank you Marshal Kincade and Deputy Sky."

They rode off on Gold Digger and Kinhuste. This case was definitely different from their regular duties. "Do you know who Dan

Cupid is, Sky?"

"No, Marshal, I don't."

"Well, you'll probably meet him soon, as it appears he's been shooting his arrows at a young lady and young man."

"Arrows? At the two lovers? Must be a renegade. What tribe is he from?"

"The Love Tribe," Kincade said as he and the boy returned home.

15

The day arrived. The grass in front of the church was trampled with happy, chatting, men and women and their rambunctious offspring.

"Marshal Kincade, we are so thrilled that you and your Deputies could come," the Mayor's wife cooed without a hint that she knew the real reason for their presence. "You're the town's celebrities, you know."

"Our pleasure, Mam. Is that your daughter over there?" She nodded. "Beautiful girl. What is her name?"

"Blossom."

Sky rolled his eyes.

"A well chosen name, Mrs. Clum."

Other townspeople approached the Marshal to congratulate him on the work the two were handling in Tombstone. Sky and Smoke wandered among the guests without much notice. The dog came to a lovely young girl in a pink flowered frock. He sniffed her sash and she pushed him away.

"Your dog has bad manners!" she told Sky in a huffy tone.

"I apologize, Miss. It's just that he thinks you're so pretty."

Blossom Clum fluttered her fan. "Have you noticed that too?"

"Excuse me, Miss. I believe the Marshal just called me." The boy and dog moved on to another group.

"Sky!" Liveryman Curley Smith called. "I want you to meet my family." The Deputy walked to Curley's side.

"My dear, this is the boy who found those stolen mares. Saved my butt - my life, he did. And this is our son Clement."

"How do you do, Mam," said Sky politely. "Clement." Sky shook hands with a lanky, pimply faced boy about nineteen. Smoke sniffed the boy's trousers and went crazy, jumping and circling the Smith family as he woofed in a low voice.

"What's the matter with your dog?" Mrs. Smith asked with concern.

"I'm sure he just recognizes your husband from our trip together to find the horses, Mam. Come along, Smoke. Nice to have seen you again, Mr. Smith." Sky grabbed the wolf by the tuff of hair at the back of his neck and they moved to Kincade.

"We can go now Marshal," whispered Sky. "Blossom's beau is the son of the livery stable man."

"You're sure?" asked Kincade.

"I myself have no idea," said Sky. "But Smoke is positive."

Kincade nodded. "I'll make our excuses to leave." Which he did, but on the way to their horses Kincade approached young Clement Smith. "I've a business deal to talk over with you, son. Could you come by my office tomorrow morning - say about ten?"

The boy brightened. "A business deal? Certainly, Marshal. I'll be there promptly at ten."

The next day Kincade and Sky waited for the arrival of Blossom's Romeo. Clement was punctual, dressed in his best suit with hair slicked down.

"I'm here, Marshal, just as you asked," he said brightly.

Kincade stood up from his desk, and began a measured walk from its edge, to the far wall, and back, stroking his chin thought-fully as he paced the plank floor. "Clement... I need your help."

"You do?!"

"Both Sky and I do," said Kincade.

"But not Smoke," added Sky. "He already has all the answers."

Kincade looked at Sky with a stern raise of the right eyebrow.

"I was saying," continued Kincade, "that all of us need your help in cracking a very tough case."

"Whatever I can do!" replied Clement, obviously excited about being involved with an investigation by a U.S. Marshal.

Kincade continued. "Speed, confidentiality and discretion are a must."

Clement eagerly nodded his head.

"Good!" said Kincade, returning to sit at his desk. "Clement, this crime took place in Bisbee, just south of here. There is this young boy... about your age... a good boy who has a girlfriend. And it seems that these two may have gotten themselves entwined."

"Like in a barn," added Sky.

"Now far be it from me, or Deputy Sky, to meddle in the affairs of these two young lovers...."

Clement's eyes began to widen.

"... but it seems, Clement, that the two young lovers are soon to have a third member join their romance..."

Clement began to nibble at the fingernails of his right hand.

"... and that the young lady's Mother is quite eager to see the two bring their third member into this world under the blessing of ordained wedlock."

Clement's armpits began to moisten.

"The boy may need to be encouraged to ask for the young lady's hand, and this boy must do the asking quickly..."

Clement's left eye began to twitch.

"... and Deputy Sky and I were unsure whether or not this certain young man realized that his physical consummation of affection within said barn was, in effect, a Legal Promise to the young lady that his intentions were honorable from start to finish..."

Clement wondered how he could get out of the door without the wolf stopping him.

"... and that if the young man were to decide not to ask for the young lady's hand in marriage, that would be a Breach of Promise and violation of Arizona Territorial Law, which would force

Deputy Sky and me to arrest the boy and throw him into our jail."

Clement swallowed.

"And so, Clement, Deputy Sky and I were wondering if you had any advice... any words of wisdom you think we ought to share with this young man as he makes his decision regarding matrimony?"

As Clement's sweat pooled in his bellybutton, Sky walked over to Kincade's desk, opened the lower left drawer, and withdrew Blossom's bloomers, holding them up to Clement as he smartly snapped the fabric to full attention. "Do you want to examine the evidence in this case?"

Clement had examined this particular piece of evidence quite thoroughly in the loft of her father's barn. He swallowed again, and squeaked.

"Perhaps you wish to think about it?"

Clement nodded his head faster than a woodpecker attacking a tree trunk.

Kincade turned to Sky who was peeking out from between the bloomer leggings. "What do you think, Deputy? Should we allow Clement to leave, and give some thought to our dilemma?"

"It's up to Smoke," said Sky.

Seeing that the wolf was fast asleep at the Deputy's feet, Sky said, "It looks like he's comfortable with that."

"Very well!" said Kincade, rising to his full six foot six inch height, walking over to tower over Clement Smith.

"Why don't you give it some serious thought, Clement" said

Kincade as he placed his very large and firm hand on the Romeo's shoulder. "We need to visit Bisbee by this afternoon, and enforce the law of the land."

Clement nodded his head and squeaked again as Marshal Kincade showed the boy to the door. "Thanks son. I'm sure you'll be able to help us."

"You sure you don't need the bloomers?" asked Sky as Clement tripped over the door's threshold.

Clement Smith stepped onto the boardwalk as Kincade filled the frame of the door opening. "Oh... and son..." said Kincade, freezing the boy's feet to the planks. "We need your ideas quickly. The father of the young lady involved is the Mayor of Bisbee. You can imagine how very eager he is to have this matter successfully resolved."

One last squeak from Clement Smith as he nodded to Kincade and Sky. The boy stepped into the dust and began his wobbly retreat up Allen Street.

Two weeks later the society column in the Tombstone Epitaph, also written by David Cook, carried the headline:

TWO PROMINENT FAMILIES JOINED BY WEDLOCK

Josephine began reading aloud at the breakfast table: "In a spectacular ceremony conducted by Pastor Jedadiah Elsea, the mayor of Tombstone, John Clum, gave the bride away....."

Sky interrupted, "Why doesn't it say that Smoke gave the groom way?"

Josephine and Kincade burst into laughter as they pictured the dog pointing out the Casanova with his sensitive nose at the ice cream social.

"That he did!" smiled Kincade. "That detail apparently escaped the journalistic pen of Mr. Cook, but yes, Smoke most certainly did give the groom away."

16

Kincade looked up from the big grey ledger in which he had finished writing CASE CLOSED next to the matter involving Mayor Clum and his newly wedded daughter. Sky and Smoke came walking through the door.

"Nice job with Blossom," said Kincade. The Mayor's wife is particularly pleased with you two. Were you able to go to the Post Office?"

"Yes, Sir. Nothing special except a new Wanted Poster."

Kincade made a final notation and closed the ledger. "Let's take a look." Sky handed him the large, brown poster and put the rest of the mail on the desk. Kincade read aloud:

"HORSE THIEVES WANTED IN ARIZONA,
TEXAS, AND NEW MEXICO"

There were pictures of two grisly looking men with their names underneath.

SPIKE JAMISON MAT MOON
ALSO WANTED BROTHER AND
KNOWN ASSOCIATE, CHARLIE MOON

IF RECOGNIZED NOTIFY ARIZONA
TERRITORY MARSHAL IN THE CAPITAL

Kincade handed the poster back. "Pin it on the bulletin board with the rest."

Sky took the paper and looked at it carefully. It suddenly struck him. "Marshal, I think these are the three men who tried to steal Curley's horses. We've got them right here in our jail!"

"What makes you think that?" asked Kincade. "The pictures are terrible."

"Yes, but I see those men every day and I know them."

"I didn't think you paid much attention to them."

"Smoke and I do," replied Sky. "We have to stand guard when old Teddy brings them food and takes away the thunder mugs to dump in the out house."

What Kincade thought he was hiding, Sky knew to be true. Kincade had avoided going back into the cells since the thieves had been locked up. Even looking at that trash had seemed to bring on the headaches.

"Look here," Sky pointed on the wanted poster. "See this face with the hair growing almost down to the eyebrows and the big fat lips? I know that's the man in the first cell."

Kincade nodded. "It does look like him."

"And the man in cell two. He's almost bald with a scar just above his left eye." Sky was right.

"I've heard them call the man in the third cell Charlie."

"Well, Deputy, you've certainly earned your pay again today." Kincade put his hand on the boy's shoulder, nodding his head. Sky smiled proudly. "I'd better get over to the Post Office and have Miss Sadie wire the Capital."

Kincade put on his black coat and hat and went into the street. The dull throb, gone since the success of finding the miner's body and Blossom's beau, suddenly reappeared behind Kincade's right eye. He winced, trying to massage the pain away.

Kincade enjoyed Miss Sadie, the spritely, little spinster who ran the telegraph and post office. She always had a cheery smile. "Mornin', Marshal. Your Deputy already picked up the mail. Somethin' I can do for you?"

"Yes, you can marry me." His eyes sparkled with his traditional teasing of this very pleasant woman.

"Oh, Marshal Kincade, Miss Josephine would have my head on a platter."

Kincade paused, bringing his right hand to his chin. "You know, Miss Sadie, she might at that. Tombstone would be in a real mess then. Who would sort the mail?!" Miss Sadie laughed, and blushed at the Marshal's attention.

"I need to send a telegram. If you'll give me the form I'll write it out."

"Here 'tis. Let me know when you're ready." Miss Sadie went back to sorting mail while Kincade pondered what to send. He finally settled on: Holding Spike Jamison, Mat and Charlie Moon in Tombstone jail STOP Awaiting Circuit Judge STOP Please advise STOP Marshal Kincade.

He handed it to Miss Sadie and she looked at it slowly. "These the boys who stole Curley Smith's horses?"

"Miss Sadie," Kincade winked, "You know you're not supposed to read personal mail."

She quickly went to her telegraph key. "Right you are, Marshal. I'm sending it as you stand there."

"Get the answer to me as soon as it comes in, okay?"

"Don't I always?" She blew him a kiss and blushed once again.

Kincade started slowly back to the Marshal's Office. His mind was racing and his head throbbing. Perhaps he should go talk with Josephine about the Wanted Poster. No, there were thoughts on his mind that even her sweet presence and understanding couldn't mitigate. He'd tell her everything after he got a reply to his telegram.

He didn't have to wait long. Late that same afternoon Miss Sadie bustled into the Marshal's Office waving a piece of paper. "I was right, wasn't I? It's those three dirty, rotten, scoundrels who tried to ruin Curley Smith."

"Miss Sadie! You read the return telegram!" Kincade said with eyes wide.

"I did not! I only copied what I heard. That's very different than reading what I write!"

Kincade had to laugh. "You have the integrity of an angel. Now let me have it."

She handed it to the Marshal and left in a fluster. He read aloud to Sky. "Capital Offenses not tried locally STOP Mob lynching too probable STOP Black Maria with guards arrive Tombstone Thursday to transport three to Capital."

Kincade handed Sky the telegram. "So we'll only have our guests until day after tomorrow."

"What's a Capital Offense, Marshal?"

"One that's punishable by death."

"You mean a man can lose his life for horse thieving?"

"Sky, what a frontier man loves first is his horse. Then his rifle. Then his dog. And then, last, he loves his wife."

"I understand the love of horse and of dog," said Sky, handing the telegram back to Kincade. "But those three would have been better off to steal Curley's wife."

Kincade laughed, in spite of his growing headache. "I don't know, Sky. Have you seen Curley's wife?"

Then they both laughed. "Marshal, what's a Black Maria?"

Kincade paused, thinking, and rubbing his fingers around on his right temple. "It's a very secure, iron jail cell on wheels. The only way to see out is through a slit window in the door."

"And that's what's coming to Tombstone! These men must have done more in their lives than we know about."

Kincade had to stop this conversation which had brought on the pain. He reached for his black coat and hat. "You want to eat something at The Josephine before we start our rounds?"

"Smoke too?"

Kincade locked the Marshal's Office before the three headed down the street.

It was a struggle to make the rounds look as normal as usual.

Kincade's mind was elsewhere. Sky and Smoke never suspected as they performed The Intimidation, even when the Marshal made an unusual suggestion. "Seems pretty quiet in Lower Tombstone. Let's call it a night."

"You in a hurry to get to The Josephine?"

"Aren't I always?"

Sky laughed. "Come on, Smoke. See you in the morning, Marshal."

But Kincade did not go to the saloon. Instead he backtracked through Lower Tombstone and climbed the dusty road that led up to Boot Hill. He found the grave of his best friend and stood over the tombstone.

"Hello Jesse," Kincade said. "I know you're in a pine box, six feet under, but I need to talk. You need to listen..."

Kincade squatted on his haunches and pulled up a milk weed that clung to the stone. "My horse thief prisoners are going to the Capital, Jesse. Their trial will be in a higher court than the municipal one I went to in Bisbee."

He twirled the weed between his hands, reducing it to shreds. "But, Jess, I know they'll pull a fast one – either escaping from incompetent guards, or bribing a jail keeper, or threatening a judge. They'll be back, getting away with the same damn things over and over again."

Kincade stood and stared at the stone with Jesse Keller carved on it. "That's not going to happen. I won't let it happen. Not again..."

Kincade turned away and looked at Wil Logan's grave so close by. "Logan, you and your kind have gotten away with enough." Kincade's headache was steadily throbbing.

"People are sick of it...."

The Other voice said, "AND YOU'RE GOING TO FIX IT."

17

Kincade lay awake most of the night thinking of what he would do to carry out his graveside threat. Or was it a promise?

The following day, after having the usual breakfast with Josephine, Sky, and Smoke, he went t o the General Store and bought a hundred and fifty foot length of hemp rope. Mr. Perkins didn't ask what it was for. Kincade threw a saddle blanket over the cumbersome coil and managed to get it into his house without anyone questioning its use.

He cut it into three even lengths and spent several hours fashioning a hangman's noose in one end of each. After cramming them into saddle bags, Kincade took them to Gold Digger's stall, leaving the heavy bags next to the palomino's saddle.

Kincade then headed to the livery stable where Curley Smith greeted him warmly. "What can I do for you, Marshal, or did you just drop by to chew the fat?"

"Just wondering, Curley," responded Kincade. "Do you still have those three horses that the thieves rode into town after we waylaid them?"

"Yeah, they're still here. Not very good horseflesh, however, and

I'd sure like to get rid of them. I'd trade all three for one good gelding."

"I might need them tomorrow, but there's no trade involved."

Curley looked perplexed. "What's up, Marshal?"

"A Territorial Marshal is coming to take my prisoners back to the Capital for trial. He's supposed to show up tomorrow, but I have no idea what time he'll arrive, how many will be coming with him, and what time they'll leave. So I thought I'd be ready in advance and get those boys off my hands as speedily as possible."

"So you want me to get those nags fit to ride, just in case?"

"You bet. You still got the tack and saddles?"

"Same as when we brought them in. You know Kincade, that was one of the highpoints in my life."

"Mine too, Curley. Can you get them ready?"

"I'll saddle them up and tie them to the hitching rail outside your office. Nobody's going to bother horses in front of Marshal Kincade's place."

"Thanks, Curley. That'll save me a trip coming here to get them." They shook hands. Though Kincade's plan was working perfectly, he felt guilty being less than honest with Curley.

When he got to the office Smoke was asleep under the big roll top, snoring softly. Sky was sitting in Kincade's swivel chair with his feet propped on the desk as he'd seen the Marshal do so often. He was reading the Farmer's Almanac and dropped it when he heard the door open.

"Sorry, Marshal. I shouldn't be reading your mail." He got up and started to move to a smaller chair pulled up to the big table.

Kincade smiled. Sky's respect and courtesy never waivered. He was so much like Jesse... the dead and buried Jesse. "Read all you want. That's a new magazine that's pretty interesting."

Sky looked relieved. "I'm going to be in and out today, Sky. Last time I rode Gold Digger he seemed to be favoring his right foot. I'm going to take him, see if I can help work it out. Will you and Smoke hold down the fort for an hour or so?" Kincade's head-throb was as consistent and rhythmic as the clock pendulum on the office wall.

"You bet!" Sky felt honored at the great responsibility Kincade had given him. "Wake up, you lazy Deputy," and Sky nudged the wolf with his toe. "Take your time, Marshal. Tombstone is in safe hands with us in charge."

In that very brief hour, Sky and Smoke proudly strode the boardwalks of Allen Street. They greeted shopkeepers and politely acknowledged the ladies who, after Sky passed, said to their companions, "They are so nice. Tombstone is lucky to have honorable men like Marshal Kincade and Deputy Sky."

Keeping track of the time, Sky and Smoke had returned to the Marshal's office minutes before Kincade rode up, tying Gold Digger to the rail outside. "Anything to report?" he asked Sky as he walked into the office.

"No, Sir," replied Sky with a note of concern in his voice. "Marshal, you look tired. You want me to put Digger in the stable?"

"No, I'm going to leave him at the livery overnight. The reason he's favoring his leg is because he's thrown a shoe. It's made the frog tender. Big Red's going to get at it before sunup in case I need Digger when the Territorial Marshal comes."

Sky looked at Kincade quizzically. Something was wrong. He could feel it, even though he wanted to deny it. The Marshal was lying. But why? He thought carefully before asking, "Should I saddle up Kinhuste too?"

"No need. It's getting dark. Let's get to our rounds." Kincade walked over to the office door that led to the cell area, opened it, took two steps inside, and stopped. Sky waited as the Marshal stood absolutely motionless for over a minute. He was looking at the three horse thieves, dead-on. They cowered under Kincade's withering stare. No one spoke.

Finally, Kincade backed up the two paces, reached down to the cellblock latch, and softly closed the door in their terrified faces. He turned to Sky.

In a nearly inaudible voice, Kincade looked at Sky and said "Let's go."

As the two lawmen and one law dog left the office, the jailed thieves heard the front door close. They were alone, again. But none of the three had yet to find his voice.

Each of the bandits knew that they had just seen the face of death.

18

A midnight moon appeared from behind slowly moving clouds, only to disappear – just as suddenly - behind black wafts as though suffocated. Sky could barely make out the Marshal's face. What he did see troubled him. Something was definitely wrong.

Kincade hadn't said more than a half dozen words to Sky. Kincade's Intimidation of Lower Tombstone's patrons and inhabitants took on a darker shade of fear. Sky could be wrong, but this night's visits to the sinkholes of town approached terrorization.

"Maybe it's his headache," thought Sky to himself. "Maybe Kincade just doesn't feel well..."

The three completed their rounds around midnight. "Goodnight Marshal," said Sky. A pause. "Is there anything else you need from us?"

"No."

"You sure you're okay?" asked Sky.

"Yes. Goodnight Sky. You too, Smoke." Kincade watched them enter the stable.

Now alone, the ache behind Kincade's right eye transformed from a steady throb into a pounding beat....a strumming anger straining to break free. It was not his deterrent, but rather his driving force.

Kincade walked down to the blacksmith shop where Gold Digger stood waiting. He led the stallion to the railing outside the Marshal's office, tying him next to the three saddled horses left there earlier by Curley.

He looked up and down the street. All was quiet. He stepped up and onto the boardwalk. Reaching into the right pocket of his frock coat, Kincade withdrew a ring of keys, fitting one into the locked door of his office, and slid inside.

What moonlight there was became even dimmer as it filtered through dusty windows. With the hush of a stalking cougar, Kincade passed the pot belly stove, the big table with the chairs around it, and stopped at his desk. He kneeled down and removed a false front board below the lowest right-hand drawer. Reaching in required no light. He knew exactly what lay waiting: a wicked Bowie knife with a handle forever stained by dried blood... a Bowie knife drenched with hideous memories... Wil Logan's Bowie knife, taken by Kincade from the floor of The Josephine Saloon the night Logan and Jesse Keller died.

Was that Kincade's dried blood on the blade? Probably not. Logan had mutilated too many people in the years since.

Kincade touched the scar on his neck – a lifetime reminder of the knife fight he'd had with Logan when they were kids. Kincade would have died that day, had Jesse not carried him to the doctor.

After the last stitch, Jesse asked the doc to slash his own arm so that he and Kincade could mix their blood together - becoming blood brothers – for ever and ever.

Kincade ran his callused thumb carefully across the blade. Still as sharp as ever. He slipped it under his frock coat and behind the gunbelt at the small of his back.

Replacing the board, Kincade rose. Fifteen paces across the room and Kincade stood at the cellblock door. He selected another key from the ring and unlocked the door to the jail.

The stink of dangerous men, sweat and urine wafted on the snores of the three caged horse thieves. In anticipation of what was about to happen, Kincade did not recoil from the disgusting odor, but seemed to drink in the nearly nauseating stench of these three very bad men. The Other Voice was only a chuckle, but it filled Kincade's ears.

Kincade reached his left hand up to the nail just inside the door, and removed the jailer's key. Moving to the third cell, then the second, and finally to leader, Spike Jamison's. Kincade unlocked each of the barred doors, their newly greased hinges assuring that all remained asleep.

Jamison lay splayed on his back, mouth slack, snoring like the filthy hog he was. Kincade moved into his cell and stood tall above this human filth. From inside his coat Kincade withdrew three dirty rags and several pieces of latigo. Keeping one rag and two strips of leather, the Marshal dropped the others to the floor.

Kincade then leaned down to within a breath of Jamison's right ear and barely whispered, "Get up you scum sucking pig."

The outlaw's eyes fluttered open. "Whaa?..."

At that split instant, Kincade rammed the rag inside his fat-lipped mouth. Jamison fully awakened with a start, but it was too late. Kincade's years of being a cowpuncher enabled his hands to move like lightning, binding Jamison's hands in seconds. Jerking the second piece of leather across Jamison's mouth, Kincade pulled the loose ends around his skull, knotting the ends together so fiercely that the edges of the bandit's mouth began bleeding.

Jamison's shocked eyes looked into Kincade's. But the Marshal seemed deadly calm, looking back at the outlaw. With his right index finger barely touching his lips, Kincade whispered "Shussh…"

The Marshal grabbed a fistful of Jamison's greasy hair and pulled the bandit to his feet. He turned the thief's body to face the other two men still sleeping soundly.

With his remaining hand, Kincade withdrew the blood-stained Bowie knife from beneath his coat. He very slowly moved the blade to where Jamison could get a good long look at its razor-sharp edge as it caught the moonlight spilling through the cell's barred window.

Gagging at the rag and riddled with fear, Jamison cried out, "Mmmmuh! Arguumuh!" The muffled screams were just enough to wake the other two thieves, who quickly sat bolt upright, rubbing their eyes in disbelief of what they saw. Seeing their leader, the two sprang to their feet and froze.

Kincade had moved the tip of the Bowie knife to within a hair of Jamison's left eye. Softly yet powerfully, the Other Voice spoke aloud to the Moon brothers. "MAKE ANOTHER MOVE AND I'LL BURY THIS KNIFE IN SPIKE'S BRAIN."

With those eleven words, the pounding headache fully overpowered a good man named Kincade.

19

Horse thieves, Matt and Charlie Moon, simply could not believe their eyes. An absolute terror oozed from Spike Jamison like puss.

Listening to directions by the Other Voice, Kincade whispered, "Matt, come here..."

Charlie started to move towards the open cell door as his brother Matt obeyed. "Not you Charlie," said Kincade. "Not unless you want to see this blade buried in Spike's eye." And Charlie stopped.

Matt walked out, and then to the opening of Jamison's cell. Kincade spoke again, "Get on your belly and crawl over here." Matt did.

"Now you Charlie," Kincade said as the end of the Bowie knife danced in front of Jamison's face. And Charlie did.

"Do to your brother what I've done to Jamison." Charlie nodded, stuffing the rag in his brother's mouth, binding it and Matt's hands with the latigo at Kincade's feet.

"Boys, we're gonna take a little ride," Kincade said in a hushed voice. "Just the four of us. Charlie, I like you. So you're gonna help me get your friends all saddled up. And then I'll help you,

Charlie. The horses are just outside.

"Oh, and Charlie," Kincade added. "It's awful dark tonight. Any distraction and I'm afraid I might lose my footing. Maybe slip. Charlie, you gotta make sure that doesn't happen. Because my hand might jerk this knife blade into Spike's head. Tryin' to catch my balance, why your brother Matt might get caught in the middle and be cut to ribbons.

"Charlie, how do you think Spike and your brother would feel about that?" Kincade waited for his response. The fear in Charlie's eyes was response enough.

"Good," whispered Kincade. "Let's go..."

About a quarter mile from the wooden gate of Boot Hill, down an arroyo and next to a creek, there stood a large cottonwood. The tree had been there for as long as anyone could remember. Its branches were thick and strong, fed by cool waters that ran through its spidery roots. One branch in particular extended far from the trunk. Thick, healthy, and capable of supporting tremendous amounts of weight. Dead weight.

This large cottonwood was Tombstone's Hanging Tree. The lives of countless outlaws, thieves and cheats had been snuffed here before taking up final residence with others of their kind beneath the weeds of Boot Hill.

Four dark men rode slowly past the graveyard beneath the light of a masked moon. Three of the four were thrown over their saddles, securely lashed down. The fourth, the Marshal of Tombstone, held the reins of the three horses and bound riders. Together, they rode down Boot Hill's windblown flank, and into the arroyo of Tombstone's Hanging Tree.

Kincade stopped the horses beneath the largest branch of the infamous tree. The three bandits strained their necks to look up.

Within seconds they understood the horrible fate about to crash down upon them. The filthy rags stuffed into their mouths stifled their dreadful moans and screams.

Kincade seemed oblivious. The pounding headache allowing nothing except the sound of the Other Voice which had taken over his every move, becoming his ears and eyes.

Swinging off Gold Digger, Kincade walked to a creek-side thicket. Hidden there were the three hangman's ropes, brought by Kincade earlier. The Marshal slowly slipped a noose over the heads of Spike Jamison, Matt and Charlie Moon. While they choked and squirmed, he released the latigo that lashed them to the saddles, but kept the leather binding their hands secure. Then, with the skillful toss of the remaining coils, one by one the three ropes snaked up and over the thick branch that loomed over the struggling thieves.

Only the wind watched as Kincade picked up the three ends of rope resting on the ground. He walked to Gold Digger who stood patiently. The stallion was a trained cutting horse and he knew what was to come next.

Kincade wrapped the ropes around the saddle horn and tested the tautness. Then he went back to the three men who had been following Kincade's every move. Their muffled voices pleaded. All three begged for mercy. But their howls were drowned out by the all-consuming, all-powerful pounding inside Kincade's brain.

Not once during all this time had Kincade spoken. But the time had come. Kincade stood before the three thieves and spoke. "You know what the law of the West is. Horse thief trash are hanged by the neck until their feet stop jerking and their tongues turn blue. You boys have any last words before your trip to Hell?"

All three were far beyond fear. Jamison, their leader and most despicable of them all, lost control and urinated down his saddle's skirts in total terror of what was about to happen.

"I thought not," said Kincade.

The Marshal moved back to Gold Digger. He removed a whip from his saddle. "So long, you thieving bastards!" With blurring speed, the whip cracked across the rumps of the three horses which bolted from beneath the wild-eyed bandits.

The three ropes sizzled over the bark of the large branch as the outlaws swung free and began their fall towards the ground. Each of them knew that within the next second, each noose would catch their throats, crushing cartilage and exploding their eyes into globs of thick liquid dripping down their cheeks.

Each fell for what seemed like an eternity. But the three did not swing. They slammed into the ground as the lengths of rope snaked up and over the branch, crashing down upon them like the strike of a diamondback rattler.

The dust settled. The air went as still as a tomb. Kincade stood there, looking through ferocious eyes at the three dazed bandits all fighting to regain their breath. He had deliberately secured the ropes to Gold Digger's saddle so that the least jerk would release the knots.

"Listen to me and listen good. Sunup today, a Territorial Marshal comes to Tombstone. He'll take you boys to the Capital, where you'll get a fair trial.

"I swear by the light of this moon, that if any of you try to bribe that judge, if even one of you lying scum gets off, I swear I'll track you down. I'll bring you back here where you'll hang by your necks. I swear on my brother's grave!"

Another pause from Kincade as the pending horror of Kincade's promise sank into the souls like quicksand. Then, in a deliberate whisper, Kincade said, "You hear me?"

They did.

Before the moon finally sank into the jagged black silhouette of the western horizon, Spike Jamison, Mat and Charlie Moon were back on the cots of their cells. No longer bound. No longer gagged. Marshal Kincade stood at the entrance of the cellblock and hung the jailer's key on the nail near the door. He turned to the three men. "Not a word of tonight's episode to anyone, do you understand me?"

The three did. They would never say a word. Not ever. The three stared into a cobwebbed ceiling, stunned by their nocturnal journey to the very gates of death. So they would remain, absolutely petrified by fear, as they awaited the Territorial Marshal and his Black Maria.

Kincade closed the cellblock door and walked to his office desk. He kneeled down, removed the false front board and returned Logan's blood-stained Bowie knife to its hiding place.

Walking out to Gold Digger, Kincade stepped up into the saddle to make one more stop that night.

Up the dark lonely road to Boot Hill. Through its worn wooden gate.

Kincade knelt on Jesse Keller's grave and in a whisper only a ghost could hear, he said, "I had to put fear into those horse thieves, Jess. What happened in that Bisbee courtroom just wasn't right. That kind of justice is no justice at all..."

Kincade could hear the Other Voice inside his head, laughing into the darkness. Then it whispered to Kincade, "DON'T TELL JOSEPHINE WHAT YOU'VE DONE."

Kincade crossed his arms on Jesse's tombstone, and rested his head. He stayed there until the first light of dawn began to appear from the east.

He stayed thus until the pounding in his head subsided and the demonic, all-powerful, all-consuming Other Voice disappeared.

20

Josephine arrived at the train station just moments after the hissing locomotive stopped its long line of passenger and boxcars. Accompanying Josephine were two of her strongest employees, Craig Hess and his son Dean. She flipped through a sheaf of papers as she scanned the tracks. "Craig, all three crates with the hotel and saloon supplies I ordered from Kansas City a month ago should be on this train." She looked up and down the tracks to see where they might be unloading cargo.

"What about the surrey, Miss Josephine?"

She flipped through more papers. "Yes, it says right here that all were to be loaded on the same flatcar."

"You're going to be the talk of the town when you go riding around in your own little surrey with your name right on the side." Craig laughed.

"She's already the talk of the town," his son Dean added. "Folk's just say, "Miss Josephine's done it again!"

Josephine blushed. "That's enough gentlemen. Mr. Albert Bilicke was very kind to send it to me, but I'll not ride in it at all if people start to think I'm showing off." She returned to scanning the tracks. "Let's just find that flatcar and get everything to the hotel."

She was suddenly attacked from behind, grabbed around the waist in an almost vice-like hug. "Oh, Miss Josephine! What a wonderful, wonderful surprise that you would meet us! How did you know we were coming?"

Josephine loosened the arms which held her and turned. There before her, jumping up and down with delight, was a lovely little girl. Josephine could hardly believe her astonished eyes. There, on the train platform, stood Melissa Wilcox, older, taller, more beautiful than ever – but it was Melissa, for sure.

What a change from the first time Josephine had seen Melissa. Then she had been pinned by the throat against the chest of Wil Logan as he used her as a shield against his twin brother and mortal enemy. She had been ragged and dirty, thin and trembling. That day so long ago, tears were pouring down her cheeks as she cried out to Kincade, "Don't shoot me mister. Please don't shoot me." Logan had laughed his beastly roar. "Why not shoot me now, Kincade? Of course I might just dodge a bit and you'd hit Melissa here." Josephine remembered each moment of that horrible night.

When Kincade's lifelong friend, Jesse Keller, sacrificed his own life that night to kill Wil Logan, Melissa had been dropped to the floor. Josephine had rushed to her side and folded her arms around the terrified child. For many weeks after this traumatic experience, Josephine and Kincade had cared for and loved and comforted the little six-year old until she could be reunited with her father in Julesburg.

Josephine remembered the day Melissa had left Tombstone, headed home to Colorado... remembered how happy and how sad she, Kincade and the little girl had been saying goodbye to one another.

Now here she was at the train depot in Tombstone. "My darling child! What are you doing here?! What a surprise! I had no idea you were coming to see me. Look at you – a grown up little lady!" Her skin was like cream, her golden curls falling to her shoulders in playful cascades, her big blue eyes sparkling with laughter. Her gingham dress was simple but spotless and obviously made by loving hands.

"I'm going on eleven, you know." She flashed that brilliant smile which had won the hearts of everyone - except Wil Logan - for her entire life. "Come, hurry, and meet my Papa and Second Mama." She pulled Josephine by the hand in the opposite direction from the box cars, and called loudly to her parents.

Josephine beckoned to the men who had come to the station and were wondering who this excited child could be. "Craig, please locate the shipment for me." She handed him the order papers. "Dean, hire a cart to take the boxes to the hotel."

"What about your surrey, Miss Josephine?"

"Just leave it here and I'll get Curley at the livery to bring it around later." Both men nodded. "Thank you. I'll be along shortly," and she looked ahead to see who Melissa was waving to.

"Papa, Mama! This is Miss Josephine here to meet us. I told you she's wonderful!"

Josephine held out her hand to the tall, middle-aged man. He shook it and then Josephine embraced the smiling woman at his side. "You must be Cissy," smiled Josie. "I simply cannot tell you how I've dreamed of one day meeting you. And now, here you are!" Cissy Dye Wilcox was petite, the top of her hair barely reaching her husband's shoulder. Kincade had told Josephine about what happened on the rim of the Dry Head Canyon years before, and the enormous inner strength of young Cissy Dye. Kincade was right.

"Melissa is mistaken about my knowing you were coming. If I had known I would have been looking everywhere for you instead of searching for my shipment from Kansas City. Jethro, Cissy, and my sweet Melissa! Welcome to Tombstone! Please tell me you're staying long!"

"Oh, yes," Melissa chimed in. "We're going to live here!"

Jethro smiled at his very excited daughter. "It's true Miss Josephine. We hope to. Melissa has talked of you and Kincade constantly for years. Her thrill at finally seeing you again has revealed the dream all three of us now share."

Josephine and Melissa hugged one another with total abandon. "I am absolutely delighted to hear of your plans. And to finally meet the two of you. Where are you staying?"

"Can you recommend a boarding house?" Cissy gently squeezed her husband's hand and their eyes briefly met. Slightly embarrassed, Jethro added, "Perhaps one that isn't too expensive."

"Nonsense, my dearest Jethro and Cissy. You will be my guests at The Cosmopolitan Hotel for as long as you wish to stay. Nothing could please me more." Josephine called to the older of the two men loading her boxes. "Craig, please get the luggage of the Wilcox family and direct them to the hotel. Tell Stephen they are to be my guests in the Columbine Suite and in the dining room as well."

Cissy Wilcox's mouth flew open. "Miss Josephine, that's very kind of you but..."

"Cissy, of all the people in this world, I wish to have your family as my guests. After all, you are the parents of my darling Melissa whom I have thought of a thousand times. I would not have you stay anywhere else. Kincade will be so happy to see all of you!"

"Do you think Kincade will remember me?" Melissa asked shyly and she blushed.

"How could he possibly forget his little angel! I can hardly wait to let him know you're here. But that must come later. Please settle into your rooms and get some rest. You've had a long train ride. Tomorrow morning, please join me for breakfast at The Josephine. Say 8:15. Will that do?"

Melissa gave her a big hug. "Will Kincade be there too?" Her blush was even deeper.

Josephine's blue eyes danced at Melissa's question and obvious affection for Kincade. "Let's surprise him, shall we? He won't believe his eyes at how you've grown so beautiful." She kissed Melissa's cheek and held out her two hands to Jethro and Cissy. "Until breakfast then?" They smiled and nodded.

Cissy ventured one last word. "Everything Melissa has said about you is true. Thank you, Miss Josephine."

When Kincade, Sky, and Smoke arrived for their usual a little after eight, they knew that something was up. Josephine usually floated down the stairs from her suite in a silky and cool dressing gown. Now she was spruced up for the day in a black and white striped suit of faille with a red rose in her long hair. She was already seated at their table.

"Going somewhere, my darling?" Kincade asked as he pulled out the chair next to her and called to the kitchen, "The usual for Sky and me."

"Smoke too," the boy added as he sat in his usual place across from them and the wolf settled under the table near his chair.

Josephine seemed excited and more than a little mischievous, looking constantly at the front door. "I'm not going anywhere, but someone's coming." And she smiled coyly at the very curious Kincade.

"Am I supposed to guess who?"

"You'd never guess – not in a thousand years."

"Will you give me a hint?"

"She's beautiful and she's possibly in love with you."

"But you're already here, Miss Josephine." Sky looked at Kincade with a grin. "Who else could be beautiful and in love with the Marshal?"

Kincade leaned over to give Josie a quick kiss on the cheek. "He's right, you know. You're the love of this cowboy's life, Josie."

She laughed. "Now you have two loves. And I may feel a little jealous when you see her." There was a knock at the front door. "She's here! Kincade, close your eyes until I say to open them." Josephine left the table.

But there was no time for Kincade to open his eyes before a bounding bundle of joy ran to him and threw her arms around his neck. "Kincade, it's me! Melissa all the way from Julesburg! Are you surprised?"

Kincade could not speak, so completely astonished at seeing the nearly-grown and absolutely beautiful Melissa Wilcox, who now smothered his face with kisses. He couldn't ever remember a surprise as glorious and as unexpected as this. "You were right, Josephine. The two loves of my life are here, together, and I... well... Melissa! Hop onto my lap, little darling, and let me look at you."

Melissa giggled delightfully and jumped onto Kincade's lap. "See Papa, Mama. Didn't I tell you he is handsome?"

Jethro and Cissy stood proudly to one side as their daughter took over center stage. "Mr. Kincade, I'm Jethro Wi..." Cissy chimed in, squeezing her husband's arm with obvious and deep affection. "It's just 'Kincade', Jethro. No Mister."

Kincade gently lowered Melissa to the floor, continuing to hold her left hand and stood in respect to the woman who had, indeed, saved him from death. "You remembered," Kincade said to the lovely woman standing with her small hand in Jethro's big one. What a great change from the bedraggled woman he had met standing outside a soddy when he was a wandering cowboy.

"Kincade... I'm Jethro Wilcox." He extended his hand and Kincade took it in a firm clasp.

"This is a great day for me, Mr. Wilcox," smiled Kincade.

"It's just 'Jethro', Kincade. No Mister," said Cissy, smiling at the two men who had changed her life forever, each in their own way.

Josephine laughed at Cissy's quick wit, appreciating her affection for both Kincade and her husband Jethro. Josie immediately recognized the depth of heart and the sensitive soul of Cissy Wilcox.

Kincade nodded at Cissy's correction and continued, "I've wondered many times about you, Mr..., I mean Jethro. Meeting you now is an unexpected and tremendous joy. Please sit down."

"Thank you," said Jethro. "And may I introduce you, please, to my wife Cissy."

"Yes, we've met before," responded Kincade, taking Cissy's hand and kissing it gently in respect. "I'm so happy to see you again, Mrs. Wilcox... Cissy." He pulled out the chair next to her husband, realizing that Cissy had never revealed to her husband what happened to her after she left Jethro standing on the porch of his Julesburg home so many years ago.

"When did you and Cissy meet before?" Jethro looked puzzled. "I've not heard that story, although Melissa has told me the saga of the shooting at The Josephine over and over again."

What could Kincade say? How should he start? It was a long story about a long time ago. He could still smell the warm bread floating from the soddy where Cissy was being held a virtual prisoner by a savage Apache. He could still see the frightened longing in her eyes as he rode away. But most vividly he remembered that she had followed him.

As the Apache was on the verge of splitting Kincade's skull with a tomahawk, Cissy had summoned her trained eagle with a shrill whistle. The bird had swooped down from nowhere and buried his talons in the eyes of the Indian who screamed and clawed at the winged attacker. Gold Digger had then pushed the blinded savage into the abyss of Dry Head Canyon far below.

"You going back to the soddy?" he had asked her back then.

"Nothin' I want there," she had responded. "...Julesburg. I hope to find my little girl's grave there." She had ridden away, and he had seen her new pride and self confidence.

Kincade now looked across the breakfast table to the woman who had saved his life, and he saw love and security pouring out of her eyes as she looked at her husband seated beside her. Jethro tenderly held her hand, curious as he waited for an answer to his question. "When did you two meet before?"

Kincade smiled at them both. "It's a long story with a very happy ending, if my eyes judge you two correctly. Save the telling for a cold, winter evening." He turned to Cissy. "Did you find your little girl Lena's grave?"

She smiled up at Jethro. "Yes, Jethro took me to Lena's graveside. She is with the angels now."

Josephine knew without a doubt that Cissy and Jethro had a love for one another like she and Kincade shared. "Is that when you and Jethro first met, Cissy?" asked Josephine.

"No." She shook her head with a sigh. "I was with a wagon train, travelin' to California. We tried to cross the Platte River at flood stage but the wagon got overturned and my little Lena was washed away. The men couldn't find her body, and the train had to move on. So I stopped by Mr. Wilcox..." she smiled shyly, "By Jethro's homestead to see if he'd be on the lookout for her body. I asked him to send me a lock of her hair and a piece of her calico dress."

"And he did?" Josephine asked with a lump in her throat, trying to imagine a mother's anguish at the loss of her little girl.

"He found her little body and buried her, but I never got the curl and dress."

Jethro continued to tell his wife's story, for he could see that Cissy had difficulty, even now, with recounting her ordeal. "Her husband, Mr. Dye, was also drowned, but she went on with her five boys. Within a few days the wagon train was attacked by Indians and all were killed except for my dear Cissy. She was kidnapped by a brave who made her his...." Jethro put his arms around Cissy's shoulders. "Anyhow, when she finally escaped and came to Julesburg to find her daughter's grave, we met again."

"And Papa married her just so I'd have a second Mama after that awful Wil Logan killed my first one," Melissa piped up.

Cissy lovingly patted the little girl's head. "If my little Lena had lived I would have wanted her to be exactly like you."

While Sky understood their excitement, he felt invisible being left out of the conversation. He cleared his throat and kicked Kincade's leg under the table. Kincade turned to Sky who wiggled his eyebrows.

"I'm sorry, Sky." He turned to the guests. "I apologize for my lack of manners, but I was so taken by surprise that I didn't introduce you to my First Deputy. This is Sky, and my Second Deputy is under the table."

Melissa squatted on her ankles to view just who had been relegated to such a lowly spot at breakfast. She giggled with delight when she saw it was a large, grey animal whose tail began wagging at seeing the girl's gleeful face.

"It's a dog and he's huge!" She inched closer. "Hello, big fellow!"

Sky wondered if he should say that Smoke was really a wolf and didn't take to strangers right off the bat. But before Sky could speak, Melissa said "I'm Melissa Wilcox, and I'm going on eleven!"

Smoke came out from under the table and poked his nose to Melissa's, smiled his big fang grin and licked her face top to bottom.

"I love him!" Melissa squealed, and she put her arms around his neck. Smoke loved her back with another big wet lick on her cheek. Sky sat there amazed. "Who is this child michamunga working magic on Smoke? He never acts like that around strangers!"

"What's his name?" Melissa turned to Sky. Her hair was the color of Josephine's. Her eyes as blue. Her smile as radiant. She was like a child Josephine.

"Smoke.... it's, uh, Smoke," Sky stuttered. "He's the Marshal's Deputy just like me."

Melissa looked them both over carefully. "Tombstone must feel very safe with three brave officers of the law like you!"

She was only a child. Why did Sky feel a tightening in his stomach? Perhaps he just needed to eat breakfast which was, at that moment, being put before him.

"Please order whatever you'd like," Josephine was saying to Jethro and Cissy. "Flapjacks, biscuits and gravy, steak and eggs – we serve them all."

"Whatever you're having will be fine," Jethro looked at Kincade's plate.

"Whatever you'll be having, Miss Josephine, will be okay with me." Cissy was sure that the lady would not order the mounds of food set before the men.

Soon all were eating including Smoke under the table with his morning steak. The conversation was light - about the climate of Arizona Territory, the growth of Tombstone, the success of cattle and silver enterprises in the area.

When a second cup of coffee had been finished, Sky looked at Cissy and then at Jethro. "Will you allow me to show your young lady our town of Tombstone while you old folks talk about whatever serious stuff you're going to talk about?" Josephine laughed.

"Since when are we old folks?" Kincade asked.

"Am I your Deputy, or not? I read you like a book."

Everyone laughed. Jethro nodded his head. "Fine with me," and he looked questioningly at Cissy. She nodded. "Fine with us both, Deputy Sky."

"Then come along, Melissa," Sky pulled out her chair and took her hand. "You and I will tour the town."

"Smoke too?" Melissa innocently asked, and Kincade and Josephine fell into a fit of laughter.

When Sky had closed the door behind them, Josephine said to Jethro and Cissy, "You two have worked a miracle. I thought she would never be able to overcome the horrific time when Wil Logan and his men held her hostage."

They both smiled and Cissy took Josephine's hand. "It was the care and security the two of you gave her when she was finally free of him."

Jethro added, "There are still a few things she can't tolerate, like being totally covered up. Wil Logan had her carried from one camp to the next tied inside a gunny sack, you know."

Cissy continued. "And she has to have lots of jam on bread and won't drink plain water. We add lemon juice. Bread and water was all she was fed for so long."

"Spunky, little darling," Kincade said. Then he folded his napkin and came to the question that had been troubling him all during breakfast. "So why are you here in Tombstone? It's not the vacation spot of the world."

"We have been talking of moving to a warmer climate. Colorado's cold winters and the hard work of heating our house with a wood stove are driving us to look somewhere else," Jethro explained.

"He won't admit it," Cissy added with a laugh, "but old age is creeping up on him."

"It's not my age, it's my rheumatism."

"Time takes its toll on all of us," Kincade assured him. "But why Tombstone?"

"That was Melissa's idea, since of course we included her in our discussions. The only thing she remembers about this town is that two people whom she loves dearly would be here."

Kincade took Josephine's hand. "And we love her back. Do you have plans?"

Jethro heaved a sigh. "I've never lived in a town, only on a homestead. But we feel Melissa should start attending a school with other children."

"Jethro has been teaching her - and me - at home," Cissy interrupted.

He smiled and continued. "Also, Cissy feels she could become a good midwife to bring in more money. She might need to live closer to town. Do you have a midwife here?"

"No, only a doctor," Kincade told him. "I'm sure he'd be delighted with some help with our ever growing population."

"Have you had any training – any experience?" Josephine asked.

"No training but lots of experience." Her smile was a little sad. "I birthed six boys and little Lena – one baby a year from the time I was thirteen. The last one was born dead."

"I'm sorry," Josephine said, realizing that Melissa was nearly the age when Cissy had birthed her first child.

"Don't matter. It was just another boy anyhow. I had a midwife and I think I could have done it all by myself. I'd be a better midwife than she was."

"Where are your sons, Cissy?" Josephine wanted to know.

"The Indians killed them – killed everybody but me. Scalped 'um too."

All at the table fell silent.

Kincade knew it was time to change the subject. "Well, Jethro – Cissy - I'll show you around this afternoon and you can judge for yourselves if Tombstone is right for you."

The tension was broken and Jethro and Cissy both laughed. "Melissa has already made that decision," her Papa said. "But we will appreciate your giving us some of your time..."

"...and your advice too," her Mama added.

So they talked of homestead properties, and job opportunities within the town, schools and churches, banks and businesses. Time passed swiftly.

When Sky, Melissa and Smoke returned, her face was aglow. "He took me everywhere," she exclaimed. "To the General Store where he bought me a peppermint stick candy, and to the livery stable where he put me on a nice gentle pony, and to the school house where I got to ring the bell." She was breathless.

"Everyone in town knows Sky. They'd tip their hats and say 'Mornin' Deputy.' They even said 'Mornin' Law Dog' to Smoke. Isn't that wonderful! I told Sky we are going to move to Tombstone. We are, aren't we?" she added anxiously.

"It's a possibility," Jethro said.

"Then we will see lots of each other," Melissa reached out for Sky's hand and he looked fondly at the little girl. Then Sky turned to Jethro. "What are your plans, Sir?"

"Haven't made any definite ones. Cissy thinks she'd like to be a midwife. Do you know what that is?"

"I do. My mother was a healer – the pejuta winyan of our tribe.

She knew how to treat with over 300 herbs and roots, flowers, minerals and muds. I learned about many things from her, including the birth of babies."

"You probably know more than I do," Cissy said shyly.

"Delivering babies was the job of women, getting women pregnant was the job of men."

"Sky!" Josephine said. "Our new friends may need a few days to understand your sense of humor."

"I beg your pardon, Mr. and Mrs. Wilcox. I didn't mean to offend."

"No offense taken by us," Jethro chuckled. "Besides, I think you may be right." Cissy poked her husband in the arm.

"Melissa might not have understood your remark," said Cissy, ruffling the girl's hair and affectionately pulling her close to her side. "She's only ten."

The child wiggled loose and stood as tall as she could. "I'll be eleven by the time we move to Tombstone, Sky."

He laughed and tussled her curls. "Then I shall hold you in my heart until you return."

Jethro smiled with pleasure at everyone's enthusiasm. He patted Cissy's hand. "It seems, my dear that the decision is made – no ifs, ands, or buts."

Kincade hired a buggy from the livery and for the next few days he drove Jethro and Cissy around the town and surrounding areas. He introduced them to people, including Doctor Thomas Saint John who was pleased at Cissy's suggestion to become a midwife.

They met the school marm who had already let Melissa ring the school bell on her first day in Tombstone. "How could I resist granting that sweet child anything," she told her proud parents. "I hope she'll be one of my pupils very soon."

While her parents were taken by Kincade, Melissa stayed with Josephine, helping around the hotel lobby and dining room. She acted very grown up and this pleased and amused Josie. Sky stayed at the Marshal's Office while Kincade spent time with Jethro and Cissy.

One quiet morning, Sky locked up the Marshal's office, deciding to take Melissa riding on Kinhuste. For safety, he put a saddle on the paint. Asking for Jethro's permission, who enthusiastically and wholeheartedly gave it, Sky lifted Melissa onto the saddle where she would sit in front of him. She sat upright and rigid, her dancing curls tickling his chin. "I won't let you fall, Melissa. Trust me." So she relaxed her body and leaned back on to Sky's chest.

The two waved at Jethro, Cissy and Josephine standing proudly on the boardwalk in front of The Cosmopolitan Hotel. Josie waved back, a warm glow filling her heart as she remembered the first time she and Kincade rode Gold Digger together, his arms encircling her waist in the saddle.

Sky and Melissa rode Kinhuste slowly at first and then, as she became more confident, they trotted and eventually galloped across the hills. Melissa laughed with abandonment. Smoke always led the way. They stopped at a stream and ate a picnic lunch Josephine had packed before seeing them off. They sat on a blanket and listened to birds which he identified for her. They picked wild flowers and he braided a chain which he hung around her neck.

"I thought I wanted to move to Tombstone because of Kincade and Josephine," she told him. "But now I want to come to be near you." She blushed, and for the first time in his life, Sky did too.

Goodbyes were said at the train depot with women hugging and kissing and the men shaking hands. "If I hear of any job opportunity worth your consideration, I'll let you know," Kincade assured Jethro.

"Please do. Our move will take time. I must sell my homestead in Julesburg and settle other business arrangements I have with the neighbor of my old homestead in Nebraska."

"But we do want to come as soon as possible," Cissy reassured them. "You have just been wonderful – everything Melissa had told us."

"And I didn't even know Sky before now." The little girl turned to him. "You're wonderful too." She stood on her tiptoes and quickly kissed him on his lips. "Don't forget me."

His first kiss – how could he forget.

Then the Wilcox family was on the train and gone.

21

Josephine's silken hair sparkled in the morning's warm sun as the light cascaded through the front windows of The Josephine Saloon. From across the breakfast table, her lustrous blue eyes looked mischievously into Kincade's. Josephine took another small bite of an orange slice, letting the juice moisten her full lips as Kincade sat mesmerized by how beautiful she was. She was teasing him. He knew it. He loved it.

"Marshal...," said Sky between bites of scrambled egg.

But Kincade was thinking about last night, all night, of her intoxicating jasmine perfume, of Josephine's arms wrapped around his chest, of her cream-colored...

"Marshal!" repeated Sky.

"Oh, I'm sorry, Sky," said Kincade. "I was thinking about something else." Josephine smiled ever so slightly, and licked the moisture from her lower lip.

Sky looked at the Marshal, at Josephine, then back to the Marshal. "Yes I can see that," Sky said, smiling at both of them. "Have either of you noticed that Smoke isn't under the table this morning?" Both bent to look at the empty place near Sky's feet.

"Is Smoke all right?" Kincade sounded worried.

"Marshal, you're not the only one who's smitten."

Josie laughed at Sky's use of the word. Kincade had once told Sky that Josephine was 'smitten' with him. He hadn't learned that English word in the Mission School. But since first coming to Tombstone and watching Kincade and Josephine together he began to understand this 'smitten'.

Sky continued. "Smoke is back at the stable. He won't eat. He seems plum tuckered out."

"I know the feeling." Kincade grinned at Josephine who dabbed at her lips with a white linen napkin. Josie looked at Sky.

"Sky, does Smoke have a lady friend? How long has this romance been going on?" she asked.

"More than a week. I usually take an early ride on Kinhuste with Smoke always leading the way. One time before dawn we were close to that high, long cliff... the one Kincade calls Satan's Citadel... and I heard wolves howling."

"Had you ever heard them before?" asked Kincade.

"No, and I don't think Smoke had either," replied Sky. "Soon as they started, Smoke made a sudden stop and his ears twitched. He was listening to them."

"So did he leave you and follow the call?"

"Not that time, but I think he seriously considered it. On the following day he deliberately led me along that same route and this time a lone wolf was howling. He stopped, threw back his head and howled in response."

"Like he does when he's pinned a thief to the ground?"

"No, this had a different ring to it. It's hard to explain."

"So you think he was conversing with a lady wolf?" Josephine loved a good romance.

"All I know is that when we rode past that spot again he took off and didn't return to Tombstone until that afternoon."

"Did he have a satisfied look in his eyes?" Kincade asked with a glance at Josephine. "All the answers to all the questions are always found in the eyes, you know."

It was apparent to Sky that while Kincade's question was directed to him, his last comment was meant for Josephine.

Aware that much was being said between Kincade and Josephine with few words spoken, Sky said "I think he's been trying to avoid looking into my eyes the past few days."

"A sure sign of guilt." Kincade nodded wisely.

Josephine turned his face towards hers. "Look directly into my eyes, Marshal Kincade." He did. "No guilt that I can see."

"Of course not."

Just then there was a scratching at the door. Josephine got up and went to open it. There stood Smoke, grinning his most disarming smile. "Come in, Smoke. You're not too late." He trotted up to the table and looked around for his steak. "The usual for Smoke," Josephine called to the kitchen. Then she lifted his muzzle and looked directly into his eyes. "Tsk, tsk, tsk. You are a naughty boy." And they all laughed.

The next morning after Sky awoke, he checked for Smoke in

the stall with Kinhuste. He was already gone. In the days that followed, Smoke disappeared before daybreak, returning to Tombstone later and later. Finally, Smoke showed up just before Kincade and Sky began their nightly rounds.

"Do you think Smoke is becoming wild again?" Kincade asked with concern for he knew how much the wolf meant to Sky.

"I don't worry about that," the boy answered. "He always comes back affectionate and obedient. He makes the rounds with us and does his job of Intimidation as perfectly as ever. I am not his keeper, only his chosen brother, and there is no more enduring vow that anyone can take – even a wolf."

Sky continued to ride by the escarpment on his morning jaunts. He never saw Smoke, but a few times a whole pack of wolves would sing a bone chilling chorus. He liked the sound. It brought back memories of his childhood with the Old Indian who told him stories. A mystical wolf called Black Dog was the subject of many legends.

Bad news came to Tombstone one Tuesday morning.

Kincade read the telegram for a second time, shook his head and rubbed his right hand across his eyes. Although Kincade seldom swore, a "Damn it to hell" escaped under his breath. He tossed the message onto his desk.

Sky picked up the wire and read aloud, "Rafe Sloan escaped Yuma Prison STOP Three guards killed STOP Convict heavily armed and dangerous STOP Alerting all Marshals within territory STOP Reward dead or alive STOP" He put the paper down. Kincade picked it up, crumpled it into a wad and threw it onto the floor.

"You act as if you know this Rafe Sloan," Sky said, picking up the telegram and putting it into the cold potbelly stove.

"I knew his brother. Piece of double-crossing garbage named Buck Sloan. He was one of Wil Logan's segundos. They tried to frame me for masterminding the robbery of a stage coach up Montana way. Logan murdered a woman passenger on the road that day."

Sky waited as Kincade paused. Within several moments, Kincade said, "I killed Buck."

"Have you heard anything about Rafe Sloan since?" asked Sky.

Kincade nodded. "He reorganized the Wil Logan gang after Jesse Keller killed my brother in Josephine's Saloon. Rafe gathered the worst bandits in the territory. They started riding together."

"Rafe must have been caught if he ended up in Yuma Prison."

"He was," said Kincade. "Rafe's gang tried to rob a train. But the Pinkertons were on to 'em. Sloan killed one of the agents. His gang tried to ride off and leave him, so Rafe turned on them. Shot three of them himself. Fourth one got away.

"When Rafe was busy shooting his own gang, one of the Pinkertons clubbed him from behind," continued Kincade. "They hauled him in chains before a judge for killin' that agent. The day I got news of that was one of the best I can remember.

"Rafe's brother Buck was real trash, one of Logan's worst. So vicious he'd stop at nothing. Rafe went crazy when he found out I'd killed his brother up in Montana. Sky, I'd lay odds that the two of them are cut from the same cloth."

Sky nodded. "Well, he's on the run now. Tombstone's a long way from Yuma. Rafe'll probably cross over into Mexico before he'd come here."

"Maybe..." and Kincade's voice drifted away as he rubbed an ache at his right temple... an ache he hadn't felt in nearly a month. "At least we've been warned. Sky, maybe you outta get that telegram out of the stove. I better look at it again."

The next Monday, a letter arrived on Kincade's desk. It was from the Yuma Marshal.

Kincade,
First the good news. We are gathering evidence which can lead to the capture of Rafe Sloan. Apparently the last member of his old gang was not far from the prison after Rafe broke out. He must have been waiting for Sloan with a horse and some clothes. We found tracks, and Rafe's prison garments. Found something else too. After Sloan got the horse and clothes, that gang member got a bullet to the head. Rafe must not have been too happy with his gang leaving him at that train robbery.

Next day, the General Store at Covered Wells was robbed. Several guns and a rifle were taken along with a lot of ammunition. The store owner was shot and killed and a young clerk was seriously wounded. Our last report was a stage coach being held up at Benson. The passengers were robbed of their money and valuables but not harmed, although he did force a young woman to kiss him.

Now the bad news. Tombstone may be his next destination. One of my prisoners was Sloan's cell mate. After a little encouragement provided by one of my Deputies, this fella said that Rafe swore he'd kill you. Told the fella he had a plan to break out of Yuma. Said he'd go looking for you as soon as he'd settled one other matter. Said his brother's name was Buck and you had something to do with his death. I presume the other matter was shooting the last of his gang... the dead man we found.

Watch your back, Kincade. Rafe is as bad as they come.

Dale Townsend, Marshal of Yuma
Kincade folded the letter. "So what do we do now?" Sky asked.

"Just sit and wait?"

Kincade thought about it. Then said, "No, I think I'll send a telegram to Dale Townsend and ask him to send us the prison garb they found."

Sky nodded. "We'll find this gunman before he finds you."

A box holding dirty pants and shirt arrived in a week. They smelled of sweat and urine. Even Smoke turned up his nose and walked away when they spread the clothes out on the office desk.

"So, unless it's a bed of roses you won't go to work?" Sky chided the wolf.

"Can't say I blame him," Kincade pushed the garments into a gunny sack. "We'll just leave this in the stable until we have some indication that Rafe is in our area."

"In that case Smoke may decide to start sleeping in here." They both laughed. The box from Yuma also held WANTED posters with Rafe's picture.

"Does that look like him?" Sky asked.

"Never met him, but he's got the same big hooked nose as his brother. Buck had red hair, so maybe this fella does too. Looks like Rafe has a beard. Buck didn't."

"Well, Smoke can recognize him whether he looks like his brother or not."

Days passed. Kincade and Sky watched for reports of crimes which Rafe might have committed as he headed south towards Tombstone. Nothing appeared. They scrutinized strangers who came to Tombstone to see if there was any resemblance to the WANTED picture. None came even close. Smoke occasionally went to the gunny sack and sniffed the prison clothes. But nobody in town matched the stench of Rafe Sloan's filthy clothing.

"Do you suppose the cell mate was lying about Rafe saying he'd get you?" asked Sky one afternoon.

"Maybe..." The ache at Kincade's temple was growing more each day.

"He could be in Colorado or Wyoming by now."

"Maybe...." The ache was becoming a throb. Kincade tried to shake it off. "Let's get some dinner at The Josephine before we start our rounds. I'm ready for another steak."

"Smoke too," Sky said as he patted the shaggy, grey head leaning against his leg.

Rafe Sloan felt lucky to find this hideout in the escarpment known as Satan's Citadel. The way in was almost impossible to get through. But once up and inside, Sloan had no intention of leaving. He'd let things cool down. The second horse he'd stolen in Benson had been loaded up with enough whiskey, coffee, beans, and tobacco to last a month. Shooting small game would give him fresh meat. The cave had a spring in the back. The water trickled out through the entrance and into fresh grasses. The horses had plenty to eat.

Rafe knew exactly what he would do when the time was right to kill Kincade. He'd rub ashes in his hair and beard so they wouldn't look so red. He'd blacken one eye and put a bandage over his big nose as if he'd been in a fight. He'd even limp a little like he was slightly crippled. With this disguise he could go into Tombstone and no one would recognize him from the WANTED poster.

Rafe had heard that Kincade had been named Marshal by Wyatt Earp... another no-good lawman. That meant Kincade would walk every night in the worst part of town. Rafe would shoot Kincade in the back and make a run for it. He'd heard talk of two Deputies – one of 'em was some kind of dog. Okay with him. He'd shoot them too.

It was all working out, and Rafe felt good about it. At night, he'd lie on his saddle blanket looking up at the stars. Avenging his brother's death would feel good. He'd also carry out what Wil Logan had planned but failed in doing - killing Kincade. Rafe was even happy. Slept like a baby.

"Sky, have you seen that gunny sack around Kinhuste's stable?" asked Kincade one morning. "The one with Rafe's prison garb in it?

"No, I haven't Marshal," replied Sky. "You want me to ask Teddy if he moved it when he cleaned the stalls?"

"I did. He said he hasn't seen it."

Sky said "Who would want it?! It stunk! Were you going to show it to Smoke again?"

"Yeah. I wanted it handy," said Kincade. "Somehow I get the feeling that Rafe will make his move soon. If he's like Buck, he's not a patient man."

Neither were Kincade and Sky but they had no choice but to continue to watch and wait.

One morning as Kincade and Sky sat with Josephine for breakfast, there came a frantic scratching at the side door. Josie went to open it.

"Well, well! Look who's finally decided to join us!" Josephine patted Smoke's head. "Did your lady friend decide there was a better looking wolf out there?"

She began to call out to the cook, "The usual for our broken-hearted Smoke," but stopped as the wolf went bounding ahead of her and came up to Sky. With great urgency, he grabbed the boy's sleeve with his teeth and pulled until Sky said, "Smoke, you're going to tear my shirt. What's the problem?"

Then the wolf went to Kincade and did the same thing. He began running back and forth towards the door.

"He wants us to follow him, Sky! Josie, forgive us. We'll get breakfast later. Whatever Smoke wants us to do, it's important."

Smoke ran back to the stable with Kincade and Sky at his heels. They saddled Gold Digger and Kinhuste, mounted and trailed Smoke as he ran out the door.

The wolf was headed down the road that led to Satan's Citadel.

22

Rafe pulled the rabbit he'd been roasting off the spit. He tore off a leg and bit into the pink flesh. It wasn't quite done but he was tired of waiting. The silence that surrounded him was irritating. He longed for a gang to listen to his brags and boasts. He wanted a segundo that he could yell at and blame for everything. He needed a good whore who'd let him stay the night for a dollar.

He threw the half-eaten rabbit into the brush and reached for the whiskey bottle that he always kept at his side. Maybe he'd waited long enough to go after Kincade. He should get back to the real world of gunning and gambling, not be stuck in these god forsaken rocks.

Rafe pulled on the bottle and settled back against a big stone at the entrance to the cave. He drank deeply, trying to find some sort of comfort from a night that was dark as pitch, no moon, no stars. "Hell has no hole like this," he thought.

Then he saw the first of them. Two yellow eyes glaring straight at him through the dimness of the dying camp fire. He shook his head thinking the whiskey was making him see things. He took another long pull on the bottle, nearly finishing the last of the brown liquid.

Now, a second set of yellow eyes joined the first. Rafe blinked, and took his index finger and thumb to both eyes, trying to clear his vision.

A third pair of yellow eyes. Now two more, slowly followed by two more, two more, two more, until at least twenty pairs of piercing yellow eyes all stabbing him from the darkness.

"What the hell?..." This wasn't funny.

Then the eyes growled. It was a slow, deep sound which began like a low rumble. It gained momentum and volume, enough to trigger an echo off the escarpment rock ledges.

The eyes began to move towards him, the sounds became even louder. He imagined feeling the hot breath of whatever was out there.

Rafe dropped the whiskey bottle. He rolled into the entrance of the cave and frantically searched for his guns which he'd left just inside. His fear became so great, that when his hands finally grasped the pistols they shook like leaves in a high wind. He tried to stand and staggered, his trembling legs giving way under him.

Crawling to the cave's entrance, he waved the gun barrels wildly back and forth and back again. "Come on you devils – come on and show yourselves!" And they did.

Twenty hungry wolves attacked Rafe Sloan. In waves they came, some leaping onto his back, others sinking their teeth into his face, still others ripping into his legs, tearing chunks of meat and bone. As the bandit screamed, he got off one shot before one of the wolves sank its fangs into Rafe's wrist, nearly tearing off his entire right hand.

One of the largest males ripped into the back of his neck, dragging him clear of the cave and into the open. In the blackness, the wolves tore and ravaged and fought over pieces of flesh. The man's screams turned into cries and then to soft moans as his dismembered body was torn limb from limb, skinned and eventually beheaded.

The attack was over. The feast began.

The moon rose and the escarpment glowed in a pale light. By dawn the pack of wolves had eaten their fill. They disappeared into the rocks and ravines as smoothly and effortlessly as the last of Rafe's blood, as it soaked into the dust and dirt.

Sky dismounted Kinhuste and took the bridle's reins. "I think it's time we left the horses," he said to Kincade. "This terrain is too steep and rocky for them to keep up with Smoke."

"You're right. Let's tie them to those pinon pine and follow on foot. He's way ahead of us as it is."

They twisted and climbed without any path. "I hope he knows where he's going," Kincade remarked as he stopped to catch his breath.

"He knows," Sky said as the two pushed forward.

They smelled it before they saw it. The maggots had started where the wolves ended. The stench was overpowering. The two men covered their noses with their bandanas as they entered the small clearing. A dozen feet in front of a cave's opening, a few chunks of red goo and gnawed bones littered the ground. Human bones. A few tufts of bright red hair clung to a skull that had been eaten from the outside in, the brains torn free.

Sky was overcome by nausea and vomited at the side of the clearing. He'd seen death before, and had taken part in the killing and harvesting of many buffalo. But this butchery exceeded anything in his experience. Convulsions racked his body. Coupled with the smell of the maggots as they wiggled through the remains, no human being could avoid becoming violently sick.

After several minutes Sky finished purging his stomach. He pushed himself, weakly, to a standing position and turned to help his friend Kincade, who Sky was certain was equally as sickened.

But no. Kincade stood over the mangled remains of what had to be Rafe Sloan, not ill, but as if he were in an elated, fascinated trance. Sky had seen this look on Kincade's face once before: the day they had captured Curley's stolen horses. That day, Sky had seen a look of evil in Kincade's eyes. This day, Sky saw it again.

As quickly as his weakened body would allow, Sky hurried to Kincade's side. "Marshal! Marshal Kincade!" Sky shook his shoulders to bring him around.

"The carcass has got to be Rafe Sloan, Marshal. Wolves got to him before we did."

"Yeah," Kincade said in a soft voice as he rubbed the area near his right temple with a gloved hand, wincing at the pounding pain. Sky could see Kincade clench his jaw in anger as the Other Voice said aloud, "GOOD RIDDANCE. LEAVE THE REST TO ROT."

Sky stood there, speechless. What was happening? Was that the Marshal's voice? He had never heard it so deep, so menacing....

Kincade turned, rubbing his temple. "Let's go..." He started the descent to where their horses were tied.

A whimper arose from the edge of the clearing. It sounded like it was coming from Smoke.

In the shock of the scene Sky had forgotten about the Law Dog who had led them there. He looked quickly around the area. His eyes stopped on a low bush. There, at the base of its branches, were the black and white striped pants and shirt of the prison garb that had disappeared from Kinhuste's stable. Smoke must have brought them here, sharing the scent of Rafe Sloan with the wolf pack... somehow communicating that this stench belonged to a very dangerous human who meant them great harm.

The whimper again.

About fifteen feet away, lay Smoke. Sky's wolf was crouched down next to the body of a dead wolf. He was nudging and trying to rouse her from her stillness. Her chest had a bullet hole and dried blood was staining her tan fur. Sky went to Smoke and knelt beside him. He put his arms around the wolf and gently drew him back. "Come, mihunka," he said, stroking his fur. The wolf whimpered and Sky shook his head. "You must not show your grief. It is not the Indian way. Come with me."

Sky found the rifle in the cave and with the butt end he dug a shallow grave. Smoke watched. He then wrapped the body of the tan wolf in the prison garments and gently slid her into the grave. She was heavy and her stomach was distended with unborn pups. With his feet he shoved the dirt to fill in the depression. Smoke came to stand beside him as he gently covered the carcass with soil, placing stones on top of the mound.

Finished, Sky knelt next to Smoke's sad face, resting his own face against the wolf's gray ear. "She was your nitawin, wasn't she Smoke. Those were your pups..."

While Smoke and Sky eventually resumed their morning rides, the wolf never again led the way past Satan's Citadel.

23

Every fall Tombstone put out the welcome mat for stockmen from all over the country. Many drives, some with a thousand head, made Tombstone their final destination. Dust billowed from the dry streets as they converged on the town. The vast stock pens near the rail station were always overcrowded. The lowing and bellowing of cattle being pushed and prodded mingled with toots and whistles of trains which came empty and pulled away fully loaded. Most beeves would go to buyers for the cavalry or meat packers in the east. A few hundred from each herd would be processed at the slaughter house in Tombstone which operated from dawn to dark. The air was odious with fumes from this butchering, as well as from the muck in the holding pens.

Business during these weeks wasn't confined to the shipping of cattle. There was a Stock Show where prize animals were exhibited and sold. For three days a rodeo was staged with wild horse and bronc busting, calf roping, young cowboys brazen enough to jump on the backs of raging bulls and even clowns who would distract the bulls as they tried to jam their horns up the behinds of those young cowboys bucked off moments earlier.

Prize money was awarded, and the events drew the best cowboys from as far away as Wyoming and Montana. Of course most drovers did not come for the rodeo. Most had been on the trail for many weeks and just wanted to let themselves go to hell with liquor, women, gambling, shooting, fighting and whatever else they could find to release pent up energy.

In contrast, this was also the social season of Tombstone because wealthy cattlemen from all over the west came to buy and sell. Often their wives and children came with them, and the rooms at The Cosmopolitan Hotel had to be reserved in advance. Parties were given during the days, balls attended at night. Horse races with betting were comparable to those in Virginia. Young people from near and far met at these functions and fell in love beneath the autumn moon.

The Josephine Saloon was at the center of it all - decorated with flags and banners. Pantomimists, jugglers and magicians entertained the small-fry from ten until lunch. At two o'clock young ladies gathered for their genre of music - sentimental ballads and witty ditties - performed by a beautiful and talented duo named Sheena and Shanti. These sisters sang in close harmony, accompanying themselves on two guitars. They had received acclaim at the Brown Palace Hotel in Denver and Josephine was delighted when they agreed to come to frontier Tombstone. At their first performance young buckaroos were allowed to attend. But they created such an appreciative commotion by stomping their feet, tossing their hats in the air, and yelling "Yee Haw!" that Josephine had to shoo them into the street where the lot of them plastered their faces against the windows of The Josephine while the girls performed.

All through the evening extra musicians kept the tempo lively. At one a.m., after the matrons had retired to their rooms, a dance troupe from San Francisco performed high-kicking Terpsichore nightly. Josephine was in her element, greeting and introducing, arranging and participating. Kincade was in awe of her prowess as a hostess.

For the Marshal and his two Deputies this season was a nightmare. Drunkenness was rampant. Kincade left many cowboys to sleep it off in a saloon chair or on a street bench. But others he took to jail for their intoxicated rowdiness. Guns went off at all hours and the undertaker, John Martin, kept busy making cheap pine caskets to fill and cart off to Boot Hill.

Kincade decided Upper Tombstone was more or less trouble free, and they stopped only briefly at The Josephine to make a show of the town being in good hands. Lower Tombstone was another story. Here they made the rounds two or three times every night. The Intimidation became more intense, and Sky and Smoke strolled into the saloon halls alongside Kincade instead of just standing by the doors. Smoke was called upon to attack-and-wait more than once every evening and the jail swelled with cowboys whom Kincade ordered to leave town in the morning.

This Saturday night had been particularly wild, but they were going to call it quits after their third stop at the Silver Dollar. Sky and Smoke were doing The Intimidation by the batwing doors. Kincade's attention was drawn to four scruffy hombres alone at the table in the rear. He passed them as he made the rounds of the room, but they kept their faces away from him. That made him suspicious. They had two empty bottles on the table and were pouring from a third.

Kincade returned to the exit. "Those men in the back, Sky," Kincade whispered. "I think they've made trouble here before."

"I can't make out their faces," said Sky, "but they look like trouble all right."

"I just can't remember who they are," said Kincade.

"I bet we'll know before morning."

"Well, they're not doing anything I can arrest them for at the moment. Let's go."

They returned to Allen Street where lights and music drifting from The Josephine were most inviting. Standing outside of the saloon, Kincade turned to Sky. "I think I'll drop in for awhile and see if Lady Luck's going to be with me tonight."

"Lady who?"

Kincade shook his head in amusement.

"Oh, I thought you said Lady Josephine's going to be with you tonight. My mistake." He touched the brim of his hat as he'd seen Kincade do so many times. "G'night, Marshal."

"See you in the morning, Sky." He went through the batwings laughing again. Kincade cared for the boy more and more with each passing day.

Kincade may not have been able to recognize the four at the Silver Dollar but they knew him. "Damn Marshal, struttin' around like he owns the town!"

"And did you get a load of that Injun kid? He's got a badge! Thinks he's big stuff dressed up like a white man. I'd like to peal back his redskin like a tater."

"That wolf's the town hero from what I hear. Should 'a twisted off his furry neck when we had 'im roped."

"Should 'a strung up the Injun kid 'long side him. Damn, I hate a struttin' savage."

"Damn, I hate a struttin' Marshal!"

"Damn, I hate a struttin' wolf!"

The three laughed and held up their shot glasses. "Let's drink to hatin' the three of 'em!" They gulped down the whiskey and refilled the glasses. The fourth man didn't join in.

"Damn it, Luke, ain't you sayin' nothin'? You was there too. How 'bout a little hate?" The silent partner looked at them with bleary eyes.

"Forget him, Micah. You know Luke can hate as good as us. He always does." The three sat for several minutes trying to clear their heads enough to continue talking.

"Let's get 'im," one finally said.

"All of 'em?"

"No, just the Injun. Damn wolf ain't worth botherin' with, and I've heard the Marshal is fast with a gun. Too fast."

"Damn Injun weren't wearin' no gun. Did ya notice that?"

"Yeah, I noticed. He's probably too dumb to aim and fire if he had one."

"Let's string 'im up!"

"What ya mean?"

"I mean string 'im up by the neck on that old Hangin' Tree we passed as we rode into town."

"Now wouldn't that be a purty picture! His feet swingin' and his Injun eyes buggin' out!"

"I'm with ya! When ya wanna do it?"

"Tonight - soon as the town's real quiet. We'll snatch 'im where he bunks."

"You know where that is?"

"You think I just started plannin' this? Been thinkin' on it ever since we hit town. I know everythin' there is to know about that redskin. You just follow me." The three headed toward the door. "Damn it, Luke! You comin' or not?" The fourth man drained the last drops from the bottle, stuck a dirty finger in his nose, pulled out a gob of snot which he wiped on the table, and staggered after them.

Later that night, Smoke awoke from his warm place beside Kinhuste. Something was wrong - he could feel it. He wandered to Sky's door and whined. Usually this brought an invitation to come in and sleep next to the boy. Tonight - silence.

Smoke walked to the rear door and pushed it open. He pattered to the outhouse and listened, but Sky was not inside. Hastily he returned to the stable and pushed open the old tack room door. Sky was not there. Smoke sniffed the blanket on the floor and became frantic. There were odors of three men here that he had smelled once before - the time when his head had been jerked with ropes and his body thrown and dragged to the ground. Sky was in great danger!

Smoke ran outside. He bounded to the door of the brown frame house where Kincade lived and yelped loudly. More silence. He put his feet on the door and pawed frantically, but it would not open. Kincade was not there.

Smoke turned and raced down Allen Street. Kincade must be where they went every morning - The Josephine. The building was dark and silent. He put his feet on the door they always entered and pushed with all his might. It didn't give an inch. Frantically, he lifted his head and howled his loudest, over and over again.

A window opened on the second floor and Kincade stuck his head out. "Smoke! What is it?" More howls. "I'm coming, boy,

I'm coming!"

In less than a minute, the Marshal threw open the door. He was wearing only his pants, boots, and his twin-rig guns. "What's the matter, Smoke?"

Smoke took off down the street like a lightening flash and Kincade followed, running hard to keep up. They came to the stable and Kincade pushed open the doors. He could see immediately that Sky was not there. Inserting a bit in Gold Digger's mouth but skipping a blanket or saddle, Kincade swung onto the palomino and galloped after Smoke, now far ahead of him down the street.

"My God," he thought. "This is bad. Whatever it is, this is real bad!"

They passed through Lower Tombstone and to Boot Hill. Then, down the hill and into the arroyo. In the light of a full moon Kincade could see the silhouettes of four men at Tombstone's Hanging Tree. Three were on horses and one stood. As Kincade neared, he saw that one of the men on horseback was directly below the tree's largest and sturdiest branch... the same branch Kincade had used when putting fear into the horse thieves. This man's hands were tied behind his back, a noose draped around his neck.

Kincade was close now. Close enough that several of the men turned at the sound of Gold Digger's charging hooves. "It's those men at the Silver Dollar!" Kincade said to himself. And then, it hit him. "Those are the three who put the rope on Smoke. Almost killed him! Now, the same bunch have someone else on a rope."

He was almost there. "God, NO!" yelled Kincade. "It's Sky! They're hanging Sky! NO!"

Something snapped. Deep inside Kincade, something larger, stronger, more violent than anything he had ever experienced... an explosion of pain dynamited behind his right eye. For the first time, the ache in Kincade's head was more than unbridled pounding. It became an enormous sledgehammer, shattering his ability to distinguish between right and wrong - a debacle that took on a life of its own. The Other Voice ordered Kincade, "KILL THEM! KILL THEM! KILL THEM!"

Kincade let the reins fall as he yanked both pistols from the twin-rig. Cocking the hammers back, he fired with blazing speed into the backs of the two bandits still on horseback. The lead slammed into their spines, arching both up and over the necks of their horses, their bodies crashing into the ground with splintering impact and instantaneous death. Gold Digger charged directly into the third outlaw on the ground, holding the rope on Sky's neck, catapulting his body into the air and straight into the trunk of the Hanging Tree, instantly breaking his back.

Gold Digger dug into the soft earth and pulled up short. Kincade leapt off and ran to Sky. Spent and sweaty, Kincade lifted Sky from the horse he was tied to, gently lowering him to the ground. "Are you all right?" The boy was in shock. Smoke circled and circled him, whimpering and nudging him but there was no response from Sky.

"Let's get that rope off your neck." No response as Kincade removed the noose and untied the boy's hands. They felt cold.

Seeing Sky so close to death, realizing he had almost lost the boy who meant so much to him, the hammering cleaved an erupting volcano inside Kincade and a river of fiery anger consumed his sanity.

He turned from Sky. He walked over to the two dead men sprawled on the ground. Slowly removing his Colt from his right holster, Kincade put another bullet into the first corpse. Recocking the hammer, another bullet into the skull of the second dead man.

For the first time, Sky spoke. "Don't. Please don't."

The molten lava within his head burned even hotter. Kincade turned and walked over to the third man, crumpled in a heap of broken bones at the base of the hanging tree. He still breathed, and muttered a few inaudible words.

Kincade kneeled down and looked into the man's terrified eyes. The Marshal whispered four words. "What did you say?"

The man strained to be heard through a death rasp. Kincade bent down to place his ear next to the man's bloodied face. "Little louder, you piece of scum."

"Hhhel... help me. Please, help me..."

"Sure friend," Kincade whispered back. "I'll help you..."

The Other Voice within Kincade's brain hissed, "HE TRIED TO KILL SKY. GO ON, KINCADE."

And Kincade shouted, "I'LL HELP YOU STRAIGHT INTO THE FIRES OF HELL!"

Then he gently pulled back both hammers so the man could clearly hear their clicking into the firing position. Kincade's index fingers went to the triggers. He pressed the end of each barrel into the throat of the gasping man, pulled both triggers. His body jerked ferociously with the horrific impact of the bullets.

"BETTER MAKE SURE," the Other Voice egged on Kincade.

He cocked the guns and shot the man again.

Kincade stood and turned towards Sky, Colts still in both hands, his bare chest splattered with the blood of dead men, all of his 6 foot 6 inches looking like some kind of walking nightmare.

Kincade looked directly at Sky.

The boy's face was filled with Fear.

24

The air around them barely moved. When a slight breeze did appear, it just as quickly moved away, as if it sensed the horror and wanted no part of it.

Kincade holstered his shooters, walked to the boy and wrapped his muscular arms around him, drawing him close to his chest. "You'll be okay. They will never be able to hurt you, or Smoke ever again."

Sky remained still as a stone, barely breathing.

"I've got to get him back to his place," thought Kincade. "Get him lying down, covered up..."

Bringing Gold Digger to where the boy stood, Kincade hoisted Sky up and on top of the palomino, sliding his right leg over Digger's back. Not having the horse saddled made it easier. Kincade leapt up and behind Sky, encircling the boy with both arms as his hands held Digger's reins. Smoke followed at the horse's heels.

"It'll be all right, Sky," Kincade said again. The Marshal of Tombstone then turned to the three dead men. "Don't go anywhere boys. I'm not finished with you." And the Other Voice laughed from deep within Kincade's throbbing brain.

Their ride through the light of the moon didn't take long. The streets were totally vacant, the window lamps snuffed hours before. Kincade carefully lowered Sky and carried him into his small room as Smoke crouched in a corner. Removing Sky's boots, Kincade laid him on several soft blankets, and put two more over his body. The boy had not spoken another word. But Sky's eyes were watching Kincade with a great intensity.

"Rest, Sky. No one will hurt you anymore." Kincade smoothed the boy's hair, rose, backed up to the tack room door and softly latched it behind him.

Returning to the stalls, Kincade removed Gold Digger's saddle and blanket from the rails and put them on the waiting palomino. Swinging up and moving into the street, Kincade looked around. Tombstone remained fast asleep.

As he rode back to the Hanging Tree the Other Voice whispered its plan for the disposal of the three dead men. Past Boot Hill, down into the arroyo and Kincade could see their horses were still there, picking at the grasses near the creek.

The three corpses were still limber, making it easy to heave each across a saddle and lash it securely between horn and cantle. Going over to the creek thicket, Kincade yanked a fully-leafed branch from the soft earth. He dragged it across the ground, obliterating his slaughter of the three men.

"YOU DID RIGHT, MARSHAL," soothed the Other Voice inside Kincade's head. "THEY WOULD HAVE KILLED THE BOY. SCUMS LIKE THEM DON'T DESERVE TO BREATHE. HAD YOU ARRESTED THEM INSTEAD, THEY WOULD HAVE BRIBED THE JUDGE, GOTTEN OFF, AND TRIED TO HURT SKY AGAIN. YOU DID RIGHT..."

Kincade nodded and said to the black night, "I did right." The

Other Voice laughed.

When Kincade got into town all remained quiet. He led the horses to within a block of the Marshal's office. After he dumped the bodies on the street, he whacked the rumps of the three horses so they would gallop out of town. Whoever found them the next day would probably ignore the blood-splattered saddles in favor of adding three horses to their own remuda. Possession was nine-tenths of the law, what law there was.

The Marshal led Gold Digger swiftly to the stall next to Kinhuste, swinging the gate closed. Reentering the street, Kincade dragged the heavy men, one to each side of the road and one in the center, about twenty-five feet apart. Double-checking the street one final time, Kincade ran from one corpse to the other, pulling their guns from their holsters and firing into the bodies of the other two, forcing the now spent pistols into their limp hands.

Just as the Other Voice had promised, it all looked like a shoot-out by desperate, drunken trash. Kincade quickly left the street, and returned to the stalls next to his office. His bare chest was now covered in blood from wrestling the three torn corpses from the Hanging Tree, onto their horses and to their final positions on Allen Street. Stepping up to the pump that fed the horse trough, he worked the handle, splashing cold water over his face and chest to remove the dried blood from his skin. So much of it covered his torso that it took several minutes to remove the thickened muck. As Kincade rubbed his flesh, the throbbing deep within his head continued like a dull thrum.

Kincade skimmed the water from his body with his hands, turned and went into his office, just steps away from the tack room where Sky now rested. He grabbed a shirt that hung from a nail on the south wall and put it on. He awaited anyone who would be aroused by the rapid gunfire from Allen Street. Kincade would emerge as though he too had just been awakened by the shots.

The Other Voice was smart. It knew. Within moments Tombstone's Undertaker, John Martin, came trotting down the street in his nightshirt. Kincade stepped from his office door, adjusting his belt as if he'd just put it on.

"Evenin', Marshal - or should I say, mornin'. You heard the shots, too, I see."

"Yeah, woke me up."

Martin walked from one body to the next, shaking his head. "Shoot-out. Nothin' you could have done. Drunk as skunks."

Kincade nodded in agreement, massaging his right temple. "Strangers in town. Appears they'll be taking up permanent residence at Boot Hill. Liquor and lead have given you three new customers, John."

"It'll take me awhile to get dressed, hitch up the team and get back here with a buckboard," said Martin.

"I don't think these boys will be goin' anywhere, John."

"No Marshal. Suppose not."

"You need some help?" asked Kincade.

"No, I don't Marshal. Thanks for offering. I'll have these three off the street and into pine boxes before breakfast." Martin turned, and ran back to his house and the morning's new business.

Kincade walked back into his office without noticing Sky standing in the shadows between the buildings. He had seen and heard everything that happened. Sky waited for the Marshal to go into his house, and then he returned to the stable.

Sky passed Kinhuste on the way to his small room. He entered the stall and stroked the horse's nose. "Mitasunke - my horse," he whispered. The animal nickered, understanding perfectly. Then the boy swung onto his back and sat straight as an arrow.

"I must not show my grief. It is not the Indian way. I must not show my grief. It is not the Indian way," He kept repeating the phrase over and over. Finally he sank his face into Kinhuste's mane and ignored the Indian way.

Kincade turned in, totally spent by the trauma of the night. He decided not to disturb Sky, hoping that rest would restore and calm the boy by morning. They'd talk about it over breakfast.

Kincade didn't have the strength to remove his clothes. Lying on his bunk, he descended into an exhausted, fitful sleep, filled with screams of men begging for mercy, of Sky's face racked by fear, of gunfire and of the Other Voice urging Kincade, guiding his every move. It thrummed a demonic litany, "DON'T TELL JOSEPHINE...DON'T TELL JOSEPHINE...DON'T TELL JOSEPHINE...."

By dawn, Kincade knew he had to tell Josephine everything. The raging headache and the Other Voice finally, and blessedly, vanished.

Around 8, Kincade came into the office expecting to find Sky waiting to go to breakfast as usual. The place was empty. He called, although there was nowhere for his Deputy to go except into the jail. No response.

He went out the back and into the stable. Kinhuste was in his stall. "He isn't riding. Who could after what happened last night?"

"Sky!" he called. No answer from the small room. He returned to the office and put the sign in the window. As he left, Kincade saw that John Martin had finished loading the three bodies onto his buckboard. A small crowd was breaking up and heading home.

Some were shaking their heads and muttering about the rabble which had come into town lately.

"Sky probably went to The Josephine ahead of me," Kincade thought as he took long strides down the street. "Poor kid went through hell last night. Wonder if he's there now, telling Josie what happened."

Kincade entered the door and saw Josephine already sitting at their usual table. "Josie, good morning. I'm sorry I'm late." Kincade removed his hat placing it on the bar. He kissed Josephine on the cheek. "Sky here?"

"He came before the cooks started the sourdough," Josephine responded. "I was still in my suite. But they told me Sky was dressed in his Indian clothes."

Kincade stopped midway while pulling out his chair. That didn't make sense. "Did he tell them why?"

Josie shook her head. "He left a bundle for me."

"Did you open the bundle?" She nodded. "What was in it?"

"All the clothes I bought him and a bag of coins. Also his Deputy star."

"His badge?!" Kincade was absolutely shocked. "Anything else?"

Josephine nodded, concerned at the distress she could plainly see in Kincade's eyes. "He left this, for you." She handed Kincade a sealed letter. As he took it, Josephine placed her hand on Kincade's arm, trying to comfort him. This couldn't be good news. He unfolded the paper and read aloud:

To Marshal Kincade,
I am resigning as your Deputy. Smoke too. We have left Tomb-

stone. I thank you for saving my life even though I wish you had arrested those men like a Marshal instead of gunning them down like an outlaw.

I am leaving because in a Sioux tribe any man who lies or withholds the truth is subject to death. You and I and Smoke know the truth about what happened at the Hanging Tree. But to all Tombstone you hide the truth of your actions. When you will not stand tall and unafraid of the truth, you die in me.

I do not want to listen to your white man's explanation.

You can call Smoke a dog, but he is still Shotahoda, the wolf.

You can call me Sky, a Deputy, but I am still an Indian.

Goodbye.

Mahpiyasa – Red Sky

Kincade dropped the letter onto the table. His hands were shaking, his head again began its throbbing.

Josephine moved her chair closer to Kincade, and leaned her head against his shoulder. Though she didn't know what Sky referred to, or what had happened at the Hanging Tree, she believed in Kincade without question. Josephine loved him unconditionally. He would explain to her when he felt he could. Time wasn't important to Josephine. Only her love for Kincade. She slipped her arm under his and waited without speaking.

Several minutes passed. Josephine could see Kincade reliving, reprocessing whatever had happened near Boot Hill. She could see confusion in his eyes, tension in his brow. Kincade took his right hand and began massaging his right temple. Josephine had seen him do this before, and knew it meant Kincade was once again suffering from the headaches.

Kincade turned to look into her eyes. She could see such pain within his. It was as if he were crying out to her. It tore at her heart.

He gradually looked away, and down at his hands. Then, across the room, but Josephine knew he was looking far beyond the walls themselves. Finally, he spoke.

"Josie...." Kincade struggled for words. She kept her right hand on his arm, trying to console him.

"...I've got to find him," he said. "Maybe Gold Digger and I can catch up with him."

Josephine nodded her head. "He's been gone several hours."

Kincade said, "He left Kinhuste behind. He'll be walking. I'll find him..."

Josephine pushed back her chair as Kincade rose to his feet. She picked up Kincade's hat and returned to his side. As he took the hat, she knew from Kincade's eyes that he would not only be looking for Sky, but for something within himself.

She placed her hands ever so gently on Kincade's face and looked deeply into his eyes. "I love you more than you will ever know," those eyes said to one another, but they spoke not a word. Rising up on tiptoes, she kissed him with all her heart.

Kincade found Gold Digger in the stall where he'd left him several hours ago, still saddled and bridled. In all their years together, in all the trails they'd ridden, Kincade had never neglected the palomino that meant so much to him. A good man always took care of his horse. But at this moment, Kincade did not feel like a good man. Not after what he, and the Other Voice, had done.

"I'm sorry, Digger," Kincade said to the stallion. Like Josephine, the horse cared and trusted Kincade beyond question.

"Chuff..." Gold Digger said. And for a moment, a very brief moment, Kincade smiled ever so slightly.

"I'll make it up to you..." Kincade opened the stall gate, stepped into the stirrup, swung his right leg over and settled himself. "I will..."

The day was warm, even though the leaves were turning yellow and gold. The road seemed long - very long - and there was no one in sight at this early hour. He rode slower and slower recalling everything that Sky had written:

...had arrested them like a Marshal instead of gunning them down like an outlaw...

The pain was clanging in his head like a blacksmith's hammer on an anvil. "Why did I do it? Why couldn't I just have told them to halt - or maybe called out to Smoke to attack and wait?"

He rode on, not looking right or left. He couldn't stop replaying the previous night in his mind, searching for answers, for justification.

"Because I was afraid that one fast slap on that horse's rump and Sky would be swinging," he answered himself.

The letter - the letter with its bitter fact:

...you hide the truth of your actions...

"Why did I make it look like a shoot-out when I could have arrested the lot of them? Eventually, they would have hung for what they tried to do to Sky..." Kincade shook his head hoping the pain would lessen. But it didn't. It wouldn't. Kincade had killed them all.

Sky's letter said:

...I do not want to listen to your white man's explanations....

Kincade had no explanation. "Sky, I don't know why I did it. I..." No words came. Only the pounding at the right temple, never ceasing its intensity and power.

For six hours, Kincade rode. But the boy and his wolf were gone. Kincade could never remember feeling so low. It was too late to tell Sky anything.

He turned Gold Digger around and started back.

The sun had set when Kincade reached the outskirts of Tombstone. Kincade rode up the lonely road to Boot Hill. Tying Gold Digger to its faded whitewash picket fence, Kincade went through the worn wooden gate.

Kincade knelt on Jesse Keller's grave and in a whisper only a ghost could hear, he said, "I love Sky, Jesse. I hated the men who tried to rob me of the son I'd never had." Never in his life, had Kincade felt so lost.

Grief and sorrow bore down on Kincade in ways he never imagined possible. He stood from Jesse Keller's grave, turned and walked a dozen paces to a second grave. He knelt down, crossing his arms on the tombstone. In a whisper only a ghost could hear, he said, "They would have killed the boy. Their kind don't deserve to breathe. They were trash... human filth. I did right. I have to punish scum like them."

He stayed at the second grave until the first light of dawn began to appear from the east.

Because this night, Kincade didn't seek understanding from the grave of his blood brother, Jesse Keller. He sought vindication by remembering the past at the grave of his other blood brother.

The one named Wil Logan...

25

"Have people been asking you about Sky's disappearance?" Josephine asked Kincade as she broke off a small piece of her French roll and popped it in her pretty mouth.

"Everybody." Kincade was having his usual breakfast. Over the last week, since Sky and Smoke left, eating didn't appeal to him much any more.

"I suppose David Cook wants to write it up in the Tombstone Epitaph."

"Probably," said Kincade. "When it comes to gathering the news, he's pushy. He cornered me yesterday afternoon."

"What'd you tell him?"

"Sky had a better offer and I felt he should take it."

"Did he seem satisfied with your answer?"   Clearly, Josephine was concerned about what happened at the Hanging Tree that night, and even more concerned about how it had affected the man she loved so deeply.

Kincade finished his eggs and wiped his mouth with his napkin.

"Josie, you're the only one who knows what really happened. I'm not proud of what I did, even though it may have saved Sky's life. I know I could have...." And his voice trailed off.

"I know how you feel, Darling. You did what you thought you had to. And Sky's alive because of it." She smiled, reached over and soothingly ran her fingers through Kincade's hair. He looked at her and realized, for the umpteenth time, of how lucky he was to have a woman like Josephine at the center of his life.

Josie stood and picked up his plate. "By the way, I saw Mrs. Clum, the Mayor's wife." Kincade watched as Josie handed his plate to the cook, and then return to sit close by his side. "She'd just come back from visiting her daughter in Bisbee. She's quite excited about her new grandson. Said he was a bit premature, but seems healthy. Named him for his Daddy, Clement Smith, but they're going to call him Bud since he's Blossom's baby."

"Sky would have gotten a laugh out of that."

They were both silent for a minute.

"You know, Josie, having Sky and Smoke as my Deputies made being Tombstone's Marshal fun. But since they've gone, I don't know. Sky made me smile and laugh... seemed like all the time."

"I know Kincade. Me too." Josephine put her hand over his and gently squeezed. "Would you like more coffee?"

"Sure, if you'll sit with me."

When she returned he took both her hands in his and looked into her glorious blue eyes. "Josie, I made a big mistake that night. While I couldn't care less about those three men, my decisions cost me Sky and Smoke. It's not a mistake I want to repeat." He paused to read her reaction. "What would you think about my learning some law?"

"I think that's an excellent idea."

"I know right from wrong, and I know good from bad. When people make havoc, I put them in jail and, if necessary, I deliver them to a circuit judge to get a fair trial. But maybe I should know what's really legal as far as the Arizona Territory is concerned."

"Do you want to go away to a law school?"

Kincade laughed at her honest question. "And leave you?! No, Josie... I will never leave you. That's one mistake I will never repeat."

She paused to let his words dance around the room. She took her right index finger and touched the end of Kincade's nose. "That had better be your answer, cowboy." They both smiled at one another. "So, what's your plan?"

"There's a fella just came into town," Kincade said. "Miss Sadie says he's a lawyer and wants to set up a law practice here."

"Jeremiah Scott. I haven't met him but he's staying at the Cosmopolitan until he can find a house and office space. Have you met him?"

"Not yet. But I left a message at the hotel desk asking that he meet me there this morning. Would you like to come along?"

"No, thank you. I'll wait 'til he comes to The Josephine." She was proud of her saloon, proud of her girls, and proud of the reputation they had all built together. "He will eventually. Everyone seems to."

"If he falls in love with you, I'll order him out of town!"

"Along with all the others who've fallen in love with me?"

"I can't do that, Josie." Kincade loved the play they made with one another. She made him feel so good.

With a fake pout on her ruby red lips, Josie said, "Why not?"

Kincade paused and moved his chair close to hers. It was his turn to touch his finger to the tip of her nose. "Because if I did that, Josie, Tombstone would be a ghost town." And he kissed her. A long, passionate, thankful-for-everything-about-her kiss.

Josie sat back a little breathless. "Well, we can't have a ghost town, can we, Marshal Kincade."

Outside on the hotel veranda, the lawyer waited for Kincade. Jeremiah Scott was a tall, well built man in his late fifties. His hair was salt and pepper gray and his eyes were the same tone. His tailored suit was of dark blue wool, his shirt a paler shade, and his vest and tie of paisley silk.

Kincade left The Josephine and stepped out on the boardwalk, catching sight of the attorney. "There must be money in this law business," Kincade thought as he came toward Scott with his hand extended.

"You must be our town's new lawyer. I'm Marshal Kincade. Welcome."

"Jeremiah Scott, and thank you, Sir." He accepted the handshake. His voice had a deep, dramatic ring as if he were used to speaking in front of a jury box. "I apologize for not coming to meet you at your office when I first arrived. But I've been preoccupied with trying to find suitable accommodations for myself and my legal practice. Please forgive me."

"Nothing to forgive. It's part of my job to welcome all newcomers to Tombstone - both the good and the bad, I'm afraid."

Scott chuckled, appreciating Kincade's humor. "Perhaps you and I both deal with the same elements in a community, Marshal. A lawyer's clientele can run the gamut of innocent and guilty. I haven't dined this morning. Will you join me for breakfast?"

"Thank you, no. I've eaten. But I'll sit with you, if I may. There's a matter I'd like to discuss with you."

"My pleasure. Shall we adjourn to the dining room?"

"After you."

Jeremiah Scott flipped his linen napkin fastidiously before placing it across his lap. The waiter appeared at his side. "Good morning, Sir. Would you like to see a menu?"

"I don't believe that will be necessary. I'll have two eggs lightly poached - don't let them get hard - one piece of dry whole wheat toast, and English breakfast tea."

"Very good, Sir. Anything for you, Marshal?"

"No thanks, Clyde. I ate at The Josephine." The waiter smiled knowingly and left.

"Excellent food here," commented Scott. "I didn't think civilization reached this far west."

"Miss Josephine, who manages this hotel, caters to many eastern guests."

"Excellent. You said there was a matter you wished to discuss with me, Marshal Kincade?"

Lawyer Scott was certainly formal, Kincade thought to himself – a noticeable contrast to most of the folks he dealt with. Kincade smiled inwardly as he turned to the waiter. "Clyde, I think I will have that cup of coffee."

"Certainly, Marshal. Say, I haven't seen your two Deputies lately. They on assignment?"

"You might say that," Kincade said, missing them yet again. "Just coffee please, Clyde. Don't let me catch you trying to slip one of your buttered sweet rolls alongside." And the two friends laughed. Clyde was a good man.

"You have Deputies?" asked Scott. "Well, well, Tombstone is an up and coming city."

Kincade came to the point. "I'd like to learn more about the laws of the Arizona Territory, Mr. Scott."

"Jeremiah, please - or Jeri if you'd prefer."

"Thanks, Jeri. Friends call me Kincade." He continued. "As Tombstone's Marshal, I try to keep the peace. More families are coming in, and that's good for our town. Gunfighters, thieves, drunks breaking up property, there's no place for them anymore - if there ever was. I've done my share of throwing men in jail or ordering them out of town."

Kincade remembered back to what happened in Bisbee, the bribed judge, and shopkeeper Perkins' thief getting off free and clear. That mess still rankled him. But now, he wanted to do what he could to prevent it from happening again. He continued. "Sometimes, I have to wait for a circuit judge to settle the matter. That can take weeks. Before that judge arrives, I want to make sure I've done my job right so a fair and just verdict can be rendered. I think I'd be a better Marshal if I knew more about a man's legal rights, and the laws that govern the Territory."

"That's why I've come to Tombstone, Kincade. Your town is growing and the law should be enforced according to legal statutes – not just putting trouble makers behind bars. I'm glad you're aware of that. We will work well together, I'm sure." Jeremiah inspected his manicured nails.

Listening and watching the lawyer, Kincade wasn't completely sure he liked the fellow. No matter. The Marshal needed to know more about law, not someone to share tequila with over at The Josephine. "I'd like your help. Maybe a few books on crime and punishment, and some of my questions answered along the way."

"That would be your special interest, of course. But you realize that I am not only a criminal lawyer, but a civil law consultant as well. I shall be drawing up wills and settling estates, making contracts, transferring titles of property - ah, there is a myriad of life's legal necessities that the citizens of Tombstone can avail themselves of at my office."

This fellow was full of himself. Kincade said, "I don't expect to know it all. Just the proper enforcement of the law."

"Certainly. I can do that - given time. But at this juncture I'm overwhelmed by the need to find permanent lodging and a place to hang my shingle." He chuckled. "I suggest, Kincade, that you learn the law as the need arises. We can review your arrests as you make them and then I shall give legal advice to the malfeasants. You'll learn from my directives." Jeremiah looked around for the waiter.

Way full of himself. "I was hoping you might have a book that could help me get started."

"Somewhere in my unpacked trunks I have a copy of Blackstone's Commentaries which was written more for England's jurisprudence than the western frontier. I practically know it by heart so I can loan it to you for a few weeks. I'll be glad to have one of the hotel bellboys run it over to your office when I come across it."

"That'd be fine," Kincade said.

"Ah, here is the waiter with my breakfast. Will you be so kind as to continue this conversation later, Kincade? I have a digestive problem that requires eating without distraction."

"Certainly. Good-day, Mr. Scott." Kincade rose from his chair.

"Jeremiah, please - or Jeri if you prefer." He was already briskly stirring his eggs and tearing the dry toast in half to dunk into the watery mix.

As Kincade walked out, he thought to himself, "People like you give me a digestive problem even when I'm not eating! Dudes! Can't live with 'em. Can't kill 'em!" While he smiled at his thoughts, he would keep these particular impressions of the pompous Mr. Jeremiah Scott solely to himself.

"So, what do you think of the new attorney in town?" Josephine asked Kincade when he dropped into the saloon after making his nightly rounds.

"Well, he talks like he's well educated, which I certainly am not. Did he come in here tonight?"

"For awhile. Threw a lot of money around, but he won a lot too. Did more talking about himself than listening to anyone."

"I got that treatment too."

Josephine was lovely tonight. A white satin dress with jet black buttons all down the front. "Did he make a pass at you?"

"Hardly noticed me at all and I have on my newest gown."

"Now I know something's wrong with this guy!" Kincade's eyes twinkled.

KINCADE'S FEAR   201

"Can you throw him out of town for almost insulting me?" Her eyes sparkled.

"No, but I'll give him a good thumping later on."

"Smoke too?" she said without thinking.

A silence fell between them. Sky and Smoke had left them both with a lifetime of love and companionship now lost forever.

Kincade briefly closed his eyes and wearily shook his head. "I miss them both Josie. That Smoke was a good dog. More times than I care to admit I've called out 'takpe ahpe' before I remembered he wasn't there to attack and wait."

She understood. She felt the same. "It's going to take awhile. For us both." She took his hand. "I'm sure Sky thinks about us too."

"You maybe."

"You too – nobody could ever stop loving you." She pressed his fingers to her lips and gently kissed them.

Jeremiah Scott opened his office two weeks later on the upper floor of the barber shop which was reached by an outside stairway. He put up a large sign at the base of the staircase where all who entered the tonsorial establishment couldn't help but see:

JEREMIAH SCOTT, ATTORNEY AT LAW
CRIMINAL PROSECUTION,
CIVIL ADJUDICATION LEGAL DOCUMENTS,
AND SOUND ADVICE RENDERED

He moved into a small house which Curley Smith had hoped his son, Clement, and his new bride would use. But shortly after the wedding, Clement had been offered a job at the livery stable in

Bisbee, owned by the brother-in-law of Blossom's mother. Curley's house had been furnished with presentable hand-me-downs, but the young people chose to set themselves up in style with wedding gift money. Curley's small house had been unoccupied for many months.

After Curley and Lawyer Scott signed a year's lease, they shook hands. "I feel very fortunate, Mr. Smith, to have such a fine little dwelling to live in. Please know that I am in your debt, and should there be any legal matter I might assist you with, I'm at your service for my minimum fee."

Not long after that Curley came to see Kincade at his office. "Marshal, can you arrest somebody for over-chargin'?"

"I don't think so, Curley. Who overcharged you?"

"I went to that Lawyer Scott fella to get my will changed to include my new grandson – Blossom's baby. He said he'd only charge me a minimum fee 'cause he's renting that house from me. Marshal, what he charged me is highway robbery!"

"Is the will what you wanted him to write? Does the will look legal?"

"How would I know? He used heavy paper with a fancy letterhead at the top and he put a bunch of seals and stamps on it. It's what he charged me that's got my dander up."

From Kincade's own experience with Scott, he wasn't surprised at what he heard. "I've never dealt with an attorney, Curley, so I don't know what a minimum fee should be. The main thing is that you've got a legal will that can't be challenged." Kincade put his hand on Curley's shoulder and said, "That's what's important. You've taken care of that new grandson of yours. Am I right?"

Curley simmered down a bit, but had to have the last word.

"Minimum fee - my ass! He's got a lease on that house of mine or I'd show him the minimum length of my left boot!"

Kincade chuckled and slapped Curley on the back. "Next time, just ask how much beforehand."

"While I'm here Marshal, you want to sell me that paint your Deputy used to ride. He turned him into a fine horse."

"Kinhuste doesn't belong to me, Curley. When I hear from Sky, I'll ask him. He's just fine in my stable for now and Josephine likes to ride him now and then."

"Okay. So long, Marshal." Curley headed for the livery mumbling, "Damn lawyers. Highway robbers every one of 'em!"

Over the next several weeks, Curley's opinion of Jeremiah Scott became the consensus of dozens of citizens who brought their legal needs to Tombstone's new lawyer – his fees were exorbitant. They grumbled, but they paid. His capabilities seemed unquestionable.

David Cook wrote a glowing article for the Tombstone Epitaph describing the attorney's place of business.

TOMBSTONE WELCOMES NEW LAWYER

Tombstone is fortunate to have attracted the services of lawyer Jeremiah Scott. His office is spectacular. A ponderous floor safe holds valuables. The walls are filled with many framed diplomas, certificates, and awards attesting his vast experience and legal expertise. There is even a personal letter from the Territorial Governor commending Lawyer Jeremiah Scott. A client will find that whatever document is needed to consummate the matter at hand, Mr. Scott can reach into his file drawer and produce the embossed legal certificate which he fills out in impressive black calligraphy. For too long a time deals and promises have been secured with nothing more than a handshake. It is high time Tombstone turned to constituted formality which would stand up in any court, anywhere.

The next morning as he shared breakfast with Josephine, Kincade finished Cook's article on Scott, put down his paper, took a sip of coffee and grinned at Josephine. "The way Cook writes, maybe he oughta take up lawyering himself!"

26

Kincade looked up from the work on his desk as Josephine opened the door to his office. She was such a stunning woman. For a brief second he flashed back to the first time he ever laid eyes on her.

Kincade had ridden into Benson at the same time the stage arrived from San Francisco. Passengers were getting off. He recalled swinging off Gold Digger, stepping on to the boardwalk, and looking straight into the startling eyes of the most spectacularly beautiful woman he had ever seen. "Hello," she had said in her soft, dusky voice. "My name is Josephine. I own the Proud Cat Dance Hall and Saloon. Would you be so kind as to carry a few packages to my room?"

And Kincade's life was changed forever.

Now Josephine breezed in waving an envelope in her hand. "I just picked up another letter from Cissy in Julesburg. Shall we read it together?" A radiant exuberance for everything always energized her.

"Together always sounds good to me." Kincade took his metal letter opener from one of the desk drawers and handed it to her as she sat down on a chair by the big table. "You two are carrying on quite a correspondence, aren't you?" He handed her the opener.

"Notes mostly. I think she likes to practice the reading and writing that Jethro has been teaching her." She slit open the envelope as Kincade sat on the edge of the office's large table. "I like her more and more all the time. She is so devoted to Jethro and Melissa."

"What do you write to her about?"

"Just local news that might interest her – the new lawyer in town, the rising price of coffee, that sort of thing." She took two sheets of neatly folded, lined paper from the envelope. Kincade loved listening.

She opened the top page and began reading.

"Dearest friend. I have joyful news to tell you. I am with child! This comes as quite a surprise. Jethro is thrilled and Melissa very excited. I was a little afraid when the doctor told me, but he says I will be just fine. I must not do heavy work or get too tired. This means we shall have to postpone our move to Tombstone. But it is still our fondest wish once the baby is old enough to travel. I hope you and Kincade share our joy. Fondly, Cissy"

"Well, well..." Kincade grinned. "A blessed event for two very fine people."

"Three, including our darling Melissa. She must be eleven years old by now."

"Eleven going on twelve," Kincade smiled as they both remembered Melissa's pride in becoming a woman like her new mama Cissy.

"Here's a note for Sky from Melissa." Josephine looked at Kincade. "Melissa usually sends him a note with Cissy's letters. I've put them in a drawer."

"Well, considering Melissa is close to family, I don't think she'll mind if you read it."

Josephine unfolded the page.

"Dear Sky. I'm going to be a sister. Isn't that wonderful! I had a birthday, so now I am going on twelve. Don't forget me. Your friend, Melissa."

"Had you written them about his leaving?" Josephine asked.

"No, and I don't know why exactly. I guess I was hoping he'd return."

She paused, and then said, "Me too."

They were silent for a moment.

Kincade rubbed an ache which he could still get beside his right eye and then cleared his throat. "I wonder if they'd still like to hear of opportunities here in Tombstone?"

"It wouldn't hurt to pass any along. Then it would be up to them to sustain their interest in moving or let the idea go." She folded the pages and put them back in the envelope.

As she started to go she remembered something and turned back. "I almost forgot. When I picked up my mail, Miss Sadie told me something in strictest confidence. But she did say it would be fine to share the news with you. She says she'll only be our post mistress for one more year. She'll turn fifty and her sister wants her to move to Denver when she retires."

"The town will miss her."

"She doesn't want the town to know until she hands in her resignation. She only told me because....well...she just did."

"She was probably longing to tell someone and you, my sweet Josephine, are wonderful at keeping secrets. She'll be very hard to replace since she's the telegrapher as well as post mistress."

"I think she wanted us to know because of our telling her about the Wilcox family, and Jethro's hope to find a good job. Maybe he'd like hers. Do you think you should tell Jethro that this position might be open?"

"Yes, I think I will."

Dear Kincade,
How kind of you to think of me when the position of Post Master of Tombstone will be opening up. I understand Miss Sadie's need for discretion with such information. The timing is really quite good. By knowing this far in advance, I can try to learn to be a telegrapher. The depot master here in Julesburg is willing to teach me and I shall have lots of time to practice during the long winter months as we await the birth of our baby. Cissy is doing just fine and sends her best. Sincerely, Jethro Wilcox.

27

Jeremiah Scott's imposing physique, refined attire, authoritative voice, and legalese diatribe won people over, and no one questioned his right to regulate their lives - except Kincade.

"Josie, am I wrong to have doubts about Scott? I don't know... there's just something about him..."

Once again they were eating breakfast alone without the interference of the busy world in which they both played such an important part.

"You've always been good at reading people," she said. "What happened after you asked him to help you with the study of law?"

"That's the thing. When we first met, he said he'd do all he could to help. He mentioned a book that he would loan me, but that never happened. Why would that be?"

Josephine listened.

"I'll think I'll remind him. Maybe I'm wrong about him. I'll give him a chance," Kincade said. "It's what I'd want if I were a newcomer to town."

Kincade knocked on the attorney's door, and there was an engaging response. "Door's open, friend. Please come in."

When Scott saw it was Kincade, a coolness replaced the hospitality. "Yes, Marshal, something I can do for you?"

"Morning. Not interrupting, am I?"

The attorney shook his head as he fussed with some papers on his desk .

Kincade entered the room, and remained standing. "Some weeks ago you mentioned I could borrow a book – Blackstone's Commentaries, I believe you called it. I appreciated your offer, and I've come by to get it."

Scott paused for a moment, as if he were trying to figure out what to say in response to Kincade's request. Kincade immediately caught the attorney's hesitation.

"Marshal," he began, "Tombstone is a jumble of legal complexities. It's a raw town, tangled in unauthorized and oftentimes illegal agreements and misunderstandings that eventually lead to miscarriages of justice at some future point. I have a demanding calling – to serve the public responsibly. I've found that many problems presented to me here in Tombstone require research beyond my vast personal experience. I've been referring to Blackstone almost daily. Therefore, Mr. Kincade, I'm sorry but I cannot let the volume leave my office. Was there anything else this morning?"

"No, thank you, Mr. Scott. Good day."

Kincade's suspicions of Jeremiah Scott only increased as he returned to the street below the lawyer's office. Something was wrong about Scott. Kincade could feel it.

Up ahead, Kincade could see Mr. Perkins sweeping the boardwalk in front of his General Store. A broad smile came over the shopkeeper's face the moment he heard Kincade's spurs. "Marshal!" Perkins extended his hand, which Kincade gladly accepted. "Good morning my friend!"

"And to you. Business good?"

"Oh yes. On the up ever since your Law Dog rescued my receipts. Have you heard from the boy yet?"

"Only a card saying he'd arrived, Mr. Perkins." An instant later, Kincade realized he had flat out lied to Perkins. It surprised him how easily the lie had slipped out. He didn't like how it felt, but it was too late to do anything about it now. Kincade continued on. "I'd like you to order something for me if it's not too much trouble."

"Come inside." The store owner put down his broom, went inside his shop to stand behind the counter. "What do you have in mind, Marshal?"

"It's a book called Blackstone's Commentaries. A law book. Seems like something I ought to have."

Perkins chuckled. "I'm not sure Lawyer Scott will appreciate any competitor in his line of work."

"Oh, I'm not going to quit my Marshaling job - just peruse Blackstone for general information. Can you get it for me?"

"Never tried such an order, but I don't see why not. I've lots of catalogs – everything from ladies bonnet's to men's suspenders. I've ordered children's books for the school marm and cook books for the ladies' auxiliary. Why not a law book? May take a week or so. You in a hurry?"

"I'm sure you'll get it as soon as you can."

"You want to know the cost before I place the order?"

"If the cost seems reasonable, go ahead. If it runs into serious wages, let me know." Kincade extended his hand. "I'm glad to know your business is doing well."

"Very well, Marshal!" The shopkeeper chuckled. "How's yours at the jail?"

Kincade liked Perkins. "Some nights I have as many customers as you. So long, my friend."

The book arrived and Kincade dove into it like it was a swimming hole on a hot summer day. Josephine recalled Kincade's stories of his passion for learning as a boy. Apparently, some things never change.

Kincade took to reading the book over coffee after their morning breakfasts together. As he turned another page in the monstrous volume, Josephine said, "You'll soon drown in those chapters. Let me take you riding in my new surrey this Sunday. I'm getting quite good at handling the reins."

Kincade looked up from the book, smiled and looked at Josie. "I'd like that."

"Might be nice to sit on a blanket under those cottonwoods by the river. I'll pack a lunch."

"And I'll read aloud to you."

"That's kind of you to offer, Marshal Kincade." With a flirtatious smile, she said, "I'm sure the laws of our land are absolutely fascinating, but if it's all the same, I'd rather explore the art of lovemaking on a blanket."

Kincade looked into her twinkling eyes. "Miss Josephine, as

Tombstone's Marshal, it is my duty to inform you that lovemaking on a blanket would be indecent exposure – very illegal."

"I beg to differ, Marshal Kincade," she replied, thoroughly enjoying their play together. "May I point out to the court, it has been my experience that our exposures together far exceed the merely indecent. They are consistently delirious. And two, the judge and jury will be quick to agree with me that your obsession with Blackstone's Commentaries is cruel and unusual punishment!" Never removing her eyes from his, Josephine moved her exquisite fingers to the side of her face, where she leisurely twirled a silken blond curl. "I rest my case."

He loved her so. "I concede." He closed the book, left it on the table, stood to take her hand and lead her to the stairs. "This case is best rested by an afternoon in your boudoir. We'll call it reduced sentence for time served."

Late that day, Kincade sat on the edge of the bed. He stopped as he started to pick up his shirt and looked at the old Indian's medicine bag which hung around his neck. He fingered it for a few seconds as Josephine watched, her head cradled in the pillow. It was apparent that Kincade was deep in thought. Within a few moments, he slipped it off and gently placed it on Josie's nightstand.

Only once had Josephine seen Kincade remove the old Indian's medicine bag from around his neck. That was when he had shown it to Sky. Surprised, she asked, "Darling... what are you doing?"

"I've been thinking about doing that ever since Sky left."

"After all the years you've worn it - why now?"

"Why not?" Kincade's abrupt response was unlike him, and he regretted it immediately. He turned to her. "I miss him, Josie."

She understood completely.

"Every day, the medicine bag reminds me that I had a twin brother. The Circle of Life revealed an opposite side to me that I despise. It was, it is, powerful enough to have cost me Sky and Smoke."

Josephine rose from her pillow, moving to be close to Kincade's back. She rested her hand on his waist and consoled, "You're the exact opposite of Wil Logan, Kincade. You're honorable and honest, and tender and helpful, and....

He turned his head to look at her, his answer nearly a whisper. "And you're in love with me - right?" He smiled.

"Do I have to tell the truth, the whole truth, and nothing but the truth?"

"So swear!" And he held up his right hand.

"Yes, I confess. I'm guilty of being deeply in love with you."

The room fell quiet, the only sound their soft breathing together. Josie returned her head to the pillow. Kincade moved his body next to hers, gently pulling the sheet over them both.

They embraced...

28

Josephine drew the surrey into the shade of the old cottonwoods. Kincade helped her down. "You're right. You handle the reins perfectly. I'm impressed." Kincade took the blanket and picnic basket from the rig.

"Thank you. I've been going for a spin nearly every day since the surrey arrived."

Kincade paused to look at how stunning Josephine was in the soft light beneath the trees. He decided to play. Bowing his head slightly, then peering up at her as would a schoolboy, Kincade said, "Alone?" He quickly avoided her eyes as he spread the blanket on the soft meadow grass.

Josephine giggled, loving this hint of possessiveness. "Well, Curley Smith went with me the first time to.... My, are you jealous?"

"Not yet, but keep going." He smiled, loving the playfulness they shared.

"...to teach me about the reins. But I'm a fast learner - or else Clementine there..." she pointed to the little black mare nodding in the warm sunshine. "...unless she's the one who learned quickly about me."

Kincade paused to look at the mare and nodded thoughtfully. "You know Josie, as I recall, it didn't take me long." He opened the picnic basket and sniffed. "All my favorites. Shall we eat now or later?"

"Whatever is your pleasure."

"Oh, I like the sound of that. Come here." She did. They kissed.

"Hummm. Delicious," Josephine whispered.

The shadows lengthened. They had their picnic in the shade of the old cottonwoods, happy in each other's company without much talk. There was no need. Kincade stretched his long body out on the blanket and put his head on Josephine's lap. She sighed and twirled his thick waves of hair with her fingers, humming softly.

"Okay, Josie, what's on your mind?" he asked. "I've heard that tune before."

"You know me too well. But you're right. I have two thoughts to share."

"I'm ready, even though this was supposed to be my day off."

"I've been thinking about your suspicions regarding Lawyer Jeremiah Scott. I may have some myself."

Kincade sat erect. "So, I'm not the only one."

"This may be nothing, but.... Several times in the last few weeks he has asked to use one of my private parlors for business purposes. He wanted no drinks or entertainment from my ladies. No interruptions of any kind."

"All business, eh?"

"I would make sure he and his guests were comfortable. Just as I closed the parlor doors, Scott would bring out several big tubes of papers."

"Like maps?"

"Or maybe drawings. I wondered who was meeting with him. The men were all from out of town – mostly from Chicago. They were staying at the Cosmopolitan."

"Anyone you'd seen before?"

"No, all were strangers. When I asked – just to be friendly – what brought them to our fair town, one boasted they were eastern tycoons. Pretty self impressed."

"You say Scott wanted no interruptions during these meetings?"

"That's right. And he always locked the door after the group had gathered."

"Did you ever hear their conversations?"

"No. Several of my ladies mentioned that as they passed this parlor, they would hear low voices and occasional laughter, but even that wasn't loud."

"I suppose they were standing in the hall with their ears pressed to the door?"

"Marshal Kincade... my ladies are aware of what occurs in many of those rooms, and use the utmost discretion when listening."

Kincade smiled mischievously. "Especially your room..."

"Especially my room!" She wrinkled her nose at Kincade and

continued. "When the meeting would break up, a very large man always escorted Mr. Scott back to his office. He'd carry a heavy canvas bag. I think it was full of money."

"They go to the bank?"

"No. One of my ladies says Scott has a big safe in his office. His money goes there, as well as the papers he fills out for clients. He encourages them to leave their documents with him because his safe is fireproof. Especially the owners of the silver mines. More and more of them are using Scott's services."

"Hmmm." Kincade slowly closed his eyes. "Well, he's not doing anything against the law, but keep an eye on him for me."

Josephine started to say 'Smoke too', and then she caught herself. She ran her fingers gently along the stress lines on his face.

"That feels good. Could you get that little soft spot by my right eye? It throbs sometimes."

"Maybe you need to get more rest at night."

Kincade opened his eyes and looked into hers. "I'm trying. But there's a businesswoman in Tombstone who won't let me." She smiled and shook her head. The sounds of the creek replaced their conversation.

After several minutes, Josephine said with some hesitation, "Kincade... the other thing on my mind – do you think you should be looking for another Deputy? You're working far too hard and when you're called out of town there's no one in the Marshal's Office."

Josie was right. Tombstone was growing faster and larger than anyone had ever imagined. More and more silver strikes, more mines, more money. Tombstone was booming. There was talk of the town becoming larger than San Francisco. Kincade did need help, and he needed it now.

He was quiet and then looked at her seriously. "You don't think Sky and Smoke are coming back, do you."

"I don't know. I hope so. Maybe it could just be a temporary position. It would be a help to you."

"I'll give it some thought." He sighed, looked up into her angelic face and smiled. "Keep rubbing. That's a great help."

It seemed a strange coincidence that a few days later a lanky boy in his early twenties came into the office. He had long stringy hair hanging from beneath a stained wide-brimmed hat, dirty overalls with only one strap hooked over his left shoulder. He was shirt-less. He had two holsters slung low on his hips with black handled guns in easy reach.

"You the Marshal?" Kincade nodded, immediately not liking him. "I heard you was lookn' fer a Deputy."

"Who told you that?"

"Well, yer last two was an Indian kid and a wolf that run off an' left ya'. Sounds like ya' need someone who ain't got no wild blood and who'll stick around." He talked with a drawl that was high pitched and irritating. His eyes were little slits that glinted with wickedness.

"Sorry, you got the wrong information from someone."

"Well, my information is from someone who saw what hap-pened at the Hanging Tree a few months back. Didn't know you was spied on, did ya'?"

Kincade went cold.

"This someone saw no reason to spill his guts 'til I tol' him I'd like a job in Tombstone. Then he says I'd be well qualified for your Deputy with what he'd tell me. Is that right?"

Kincade went colder.

"Look... I got no beef with you. What I do have is these two pistols and my rifle hangin' on Flo out there." He pointed to a mule tied to the hitching post. "I can shoot the ears off a prairie dog at fifty yards. You want a demonstration?"

Kincade did not like this boy, and he liked being blackmailed even less. Kincade thought, "It must have been the fourth man at the Silver Dollar's poker table that night, the one the other three called Luke. He must have been at the Hanging Tree the night they tried to lynch Sky." Kincade shook his pounding head realizing that one of their trash had gotten away.

The boy looked at Kincade, waiting for a decision. "Damn that night!" Kincade said to himself. "Damn the decisions I made, and damn the lies I've told since!" The pain that often plagued Kincade began.

He put his fingers over his eyes as if considering and turned in his swivel chair. Kincade's head had begun to swoon with the throbbing in his right temple. He shook his head and stopped his chair. What was done, was done.

"What's your name?"

"Folks call me Polecat. My mule is Flo."

Kincade was used to the roughness of the men who populated Arizona Territory. This boy was like most of them. Unfortunately, it often took rough men to deal with rough men. Kincade clenched his jaw. He didn't want to do this, but if he kept a close eye on the boy, then maybe he'd be able to buy enough time to come up with an answer. The town's growth demanded an additional Deputy be hired, and the pickings of qualified applicants were slim to none. Josephine suggested any hiring could be on a temporary basis. "I'll give you a try for the position, but only until my former Deputies return."

Polecat chortled. "Oh hell, they ain't comin' back. I know all about that dirty, little secret too." He fingered his guns.

That was just about enough. Kincade stood, his six and half feet towering over the boy. "Listen to me, and listen to me good. My name's Kincade. I'm a U.S. Marshal. You make one step out of line, and you'll not only be out of this job, but you'll have to deal with me." Kincade lowered his voice. "And if you have any questions about what dealing with me is like, why don't you ask your friend Luke to describe, in detail, what happened to his three friends underneath the Hanging Tree."

Polecat kept still. He knew when to keep his mouth shut.

Kincade's temple pounded. "Tonight, I start my rounds at seven." He looked at the boy. "And one more thing, I'm calling you Pat Cole – Polecat is exactly what you smell like. Get a bath, put on a shirt, and hook up your overalls before tonight."

"Fine." Muttering to himself so Kincade wouldn't hear, Polecat added, "You don't have to get your tail in a twist."

The boy looked around the office. "You got any place for me to sleep here?"

"Don't push it!" Kincade said.

"Don't matter. I'm bunked with my Uncle Luke down in the holler. Guess I can stay there 'while longer. See ya tonight." Polecat slammed the door behind him.

"My God! What have I done to deserve this?" Kincade asked himself, but he knew full well. Sky's last letter had spelled it out plain and simple: "When you will not stand tall and unafraid of the truth..." Kincade knew he was living a lie – every day – and Polecat was making him pay for it. Maybe it would be better to confess to the people of Tombstone – give it up. But then he'd be leaving Josephine, and that would kill him.

No, for today, at any rate, he would deal with this blackmailer. But it would be on Kincade's own terms. "Damn!" he said out loud. "What should I tell Josephine?" He knew that with her he could bare his soul and she would understand.

He hesitated.

For a brief second, the Other Voice appeared and just as suddenly disappeared, but not before leaving an answer to Kincade's own question. "PERHAPS FOR NOW, GIVEN THE WAY JOSIE FEELS ABOUT YOU, YOU'D BETTER DO YOUR TALKING TO THE GRAVES ON BOOT HILL."

For the first week, Polecat walked with Kincade through all of

29

Lower Tombstone, learning the names of the saloon keepers and carefully remembering which ones made the most money and had the most cash. He kept his mouth shut.

That week went better than Kincade expected. The boy stayed in line. Almost quiet. The persistent pain was there at his right temple but it hadn't escalated to a throb, a pound, or the Other Voice. So on the eighth day Kincade decided that he and the boy should split up so that all the saloons could be covered. Too many people, too many stops, too much time to handle it all if they stayed together.

"Remember what I told you," Kincade warned Polecat. "You just do your job and do it right."

As Kincade left to begin rounds of Tombstone's south side, Polecat smiled. "Yeah, I'll do it right," he sneered to himself. "I'll do it just right - for me!"

That first week when he and Kincade had worked together, Polecat stayed back at the entrance to the saloons to serve up The Intimidation exactly as Kincade ordered, just like Sky and Smoke had done. He watched Kincade walk the floors and saw the reaction of these rough men, and their submission to tough talk from a man who wore the badge.

But now he'd do things his way. He'd make his own mark on the saloonkeepers of Lower Tombstone. Polecat would crash through each saloon's batwing doors and yank both shooters from their holsters with great bravado.

"Howdy boys!" he would yell across the room. "Deputy come to visit 'ya all!" He would then twirl the guns around his triggered forefinger, snapping them forward and then back in a blur, twirl both again but in opposite directions, finishing the display with a quick cock of both hammers as the guns were slowly panned from one side of the room to the other. Then, a thumbed release of the hammers, a three revolution spin backwards to drop both pistols into their holsters.

"Anyone here think they can outdraw me?" he asked with a malicious grin. No one volunteered. Not until late that first Saturday night of his patrolling alone.

A bulldogger from the Rockin' R spread had been drinking steadily since three that afternoon. When Polecat banged through the saloon's doors around midnight, the cowboy had turned into one mean drunk.

"You may be able to do some mighty fancy twirling with them shooters 'a yours," his slurred voice boomed across the room. "But I hear you can't hit a bull's butt with a banjo!"

Before the words were out of the wrangler's mouth, Polecat drew and fired through the top of the man's buckaroo hat, sending it flying off his head. Men dove under tables like prairie dogs scrambling for holes. Glaring, Polecat walked up to the dazed cowboy and leaned into his face. "I don't think I heard you," the Deputy hissed. "What was it you was sayin'?"

The room was silent. The cowboy answered. "Nothin'. I wasn't sayin' nothin.'" He bent over to pick up his hat and turned to leave the saloon. Polecat lifted his boot and kicked the man in the butt, hard. "Well, well," Polecat said to the room. "It appears I don't need a banjo to hit a bull's butt!"

The Deputy looked around the hushed room. "Anyone else have somethin' ta say ta me?"

No one spoke.

"Didn't think so." Polecat turned his back to the crowd and stepped up to the bar. He motioned to the saloon's owner to get himself over there and over there fast. "It's time I started doin' something right," Polecat thought to himself. "Right... for me!"

"How'd ya like my demonstration, Sam? 'Nough to make ya a little jumpy?"

Sam stammered. "You'se a sure fire tough Deputy, Pat Cole. Yeah, ya sure is."

"Knew you'd be impressed. Why yer jumpin' like a speckled-legged frog from a dry lake. Lemme tell ya somethin', Sam. If I'd had bristles, I'd resemble a wild hog. Why, I can shoot every bottle off that likker shelf. I can bust out them front windows 'a yours faster than a cat with his tail on fire." Polecat grabbed a whiskey bottle from the bar, bit the cork, yanked, and spit it over the bar to land on Sam's foot. He took three deep pulls, coughed and regurgitated on the saloonkeeper's vest.

"Whatever jackass yuh got yore likker from shore musta' had kidney trouble. I kin get better likker by holdin' a bottle under a mare till she has ta pee!" Sweat began to appear on the owner's brow.

"Ya know, Sam, if'n I wanted, I could bust yer place up so quick you wouldn't last as long as a grasshopper in a chicken yard. You get the picture, Sam? Your place can be a real piece of shit in nothin' flat."

Polecat looked directly into the eyes of the frightened saloon keeper. Suddenly he shot his hand to Sam's neck, grabbed hold of his string tie, and pulled the man's head inches from his foul-smelling mouth. He whispered, "Sam, how's about $25 a week to keep this from happenin'? Sound okay to you?"

The owner was too terrified to reply.

Polecat chuckled. "Sounds 'bout right to me too." He loosened his grip on Sam's throat. "Sunday's a good day to start - beginnin' of the week. I'll be 'round 'bout nine tomorra' night. You'll be 'spectin' me, won't you, Sam."

The Deputy released his fist while Sam regained his balance, swallowing deeply. Polecat put both hands on the bar and stared unblinkingly at the saloon's owner for a full minute. He then turned, took long steps towards the batwings, turned back and looked one final time at the bartender who hadn't moved. "Nice doin' business with you, Sam."

The Deputy walked out of the saloon and onto the boardwalk. The night was warm and clear. Polecat looked up at the stars and took a deep satisfied breath. This was working out better than he'd hoped.

He pulled on the shoulder straps to hoist up his coveralls and he adjusted the gunbelts on his hips, squaring them both so they set just right. He took a look to his right, down the boardwalk, across the alleyway, and into the next block of Lower Tombstone where more saloons awaited the Deputy's Saturday night visit and the new "Sunday understanding."

"One down," Polecat said to himself. "So many more ta go!"
It took less than a month of Polecat's coercion before word got

back to Kincade. It happened on a Monday afternoon.

General Store's Mr. Perkins caught up with Kincade as he walked down the street. "Marshal, just a minute of your time." He sounded really angry.   "I've always liked and respected you, Marshal, especially after what you did for me when I was robbed. But this has just got to stop. The saloonkeepers are too frightened to speak out, but your Deputy has started up with the other business owners. He threatened me again this morning!"

"Whoa, hold on Mr. Perkins," Kincade said. "Slow down, tell me what's happened."

"Your Deputy is collecting what he calls "protection money" from the saloons. Now, he's started in with the other shop owners, demanding we pay him money or there will be big trouble to follow!" Perkins was out of breath and fairly shaking in his boots.

"He did what!?" The headache started.

"It's the God's truth, Marshal. It's robbery! We're all gettin' together at the Grange at 4 this afternoon."

"I knew nothing about this, Mr. Perkins." Kincade reached out to put a reassuring hand on Perkins' shoulder. "You tell everybody that I'll be at your meeting to refund every dollar. You tell 'em that I'll see that it stops."

Perkins calmed and nodded his head. "Thanks, Marshal. Everybody knew you had nothin' to do with this. You've always been good to everybody in town. We all knowed you'd take care of this."

Kincade thanked Perkins, feeling ashamed for the mess now placed at his feet – the mess he'd been responsible for by letting Polecat out on his own. The ache was now a throb.

Polecat was at the office when Kincade opened the front door.

The boy was cleaning his guns. At the sight of his Deputy, Kincade's pain pounded and the Other Voice said, "GET HIM! GET HIM GOOD!"

Using every bit of his self control, Kincade said, "Get up!"

Polecat could see fury in the Marshal's eyes. The boy immediately remembered his Uncle Luke's description of what Kincade had done to the men who had tried to hang Sky. The boy remembered how Luke had described Kincade's enraged eyes that night beneath the moon.

As fast as the boy believed he was, everyone knew of Kincade's skill with guns, and the reputation he held across the frontier for his lightning draw and deadly accuracy.

The boy placed both of his guns on the desk stop, slowly rising from the chair. "Okay, Marshal. I know what you've heard. But I was just foolin' around, doin' a little Intimidation just like you taught me."

With one incredibly fast sweep of his arm, Kincade yanked a chair from the floor, bringing its four legs to slam Polecat backwards and pin him against the wall. One of the chair's rungs was pressed into the boy's throat, turning each breath into a retched gasp for air. It had only taken two and a half seconds.

"Where is it?"

Polecat knew that he was within inches of being torn apart. "Hid right here in your office," he croaked.

"Get it."

Kincade released the chair from the boy's neck and dropped it to the floor. Regaining his breath, Polecat went behind the potbelly stove and lifted a stone slab from the floor. There was a newly dug hole and he pulled out a canvas bag and handed it to Kincade.

"All of it," Kincade said.

"That's it. I swear."

"You be here when I get back," Kincade warned. "Don't make me do to you what I did to your Uncle's friends."

Kincade walked to the office door and turned. "You're real close to hells' gate, Polecat. So close, it wouldn't matter to me if you told the entire town what happened that night. Ripping you apart would be worth whatever ended up happening to me."

Kincade stopped to let his words sink into the boy's skull. And in the silence, for the second time in a matter of minutes, the Other Voice inside Kincade spoke. "MORE THAN WORTH IT, KINCADE."

The Marshal quietly closed the door in Polecat's terrified face.

After first stopping by the bank, Kincade entered the Grange and took off his hat. Merchants and saloonkeepers filled the room. The Marshal strode to the front, setting the bag on a large table at the head of the room. "I've got the money, Mr. Perkins, every cent of it." Kincade then turned to the other merchants. "I have all your money. If any of you paid my Deputy one nickel of protection money, I'm here to give it all back to you – with interest."

Kincade opened the satchel. "Gentlemen, I deeply regret what my Deputy did to you. It makes no difference that I wasn't aware of what he was up to. I take full responsibility for Pat Cole's behavior."

"Ain't your fault, Marshal," one old timer shouted. "He's a dirty, thievin' polecat – that's what he is!"

"I must agree with you and I wish I could send him packing." Suddenly and without Kincade having any forewarning, the Other Voice appeared within his head, whispering, guiding Kincade into another series of lies. "Unfortunately I'm under a lot of pressure from a congressman in the Capital to keep him under my wing and try to straighten him out."

"You know why?" another shouted.

"I don't, gentlemen. But for the time being I must comply with the request. Either I will succeed with turning the boy around, or I'll tell the congressman I failed and resign my job."

A gasp rose up in the room.

"Now if each of you will step up to the table and tell me the amount of his extortion, I'll return it to you. On top of what was taken from you, I'll add another ten percent of my own money. Mr. Perkins, since you brought this to my attention, why don't you come first."

The General Store owner came to the table. "How much?" Kincade asked him.

"All told, a hundred dollars over a couple of weeks."

Kincade was shocked that the bribery had been going on so long. "Here's a hundred and ten."

"Kincade, you don't need to fork out any of your own money. You wasn't the one."

"I insist – ten percent. Who's next?"

Mr. Perkins took the hundred and left the ten on the table.
One by one the merchants and saloonkeepers of Tombstone filed before the table and received their amounts. Not one accepted the

interest Kincade included in the bills he laid before them.

When all had returned to their seats, he stood and addressed them one last time. "Thank you, gentlemen. I'll keep a close eye on Pat Cole. This won't happen again. If he ever tries anything like this, please tell me straight away.

"Now if you'll excuse me it's time to make my rounds. Good night, gentlemen."

He left and the group slowly disbanded, commenting on how honest and fair their Marshal was.

30

When Kincade picked up his mail the following day, the postmistress caught his arm. "People been talking about the meeting last night. They're right pleased, Marshal."

Kincade knew Miss Sadie was doing her best to cheer him up. The lines on his brow revealed the pain he felt over the entire matter. "I'm happy to hear of that, and I thank you for telling me. I must admit to feeling bad, and embarrassed for what Cole did." Kincade smiled his appreciation, and began flipping through the mail she handed him.

"I was told that you'd like to know if any of us suspect him of far-from-honorable intentions." She blushed pink.

"My God," Kincade thought. "What's he done now?"

Miss Sadie continued. "I may just have the jitters of an old spinster, Marshal, but your Deputy's been looking too much at Mary Beth Hobbs. You know her folks, Dutch and May?"

"I do. Live about five miles out of town on Old Stone Wall Road. Right?"

"That's them. They come in ever so often to get supplies and pick up their mail. Pretty little girl's always standing between her Mama and Papa."

"My Deputy ever speak to them?"

"Not that I've noticed. But the way he looks at Mary Beth gives me the shivers. Course, I'm just a jittery old spinster."

"Not at all, Miss Sadie. I appreciate your concern. Anything else for me?"

"Yes, this telegram. A Circuit Judge, Simon Simpson, says he'll be here in two weeks." She handed it to him.

"You been reading my mail, Miss Sadie?" He gave her a mischievous wink.

"Now, Marshal Kincade, you know I'm the telegrapher as well as the post mistress. How'm I supposed to copy messages without knowing what they say?"

"Only joking Miss Sadie. You can read all my mail any time you want – unless it's from Miss Josephine."

The post mistress blushed even pinker. "Good day, to you, Marshal," she said and went back to sorting envelopes.

Kincade sat at his desk, thumbing through the mail, but his mind was on the news that Polecat had a lecherous eye. He wondered what Josephine would suggest? He trusted her judgment completely.

Then a WANTED poster caught his attention:

FERNANDO FRISCO
WANTED DEAD OR ALIVE FOR MURDER
CONSIDERED ARMED AND DANGEROUS

LAST SEEN HEADED FOR TOMBSTONE
$ 1000 REWARD OFFERED
IF APPREHENDED CONTACT
PINKERTON AGENCY IN PRESCOTT

"Polecat, get in here," he called to the Deputy who was lounging on the porch. "I've got an assignment that's right up your alley."

When the boy came inside Kincade handed him the poster. "Can you read this?"

"Yeah – so what?"

"You claim to be a dead shot. How'd you like to go searching for Frank Frisco? Might even earn some reward money."

"Money I keep, or turn over to you?"

Kincade ignored the remark.

"Why ain't you goin' after him?"

"The Circuit Judge is coming and I've three men to go on trial. You want the assignment or not?"

"Better than hangin' around this berg."

"Then get going. And remember, I'd rather have him taken alive than dead, especially if he can go on trial during the Judge's stay here."

Polecat went through the office door, untied Flo from the rail. "I'll put my travelin' supplies on your tab, Marshal." He trotted towards the General Store.

"Anything to get rid of him for awhile," Kincade thought.

Polecat had been gone four days. It was time Kincade tracked down his Deputy and see if Frisco had been apprehended. "The boy's a good shot, I'll give him credit for that. And the reward should be an incentive. Now where the hell would he go?"

Kincade left the familiar roads leading out of Tombstone. A fugitive from the law would be hiding where few people traveled - maybe in the foothill forests or where Fred Wappler's abandoned mine was located. Kincade let Gold Digger set his own pace. It was a beautiful day for riding and he only wished Josephine were with him. But then he remembered he was looking for Polecat and he wouldn't want her anywhere near his Deputy.

He was traveling down Old Stone Wall Road and barely glanced at the tidy ranch house on his left. Then he brought Digger up short. That was Flo, Polecat's mule, tied to a post. And Kincade knew that Frank Frisco was not hiding inside. He quickly turned Gold Digger and galloped up to the house, hoping he was not too late.

Kincade kicked open the door to absolute horror.

At the far side of the room, May and Dutch Hobbs were bound and gagged. On the floor in front of them, daughter Mary Beth was curled up in a fetal position, her naked thighs splashed with blood, arms crossed over bare breasts. She didn't even look up at the sound of the crashing door.

Polecat stood over her, his overalls dropped to the floor beside him. He turned sharply.

"Marshal!" was all he said – all he had a chance to say.

Faster than a ricochet, a firestorm of anger immediately engulfed Kincade. The headache appeared so quickly it seemed the pain had dropped into Kincade's head like a falling anvil. Simultaneously, the Other Voice rang out, "KILL HIM – KILL HIM –

KILL HIM!"

He was firing before he even realized the Colts were in his hands. Polecat dropped to his knees, blood spurting from his chest.

"Damn, Marshal, you done kill't me! Shot me just like Uncle Luke said you did to my Pappy at the Hangin' Tree. You murderin' son-of-a..." But his mouth began to fill with blood. His eyes went to the back of his head, and he lay still.

Kincade quickly grabbed a cloth from the table and covered Mary Beth. Then he rushed to pull the gag from the mouths of her parents and cut the ropes which bound them tightly.

Mrs. Hobbs rushed to her daughter and rocked the little girl in her arms. The child seemed almost comatose. "There, there, my baby. It won't happen again. The Marshal came. It won't happen no more." Mary Beth rallied a little and began to weep.

Kincade took Mr. Hobbs aside. "How long was he here?"

He was hardly able to answer. "Came last night before full dark. Ain't left Mary Beth alone since. Thank God you came, Marshal. You gave him what he deserved."

"Put her to bed, Mrs. Hobbs, and then both of you sit down. I want the two of you to hear what I'm going to say."

The father lifted the girl onto her bed and the mother covered her tenderly while Kincade dragged Polecat's body onto the porch.

The fire in Kincade's breast was replaced by ice. The head pounding was gone and his thoughts were so quiet that they echoed. When the three were seated around the table, Kincade spoke without emotion.

"I must speak frankly. Is there any chance that Mary Beth will get pregnant?"

Mrs. Hobbs shook her head. "She ain't started...you know...."

"Good. No one must ever know what happened here."

Mrs. Hobbs started to cry. "No, they mustn't know my little girl was ra...." She couldn't say the word.

Mr. Hobbs put his arms around her. "It's our secret, dearest. Isn't it, Marshal."

Kincade nodded. "Absolutely. Mary Beth must realize that. And she should never think it was her fault in any way. You must help her overcome any guilt. That boy was human filth."

"What about him?" Mr. Hobbs nodded towards the porch.

"He's my problem. Don't worry." Kincade stood and put his hand on Hobbs' shoulder. "I'll get back to town now."

Kincade went outside, threw Polecat's body over Flo, and secured it with his lasso. He held the mule's reins and mounted Gold Digger.

"I'm so sorry, Mr. and Mrs. Hobbs." He could think of nothing else to say. They stood in the doorway with their arms around one another, and before Kincade was out of sight, Mary Beth joined them trailing the bedcovers behind her.

News hound David Cook saw Kincade leading Flo with his burden of a body before Kincade had a chance to drop off Polecat at the undertaker's.

"That who I think it is?" the reported asked, quite excited.

"Probably," was all that Kincade would say.

"Marshal, this smells like a big story to me. Can I talk with you about what happened?"

"After I make arrangements for his burial." Kincade lifted Polecat off Flo and headed for the back door of the undertaker.

"I'll be waiting at your office."

"I'm going to The Josephine first."

"I'll be waiting."

He'd have to tell Josephine before the entire town started speculating.

The Epitaph's headline the following day read:

DEPUTY MARSHAL KILLED IN GUN FIGHT WITH WANTED OUTLAW

Josephine looked at Kincade over her cup of breakfast tea.

"Go ahead…" and he pushed his eggs around his plate.

Josephine continued. "Four days ago Marshal Kincade received a Wanted Dead Or Alive notice for Frank Frisco, a murderer who, at last report, was headed for Tombstone. Since the Marshal had to remain in town during the brief time that Circuit Judge Simon Simpson would be conducting trials, he sent his Deputy Pat Cole on the search-for-and-arrest mission. Cole was an excellent gunman. Yesterday morning the Deputy's mule returned to Tombstone without a rider. Marshal Kincade immediately set out to find his Deputy. After an extensive search, he found Cole Pat's body in a canyon where a gun battle had obviously taken place. The Deputy had multiple gunshot wounds and had been dead for many hours. There was no sign as to which direction Frank Frisco might have gone, but the Marshal is sending telegrams to neighboring districts. Pat Cole will be buried on Boot Hill on Thursday at 4 p.m."

"Sounds believable, doesn't it?" Kincade said.

"Good enough for those really interested. Polecat wasn't popular in this town," she replied.

"I'll have to see him buried just to keep up appearances."

"I'll go with you."

John Martin, the undertaker, lowered the cheap pine coffin into the grave without words. Kincade and Josephine were the only ones attending. Just the three of them standing silently as the corpse of Polecat disappeared into the ground.

Just the three of them. And the Other Voice. It whispered inside Kincade's head, congratulating him on killing the Deputy, praising him for the ever-expanding web of lies Kincade wove, now urging the Marshal into more deception, more death under the guise of enforcing the law.

The Other Voice told Kincade to look just across the way - just a dozen yards or so from where Polecat was being laid to rest. The other fresh grave had a wooden marker that said:

LUKE SHOT

Kincade rubbed the pain drumming near his right temple. From its center, the Other Voice spoke, "UNCLE LUKE AND NEPHEW POLECAT. TOGETHER IN HELL! YOU DID IT RIGHT, KINCADE."

As Kincade looked away from Luke's headstone he saw Josephine move to the grave of Jesse Keller. She took a red rose from her hair and placed it on the final resting place of his dearest friend whom she had barely known. Kincade loved Josie so deeply. A tortuous, hollow ache racked him. Ashamed, Kincade realized for the third time in their life together, that he had not told her everything.

31

Dear Josephine,

I have birthed a beautiful baby girl. Jethro said I should pick her name since I did all the work. She is named Emily for Melissa's mother and Lena for my drowned angel. I am doing well and I am so very, very happy. Cissy

Dear Kincade,

Thank you for the letter of recommendation to the Postal Department for my employment in Tombstone. I also have letters from the Julesburg Postmaster who has been my friend for years and from the telegrapher at the train depot who has taught me very well. I shall send these to the Postmaster General in the Arizona Territory and hope they arrive shortly after Miss Sadie tenders her resignation. Wish me luck. Jethro

Dear Sky,

Mama says I am not to write you any more. That was all right for a little girl to do but young ladies do not chase after boys. I am now a young lady and know all about babies and that sort of stuff. I wish you had answered my letters but I guess you did not like me as much as I liked you. Melissa Wilcox

Dear Kindade,

I have been in touch with a lawyer there in Tombstone named

Jeremiah Scott about buying Miss Sadie's house. I can understand her wanting the full purchase price immediately in order to buy a home in Denver with her sister. I have taken a mortgage on my homestead in order to send the money. But I shall be able to pay it off without difficulty when I sell this property. Wish me luck in finding a buyer soon. Jethro

Dear Josephine,
Everything goes well with us. Jethro has a job waiting for him in Tombstone. We have bought Miss Sadie's house. We already have good friends there. And we are blessed with a healthy, beautiful baby girl. I am so very, very happy. I love you, Josie. Cissy

32

Kincade stood looking out the front window of his office. Josephine would arrive any minute for their surrey ride and Sunday picnic under the cottonwoods.

It was an irritation to have a scruffy old codger ride up Allen Street and pause before the Marshal's office. This stranger threw the reins of two horses over the hitching rail. On one were two bearded and filthy men, tied back to back, their feet roped under the horse's belly. The stranger came in the office.

"Marshal, Harvey Horvath, bounty hunter." He jerked his dirty thumb up and over his shoulder. "'N them's my prisoners, Jenson and Jackson McCord. You heard of 'um?"

"I've seen the posters," said Kincade. "Where's their brother Johnson?"

"I shot him 'bout a half day's ride away from here. Don't matter he's dead since they's Wanted Dead or Alive."

Kincade had never liked bounty-hunters. He had been dogged by them himself after Wil Logan had set him up for the robbery of the Wells Fargo stage between Helena and Corinne... the same robbery where Logan had murdered a lady passenger. Bounty-hunters were not much better than the badmen they chased. Mongrel ravaging dogs who had no qualms about torturing their captives just for the fun of it. "So why are you stopping here? You'll have to get your reward money at the Territorial U.S. Marshal's Office."

"Got to go back and get Johnson. Shot their horses so I didn't have none left to bring down his body. Now Marshal, I got to do somethin' with these two whilst I go get what's left of Johnson or I won't get the reward money for all three. You get my meaning?"

"Not exactly."

"Could you put these skunks in your jail for a day, two at the most? Shouldn't take me longer than that, and I'll be back to take 'em off your hands."

Kincade could see Josephine only two blocks away, loading the blanket and picnic basket into the surrey. "All right. Bring them in. But you better show up no later than two days from now, or I'll claim the reward myself."

"I'm plumb tuckered out, Marshal. Anyplace I could camp out for a few hours before startin' back?"

"There's water and shade just west of Sawmill Road. Get your boys in here. I've got business to attend to."

Harvey Horvath led in his captives and didn't untie them until they were in the cell. "Much obliged, Marshal." He shook Kincade's hand and left. Kincade left for the pump outside to wash off the bounty hunter's sweat.

When he came back in the two men were clinging to the bars. "Marshal, could you get us a drink of water and somethin' to eat. That old buzzard ain't give us nothin' at all for three days. We's about to die."

They did look in terrible shape and Kincade nodded. "Don't go away," he answered, and left for his little house at the rear of the jail. In a few minutes he returned with a large pitcher of water, a glass, and some bread and cheese that had been his lunch the day before. "I'm locking up the office for an hour or two. No use yelling. Tombstone's used to my prisoners putting up a racket and they won't pay any attention to you."

Josephine was outside waiting for Kincade. She was visiting with some wives who were her friends but bid them adieu when Kincade stepped up to the seat beside her.

"Josie, I hate bounty hunters," he said as they rode out of town.

"Certain memories never really go away, do they? But it's best to remember the happy ones – even after they're over."

"Being accused of stage coach robbery and murder was maybe the worst memory I have."

"And having Sky and Smoke, the best – right?"

"No." Kincade reached down and took the reins from her hands. He pulled Clementine to a stop and turned to face Josephine. "The best day of my life was the first day I saw you. I knew you were going to be mine – even though I had to give you time to find out." Kincade leaned over to kiss her.

"Not very much time, as I recall." She took the reins, flicked them over the mare's back and the surrey left a cloud of dust behind. He laughed at her playfulness.

"What made you think about bounty hunters?" she asked as they slowed down.

"One showed up at the office just before we left town, asking for a favor."

"A favor – from you – The Marshal?"

"Wanted me to lock up his prisoners."

She laughed. "So now you're running a hotel."

"Only for a day or two."

"Oh my darling, you can't say no to anyone."

"Especially to you."

That night Kincade brought the McCord brothers beef stew and biscuits. Gold Digger's caretaker, Old Teddy, cooked up the prisoners' meals, and what they lacked in tastiness they made up for in quantity.

"We ain't et this good since our Ma died," Jenson said. "Thanks, Marshal."

"...maybe not even then," Jackson added. "When'd that old buzzard say he'd be back for us?"

"Tomorrow – next day at the latest."

"Eat up, little brother. This could be our last meal."

Three days went by and no sign of Harvey Horvath. Kincade was tired of furnishing room and board for the McCord brothers, Wanted Dead or Alive. He had no other prisoners except several drunks whom he let go after they'd slept off their meanness.

"Tonight after I make my rounds I'm going out to Sawmill Road and see if Horvath ever camped there," he decided.

Although it was quite late when he arrived, there was still a small fire between stones at the campsite. Harvey Horvath was curled up in a blanket, snoring loudly. Kincade kicked the bounty hunter in the ribs.

"Wake up, you filthy leech!"

Horvath sat up with a jerk and blinked his eyes. "Marshal! You sure surprised me! I was comin' to see you in the mornin'."

"I bet you were! Where's Johnson McCord?"

"Wrapped up neat as a baby over there under the tree. How's my two other prisoners?"

"Alive, no thanks to you. Don't you know you have to give men water and food if you're going to bring them in alive?"

"So who says they have to be alive? I would'a killed them along with Johnson 'cept I wanted to have 'um suffer a little first." He laughed. "Should 'a seen 'um when old Johnson got his belly shot full of led. Jenson cried like a baby."

Kincade's head began to ache next to his right eye.

"Those boys had their tongues hangin' out like hound dogs after couple days tied to my pack horse. And me? I was drinkin' my fill of sweet well water right in front of 'em." He laughed and wiped some spittle from his mouth. Kincade's temple began to throb.

"Hell, Marshal, don't feel sorry for 'um. They's Wanted Dead Or Alive. They's as bad as that Wil Logan gang. You ever heard 'bout him?"

The throb was now pounding. Kincade drew his gun. "Heard of him? He was my twin brother!"

"My God – your ..."

The pounding turned into the Other Voice, "KILL THE SON OF A BITCH!"

And Kincade did.

Kincade loaded Johnson McCord's body on Harvey Horvath's horse. It was very dark by the time he reached the jail. Not a sound from the street. But Kincade could clearly hear the two prisoners talking very softly as he quietly opened the rear door to deposit his burden inside.

"Hell that Marshal's a push over – feedin' us like we's royalty."

"He ain't got the guts to be a Marshal. Bet he only draws his gun to take a shit." They both laughed. Kincade's throb began again.

"So what's the plan?"

"Easy. When he brings breakfast tomorrow we'll act real lazy and slow til he gets the cell open. Then you jump him and I'll get his gun."

"We gonna shoot 'im or just tie 'im up?"

"Shootin's too noisy. We'll stick a gag in his mouth and rope him good. Then we'll lock him in the cell."

"Sounds right to me," Jenson said. "But you always was the smart one."

Kincade stepped into the dim light. "But not quite smart enough." He pulled his guns. The two outlaws stared into the barrels leveled at each of their heads.

"Somebody's gonna hear that, Marshal," Jackson said.

"The sound of gunfire this time of night is nothing new in this town." The throb had changed to a pound. It was growing louder. Then the Other Voice said, "KILL THEM!"

And Kincade did.

"David Cook is making quite a name for himself over your exploits, darling. Have you seen the paper?"

"Don't need to. I was there."

"There's even a photograph of the three dead McCord brothers," Josephine said as she sipped her morning tea. "You want to see it?"

"No, I've seen them. But read me what David Cook says anyway."

Josephine placed her cup in its saucer and began.

MARSHAL IS HERO IN DARING JAIL BREAK

"The three McCord brothers, Jenson, Jackson, and Johnson, who have been Wanted Dead Or Alive, were killed last night in an attempted escape from the Tombstone jail. Marshal Kincade had been holding Jenson and Jackson for a bounty hunter named Harvey Horvath who returned to the hills hoping to capture the third brother. Apparently he was unsuccessful, for Johnson McCord found Horvath camped near Saw Mill Road and killed him. Johnson then proceeded to the Tombstone jail to free his younger brothers. He held the Marshal at gun point while he unlocked their cell. The three were about to mount horses when Marshal Kincade bravely risked his life to shoot them from the jailhouse doorway. His spectacular marksmanship was proved again. The body of Harvey Horvath was found this morning at Saw Mill Creek."

She folded the newspaper and placed it on the table, smiling proudly at Kincade. "You are most certainly a Hero. I'm so proud of you!"

Kincade ate with one hand and rubbed his right temple with the forefinger of the other. This was the fourth time that he hadn't told Josephine everything.

Kincade asked David Cook a favor. "Do you suppose I could get a good copy of the photograph your paper ran of the McCord brothers? I should let the Territorial Marshal in the Capital know they're dead."

The reporter grinned all over. "Right away, Marshal. Maybe you'll get a reward. After all, they were Wanted Dead Or Alive."

No one knew that a thousand dollar reward arrived for Marshal Kincade of Tombstone Arizona.

No one, but the Other Voice.

33

The morning sun felt good as the light splashed through the window panes of The Josephine. The butter knife slipped into the petite glass bowl of apricot jam. Josie placed a small amount on her breakfast roll as she quietly watched Kincade seated across from her.

"Does it hurt all the time?" she asked softly.

"What? I'm sorry, Josie, what did you ask?"

She smiled at Kincade. She thought she knew everything about him but lately she noticed a new habit. "When we're at breakfast, you eat with one hand and rub a little circle around your right temple with the other."

"Oh that. Guess I'm just absentminded."

"Does it hurt?"

"Not really. It's a strange feeling. It's probably just the stress of my job."

"Would you like to tell me about it? I love listening to you." Josephine meant it. Even when he had nothing of importance to share, it all seemed important to her.

Kincade looked at her as she waited for his response. In a few moments, he put down his fork and wiped his mouth with the napkin. "Josie, word has gotten out that I'm studying the law. Sometimes I wish I'd never bought Blackstone's Commentaries."

She smiled, relieved that perhaps that was all it was. "People are probably hoping you'll be cheaper than Jeremiah Scott." She laughed, and suddenly Kincade's head felt much better.

"I don't charge because I don't give out advice, but I am a good listener. Homer Henry came by yesterday asking if I could arrest somebody for writing a bad will. 'Whose will?' I asked him. 'My Pappy's,' he said."

Josephine thought a minute. "It's been a year since old Mister Henry died. Didn't he have a will?"

"Oh yes. He made a will as soon as Jeremiah Scott arrived because he knew he was in poor health."

"What happened?"

"Since there were only two sons, his estate was to be divided equally between Homer and his brother, Tad. The old man made it definite that Tad's boy, Julius, was to get absolutely nothing. He's a drunk, a cheat, and womanizer and his Granddaddy hated him. According to Homer, old Mister Henry made that very clear to our Tombstone lawyer."

"Tad Henry – that name rings a bell. Oh yes, he was killed in a mine cave-in last week. David Cook wrote a story in the paper."

"That's the one. Now his son, Julius, says half of everything the old man left is his and he wants to sell out and move to San Francisco."

"Is that true – that it's legally his?"

"That's what Homer came to see me about. His Pappy certainly would turn over in his grave if he knew Julius would get one penny."

"Did you look at the will?"

"Scott keeps it in his safe. But Josie, even though I've been reading as much as my time allows, I probably couldn't understand all that legal jargon any better than Homer. I'm just a Marshal – I'm no lawyer."

"Did Homer ask Jeremiah Scott for an explanation?"

"He did. Scott pointed out the one little sentence that gives Julius a legal claim. It says: ...his share will pass to his legal descendants..."

"And Julius is the legal descendent of Tad Henry so he's entitled to his father's share of the inheritance. Oh my, didn't old Mr. Henry read the will and see that provision?"

"He couldn't read at all, let alone figure out all the meanings. He trusted Jeremiah Scott. Homer claims his nephew paid Lawyer Scott to write in that part."

"Does he have proof of a bribe?"

"He's asking me to find proof and arrest Scott."

"Can you do that? Is that the job of a U.S. Marshal?"

"That's what I told Homer. His only recourse is to get the circuit judge who's due here next week to take a look at it."

"Do you think he'll do it?"

"Probably. Homer's fighting mad," said Kincade. "And I can't say I blame him."

She was silent for a moment as if wondering if she should say what was on her mind. But she always had with Kincade. "Kincade, do you trust Jeremiah Scott?"

"Josie, that's what starts this pain in my head." He looked at her with a smile. "No use laying my troubles on you." He took her hand. "May I have another cup of coffee?"

"You may, sir, along with a kiss from me. That should make the rest of your day beautiful."

"Kiss first, if you please."

Homer Henry wasn't the only one to approach Kincade with a legal question. Martin Hatcher found out that when he bought property, the mineral rights were not included and the seller could claim any findings as his own. Sam Coombs said his property boundaries were being questioned, including water access rights to his ranch. On and on complaints were brought to Kincade's attention, and each and every one had Jeremiah Scott as the villain.

"Why do people go to him?" Kincade wondered out loud to Josephine.

"He looks and plays the part of a big city lawyer. People can be easily fooled."

"I get the feeling he'll swing a deal any direction if enough money is laid on the table."

"You've always been able to read people well, Kincade. You may be right." He sighed and shook his head. Josephine continued. "If he really is dishonest it will catch up with him one of these days. You'll be there when it happens."

"I hope I don't have to wait too long. My head aches every time I hear a new story."

"You know what your problem is, Marshal Kincade?" She put her arms around him. "You care. You want to make everything right for everybody." She drew him close and looked up into his blue eyes. "Just make things right for me."

"Now?"

"Why not?"

Judge Simon Simpson and his court bailiff, Bowdrie, arrived on the morning train. The Judge insisted they have two of the best suites in the Cosmopolitan Hotel. Josephine was pleased to oblige, as she had decorated both herself. In one of the two suites, Josephine had placed a porcelain vase. This vase had survived the destruction and fires at Josie's stage stop on the Cherokee Trail, and the inferno at the Proud Cat Dance Hall and Saloon in Benson. It was one of her most precious possessions, and she was proud to display it.

After the Judge and bailiff checked in, Simpson sent a message to Marshal Kincade that he would appreciate meeting with him as soon as convenient, preferably before noon so that an announcement could be put in the next day's Tombstone Epitaph.

Kincade was not surprised at the Judge's appearance. He looked the part, with a portly belly, white mutton chops along his cheeks, and a practiced smile. "Come in, Marshal. Please sit down. Will you have a cigar?" Simpson's bailiff, who looked more like a rough hewn prison guard than an officer of the court, held out a beautiful wooden box with an Egyptian lady painted on the lid. The Judge opened it and extended it to the seated Marshal. "They're my favorite brand which I order directly from Havana. Quite expensive but I'm addicted."

Kincade took one and ran it along his nose. "Very fine. Thank you." He put it in the pocket of his white shirt, as the bailiff returned the wooden box to the side table. Seeing Kincade's quizzical look at the bailiff, the Judge explained. "Bowdrie is my body guard as well. A wise precaution in my position."

Kincade nodded. "Now, what can I do for you, Judge?"

"Will you arrange for the local newspaper to print a notice about my arrival and availability to judge civil matters as well as any criminal felons you may have in your jail? Then if you will find a suitable setting for these hearings, I shall be most grateful."

Kincade rubbed his chin and thought for a moment. "The Grange would be best. It's large enough. When do you wish to begin?"

"The Tombstone Epitaph comes out in the morning?" Kincade nodded. "Then let us hold preliminary hearings tomorrow afternoon and the final judgments on the day after. I shall need time to study the cases before rendering decisions. Have the announcement read that any persons wanting an audience should leave their names at the hotel desk tomorrow morning. My bailiff will arrange the docket."

Looking at the dark, enormous and silent bailiff, Kincade wondered to himself if the man were better suited to lay steel for the railroads. "Of course. Sounds good. Now if you will excuse me, I'd better get over to the Epitaph office to be sure this makes any deadline." They both stood and shook hands.

"Will I see you tomorrow?" the Judge asked.

"Yes. I have three men in jail. Would you like to have them appear before you on the first or second day?"

"The second will be better." He took one of his cigars from the box, lit it, and blew out the match. "Until tomorrow then." The bailiff moved to the suite's door to hold it open for Kincade to step into the hall. He looked back for one more goodbye and he saw the Judge share a strange grin with his court steward. The grin was quite different than the one he had first greeted Kincade with.

The Grange was full, some people wanting to have legal matters reviewed, others just curious. A big table had been set in front of the group with a swivel chair, and tacked to the wall behind it was a large Arizona Territorial Seal painted on white muslin. It showed a miner in front of a wheelbarrow with a pick and short-handled spade. There were two mountains in the background.

There was chattering, but everyone fell silent when Judge Simon Simpson entered. "All rise!" commanded Simpson's bailiff. His Honor had on a black robe which made him look quite distinguished. He sat and banged the gavel three times.

"We will begin these proceedings with a prayer. Is there a pastor in the room?" Pastor Elsea stood. "Very good. Will you please offer a blessing and petition the Almighty that righteousness will prevail?"

Jedadiah had not prepared for this request but he managed to clear his throat, and recite one of his stock prayers that many had heard a hundred times. Then he sat and several nodded their approval in his direction.

The Judge banged his gavel again and said in a loud voice, "This court is now in session." He looked down at a list before him. "First I call upon Homer Henry. Will you please rise."

Homer stood.

"What is your matter before this court?"

"It is about my father's will, Sir."

"May I have the will please?"

"Well, I don't have it. Lawyer Jeremiah Scott keeps it in his safe."

"I will procure it from him and study it this evening. I will render my opinion tomorrow. There is a $25 court fee which you must put in the empty cigar box on this table before leaving this afternoon." The bailiff glared at Homer Henry and pointed his finger at the box.

Homer's surprise was evident as he looked around for Kincade who sat in the back row. The Marshal rose a little in his chair and saw that the cigar box was similar but not the same as the one the judge had in his suite. The painting on the lid was of an Indian maiden. The cigar brand was the same.

Homer reached in the high pockets of his overalls and counted out the money. Twenty-five dollars was a considerable amount. He laid it in the box and started to ask the bailiff for a receipt, but the frown on the Judge's face stopped him.

Homer gave Kincade a bewildered look as he left the Grange and Kincade shrugged and whispered, "Maybe this is customary." Homer shrugged back.

"Will Martin Hatcher please stand," the Judge ordered. "State your case, Mr. Hatcher."

"I've been told I don't have the mineral rights on my property."

"Where is the deed to this property?"

"Lawyer Scott keeps it in his safe, just like Homer's papers."

"Then I shall request he give it to me before the day is over. Place your $25 for court costs in the cigar box. I'll review your case before tomorrow. Good day, Mr. Hatcher."

Kincade got up and left before Martin Hatcher could give him a look similar to Homer's.

The next day Kincade was deliberately late in arriving at the Grange. His excuse was the three jailed men whom he needed to take to their trials. When he got close he knew that things had not gone well for the men who had presented their complaints the previous day. They stood in a cluster at the Grange steps talking in angry voices. When they saw Kincade leading his three prisoners in handcuffs, they stopped talking and went up to him.

Homer Henry was their spokesman. "Marshal, why don't you become a lawyer, maybe even a judge. Then we'd get some real justice in Tombstone."

Another man spoke up. "Where's all this court cost money going? Any idea, Kincade?"

"I asked Jeremiah Scott that very question. He assured me it will go into the Tombstone General Fund, with a small deduction for Judge Simpson's expenses." Kincade pushed the three prisoners through the Grange door. Actually he had not thought to ask the lawyer any such thing, but it seemed to reassure the men. The more Kincade thought about it, the more he thought that he would ask. Something just didn't feel right.

The afternoon session was for criminal trials. "All rise!" said his bailiff. The Judge entered in his robe and seated himself with all the assurance of one who is doing his duty.

"First prisoner, Marshal."

The young man was given 30 days, not counting time served, for beating his wife and a fine of $50.

The second was an old fool whom Kincade had only arrested because his daughter-in-law had insisted he was stealing money from under her mattress.

"Return of the stolen money and $50 fine," the Judge pronounced. Kincade saw the daughter-in-law smile.

"But I never stole nothin' and I ain't got no money to pay no fine!" The old man shouted.

The Judge banged his gavel. "Then ten days in jail and your son and his wife must pay the fine before leaving this courtroom or they will be held in contempt." The daughter-in-law stopped smiling.

Lawyer Jeremiah Scott was there to represent only one client – the son of a wealthy ranch owner who had stolen some of his father's cattle and sold them to an army buyer. The father was present when Scott pleaded his case as a neglected youngster who was only striving to get his father's attention. The Judge banged his gavel and said, "There will be no jail sentence. I place the son in the father's custody. He shall surrender the profits of the sale to this court as a punitive fine. Step forward with the money, Sir."

The duties of Judge Simon Simpson had ended and the two would depart tomorrow. Kincade breathed a sigh of relief. He wondered what Sky would have thought about his first judicial proceedings. Smoke might have intimidated His Honor when nobody else had been able to. Kincade felt so uncomfortable with how the Judge and his strong-armed bailiff worked the law, and the pockets of Tombstone's citizens, that he probably would have told Smoke to "attack and wait."

He made his regular nightly rounds. It was late and dark when he finished but he still heard the honky-tonk piano music coming from The Josephine. "I wonder if my sweet Josephine would be agreeable to a gentleman caller?" he mused as he quickened his step.

As he passed the barber shop, a light was coming from the upstairs office of Jeremiah Scott. He slowed and stared at the drawn blind. "He's working late after a busy day. But there's nothing wrong in that."

As he started to continue walking, he saw two dark shadows at the top of the stairs. A third man stood inside Scott's open doorway. The night was quiet and he heard one of the two standing outside say, "Thanks, Gerry. Keep in touch."

Kincade did not hear a reply. He stepped into the shadows as the two men came down the steps and disappeared into the dark street. He could not see who they were.

There was a soft knock at the door of Josephine's suite and she rubbed the sleep from her eyes. She gently pushed Kincade's arm from around her waist and slipped out of bed. She tiptoed to the door. "Yes, what is it?"

"Sorry to disturb you, Miss Josephine," came a man's voice from the hall. "The desk clerk from the Cosmopolitan is here. There is a matter of some urgency and he needs to speak with you."

"I'll be down in just a minute. Thank you, Robert."

Josephine turned and saw Kincade still in bed but leaning on one elbow. "There trouble?"

"I don't know, but it sounds like it." She was hastily putting on a black velvet robe. "Sorry to wake you."

"Oh, Josie, that's okay. You go ahead. I'll dress and shave and be right down. If you need me, just call and I'll skip the dressing and shaving."

When Kincade came down the stairs, Josephine was listening to her night clerk. She was clearly distraught and confused. "Are you sure, William?"

The night clerk nodded. "Quite sure, Miss Josephine. We checked their suites. They're both gone."

Kincade came to Josephine's side. "What's wrong? What happened?"

"William says that the Circuit Judge and his bailiff have both left town without paying their room or bar bills!"

Kincade turned to the night clerk. "Maybe they're just out for an early morning walk."

William shook his head. "All their luggage is gone, Marshal." Embarrassed, the clerk stopped. He was clearly uncomfortable as he turned to Josephine.

"What is it, William?" Josie asked.

"I..., it's the suite that Judge Simpson's bailiff had, Miss Josephine. "He, uh... we're so sorry!"

"What?" Kincade almost shouted.

"He tore it apart!" the clerk blurted out. "Must have been drunk as a skunk from all the whiskey bottles on the floor. Slashed the bedding, broke two of the armchairs, and..." William swallowed, knowing how much this would hurt her. "... your vase, Miss Josie. The bailiff shattered your lovely vase."

It was like Josephine had been slapped across her face. Not once, but twice, this porcelain vase had been rescued from the destruction wielded by Wil Logan and his gang of marauders. After they had burned the Proud Cat Dance Hall and Saloon, Josephine had returned to Benson. Sifting through the rubble, she found the vase blackened with soot, but otherwise unharmed. For Josephine, the vase signified the proof of good triumphing over evil. She realized that this was a somewhat childish notion, but one she had secretly held since the vase first survived the burning of her stage stop years before.

Looking at Josephine, and seeing the pain in her eyes, there was a sharp throb in Kincade's head. It had nothing to do with the broken vase. It had everything to do with Kincade's wish to protect her from any and all harm and heartbreak. The Other Voice shouted silently, "SOMEHOW, SOMEDAY, YOU WILL MAKE THIS WRONG RIGHT."

Kincade brought Josephine to his side. She sighed and rested her head on his shoulder. "Oh, it was only a vase..."

William tried to do his best to sooth her. "We'll clean everything up, Miss Josie. We'll make it all good as new."

She nodded her thanks. Kincade said, "Josephine, I'm going to pay an early morning visit to our lawyer friend, Jeremiah Scott. I have a feeling he has an associate who just left town in a hurry." Making sure she was safely in her suite, Kincade left. Judge Simpson leaving without paying was despicable. And his bailiff destroying the second suite spoke of a wanton disrespect for the woman who had shown them her best hospitality and warmest welcome. If the Judge and his henchman were a fraud, some kind of bandits in black robes, Tombstone had been maliciously robbed. And where was the money that had been put in the cigar box?

Lawyer Scott had just pulled up the shades in his office window when Kincade opened the door without knocking. "Marshal Kincade! You're here early this morning."

Kincade came straight to the point. "When was the last time you saw Judge Simpson?"

For a split second, Scott's neck twitched. Kincade saw it plain as the morning sun. The Marshal kept his eyes locked onto Scott's, who clearly became uncomfortable at Kincade's withering stare. Over a great many years, Kincade had learned that The Wait reveals all secrets.

"I... uh... why it must have been in court. Yes, when court adjourned."

Kincade remained silent, looking hard at Scott.

"I haven't seen the Judge since, Marshal Kincade."

He waited.

"Is there anything wrong?"

Waited. Lawyer Scott began to perspire ever so slightly.

"It appears, Mr. Scott, that Judge Simon Simpson and his man Bowdrie left Tombstone in the middle of the night, taking not only the court fees collected but failing to pay their charges at the Cosmopolitan Hotel."

"Marshal Kincade, I am shocked! Truly shocked! The credentials he showed me appeared perfectly legal in every respect. Didn't you think so?"

Kincade watched Scott's eyes.

"Yes, they are bandits! My God!" Scott was scrambling for words. "Why, they must be frauds! His judicial credentials must have been a clever forgery! Yes, they are bandits! My God! They must have gotten away with several thousand dollars!"

Watched the eyes...

"At least that much! Have you sent a wire to the Chief Territorial Marshal for their arrest?"

The eyes...

"Why, we must notify the judicial authorities in the Capital about the impersonation." Beads of perspiration formed on the lawyer's brow, the color drained from his face. "It sickens me when men demean the dignity of the law by such deceit."

Kincade looked down at the desktop of Lawyer Jeremiah Scott. There lay the beautiful cigar box with the Indian maiden on the lid – the very box that money had been put into during the Judge's trials.

An explosion of pain burst in Kincade's right temple. For a moment, everything else on the table went out of focus. But the evil collusion between Lawyer Jeremiah Scott, Circuit Judge Simon Simpson and his outlaw bailiff Bowdrie began to become quite clear. And with this realization, a third presense joined Kincade. The Other Voice said, "KILL HIM!"

Instinctively his hands went to his hips, but he felt nothing there. Kincade's guns were still at Josie's bedside. In his haste to join Josephine, he'd left them.

Unable to obey the command to kill, Kincade shook his head, trying to still the Other Voice. Focus returned to his eyes as the explosion subsided. Kincade became aware that Scott was talking to him.

"..... sure you'll find them. And I thank you for coming to me directly, Marshal. Please don't hesitate to ask if I can help you in any way." He extended his hand.

Kincade shook his head again. He looked at Scott, down to the cigar box and back to Scott's extended hand. He took it, but held Scott in a vice-like grip, perfectly rigid. Without shaking the lawyer's fleshy paw, Kincade looked hard into Scott's eyes. "Yes. I'll find those responsible. Let there be no doubt, Mr. Scott. I'll find them."

Kincade held fast to Scott's sweating palm, causing several of the lawyer's knuckles to pop under the pressure. "And once I do, they'll pay!"

34

Judge Simpson, or whoever he really was, and his bailiff had taken the people of Tombstone for a judicial ride, stealing well over a thousand dollars of their hard-earned money with the pounds of his gavel. The men who claimed to be instruments of the circuit court were far worse than the trash Kincade dealt with in the back alleys of Lower Tombstone.

That night after his rounds, Kincade sought the advice of his friend Jesse Keller. Kneeling at his Boot Hill tombstone, Kincade wondered how he would find the crooked Judge to make him and his man pay for what they'd done. He rolled a marble-size stone between his fingers.

As he started to leave the graveyard, the Other Voice said, "LISTEN. I'LL TELL YOU WHAT TO DO." Kincade spun and stared back at the silent headstone of Kincade's brother, Wil Logan.

Unable to get much sleep, Kincade rose before the sun. The Marshal was waiting for Tombstone's post mistress as she arrived at her office. "Well, you're up early this fine Tuesday, Marshal," said Miss Sadie as she unlocked the post office door.

"This morning's sun just wasn't bright enough," Kincade smiled.

"But I knew seeing you would make up the difference."

Miss Sadie shook her head, always amused at Kincade's playfully innocent flirtations with her. "Okay, Marshal, you have me in the palm of your hand. How may I help you this fine day?"

"Did Judge Simon Simpson place any telegrams during his short stay here?"

"As a matter of fact, yes. Three I believe." She took off her hat and placed it carefully on the shelf above her desk.

Kincade cleared his throat. "I suppose it would be terribly unethical for you to tell me who they went to and what they said."

Miss Sadie straightened herself up to her full five foot two inches. "Marshal! Shame on you! You know how I follow the rules of my position to the letter!"

"Well, would it be against those rules for you to tell me where the wires were sent? Those transactions are public record, are they not?"

Miss Sadie furrowed her eyebrows as if pondering his suggestion. "Nothing wrong in that, I suppose, since I record every telegram in an open ledger." She pulled a big, grey book from her top drawer and scanned the lines. "Here it is. Three on the day after he arrived here. Sent to Benson, Elfrida, and Tubac."

"Humm," Kincade stroked his chin. "North, east, and west of Tombstone." The Marshal's plan just might work. "Miss Sadie, I need to send three wires myself. Forms and a pencil please?"

Carefully he wrote out the message: "Do you anticipate arrival of Circuit Judge? STOP Need name and dates of arrival and departure STOP Appreciate immediate response STOP Kincade U S Marshal Tombstone"

He handed the paper to Miss Sadie. "Send this same message to the Marshal of Benson and the sheriffs of Elfrida, and Tubac, okay?"

She read his bold printing. "Why, Marshal, I could have told you all this stuff without asking them."

He broke out laughing. "Not without breaking the rules, Miss Sadie. Wouldn't want my second sweetheart to get in any trouble." He left her at her telegrapher's key and hoped the wait for responses wouldn't be long.

By that same afternoon Miss Sadie brought him a telegram from Elfrida. "Judge Jasper Peterson arrived today STOP Staying three days STOP Sheriff Myron Sutton"

Folding the telegram in his weathered hands, Kincade said to himself, "Judge Jasper Peterson, huh. And here he introduced himself as Simpson."

Kincade would not wait for the responses from Benson and Tubac.

Elfrida was all he needed to know.

35

Gold Digger stood patiently as Kincade tightened the cinch, pulling down on the strap, up and down again as the stallion relaxed to release the air in his belly. Pushing the saddle's horn forward and back again, Kincade checked to make sure the rig was secure. Satisfied, he turned to Josephine.

"You're going after them, aren't you," she asked quietly.

Kincade looked at her concerned eyes without speaking. She already knew the answer.

She looked at the ground, her knuckles rubbing her lips as she considered what would happen when Kincade came face to face with Simon Simpson and his sidekick.

"You could bring them back," she said. "They could stand trial for what they did." She believed, and had always believed, that right would prevail. It was one of the things he loved most about her. But something horribly powerful was eating his insides away, carving up his soul, gaining strength and intensity and control with each passing day.

For several minutes the two looked into one another's eyes, past the blueness and into the center of why they loved one another beyond words. Josephine could feel that something was troubling Kincade – something much greater, far deeper, than the crimes of Simpson and Bowdrie. What ever it was, she realized there was no stopping him.

"I don't suppose it would do any good to ask you to be careful." Kincade put his hands on each side of her concerned face without speaking. He shook his head.

Kincade turned, stepped into Digger's slick fork tapaderos and swung up, the leather creaking as he settled in. Kincade's Colts were holstered in his gunfighter's twin rig, fifty cartridges per belt. He pulled gloves onto his fists, flexing the fingers, and pickled up the bridle's reins. His U.S. Marshal badge peeked from beneath his frock coat.

She reached up to put her hand on his thigh. "I'll be here – watching – waiting."

Josephine was so beautiful, so precious to him. On impulse he leaned down and swept her up with his right arm, lifting her to the saddle in a fierce embrace. He kissed her as she threw her arms around him – but not so far as to feel the large Bowie knife secured in a sheath at the small of Kincade's back.

From his second floor office window, lawyer Jeremiah Scott peered down at them both. "How touching," he smirked. "How very touching..."

A half hour after Kincade rode out of Tombstone, Scott left his office and headed for the blacksmith shop. "Good day to you." Scott tipped his hat to Big Red. "Have you seen Kincade?"

"If you need the Marshal, he ain't here." Red stood over a white-hot fire, working his huge right arm to pump the forge bellows, stoking the coals for the iron about to be bent. "He's gone. Back Saturday night. Maybe Sunday."

"It can wait," said Scott. Another tip of his hat as Scott exited through the tall doors to the street, but Red was too busy to notice.

Jeremiah Scott quickly returned to his office. In his center desk drawer, he retrieved a paper that looked like a telegram. But it wasn't. He had forged the document. Carefully folding it, he slipped the paper into his coat's inner pocket and left for newspaperman David Cook's office at the Epitaph.

"Oh no!" said Cook after reading the telegraph produced from Scott's coat. "This is horrible!"

Scott gravely nodded his head.

"You say you just received this?" asked Cook incredulously.

Scott nodded again.

"This news will shake Tombstone to its bones!" said Cook. "Tomorrow's edition is already being printed. But rest assured Mr. Scott, that this story will be on our front page Thursday!"

"Mr. Cook," said Scott. "You can well imagine how Miss Josephine will react to this tragic news."

Cook sadly agreed, shaking his head with dismay.

"I know that you are a consummate professional," continued Scott. "So, I respectfully ask that you not mention this matter to anyone until I have the opportunity to visit with Miss Josephine myself. I think Thursday morning, before the town begins reading your story, will be a perfect time for me to break this sad news to her. I can count on your discretion, Mr. Cook?"

"Oh yes," he said quickly. "It is I who wish to thank you for bringing the story to our paper."

Scott extended a handshake to Cook, assuring their agreement of absolute discretion would be followed. Josephine would hear of the tragedy from Scott's lips first, with the news immediately verified by the appearance of the story in the town's paper just moments later.

Scott smiled broadly to himself as he casually strolled down Allen Street. He had plenty of time. His plan for the ultimate prize was working perfectly.

Late Thursday afternoon, Gold Digger crested a ridge and Kincade saw the town of Elfrida. It straddled a rust-colored creek, its bed lined by a row of thin cottonwood trees. Most of the town was made up of tattered miner's tents. The main street, if it could be called that, had several wooden buildings that included a rooming house, a General Store that housed a post office and town offices, and a livery across the muddy street. All were ramshackle and in disrepair.

Kincade reined Digger to a stop. Simpson and his bailiff had to move fast through the small towns of Arizona Territory, holding Court for two days and disappearing in the middle of the third night - this night. They would now be preparing to skedaddle. Kincade would wait for darkness. The Judge and his man would be inside that rooming house, refusing to stay in some windblown tent.

Just as Simpson and his bailiff had done in Tombstone, while Elfrida slept the two would suddenly vanish, stealing not only the money but the belief in the law held by the men and women who eked out their livings there.

When that happened, Kincade would be waiting.

The sun sank to eventually be swallowed by the far horizon. Darkness fell. A few campfires sprang up here and there around Elfrida as shadowy forms stirred about. Within hours, those same fires died out, movement ceased and Elfrida grew still as the dead of night descended.

Kincade hadn't moved from the saddle. His headache thrummed behind his right eye as though the Other Voice were warming itself for what was about to happen. In the blackness, he moved his hand to his heart, removing the U.S. Marshal's badge and placing it in the frock coat pocket. "YOU DON'T NEED IT," whispered the Other Voice. "NOT FOR THIS."

He nudged his spurs into Gold Digger. They moved off the ridge and down towards the sleeping town of Elfrida...

36

Josephine sat at her breakfast table utterly stunned at David Cook's headline screaming from the Thursday morning edition of The Tombstone Epitaph:

OWNER OF THE COSMOPOLITAN HOTEL DIES IN BOATING ACCIDENT

"The entire Albert Bilicke family was drowned last weekend when their yacht capsized in a sudden storm just off Catalina Island. The cruise down the Pacific coast was to celebrate the sixtieth wedding anniversary of Albert and his wife, Juanita, and four generations of the Bilicke family were aboard. No bodies have been found. Albert Bilicke's vast holdings include the Cosmopolitan Hotel in Tombstone. We await news of the future of our famous landmark."

Lawyer Jeremiah Scott sat across from her, fingering the stem of his gold pocket-watch, snapping the cover open, clicking it closed, slowly snapping it open again. He had hoped to make his escape to the Territorial Capital on that day's train, but if he rushed her, she might sense that something was amiss. Friday's train departure at noon tomorrow would have to do. Kincade wasn't expected to return until late Saturday or Sunday. Scott would be long gone by then, so all would be well.

Scott's eyes were riveted on Josephine, judging her reaction to the news story he had brought to her that morning. Over time in countless courtroom settings, Scott had developed an ability to read people well.

Josephine's morning tea turned cold. Finally she laid the paper on the table, gently closed her eyes in utter disbelief, and said, "Albert was a good man. He treated people very well."

Scott nodded, closing the watch, smoothing the gold chain into a perfect half-circle, running his forefinger along its tiny links before slipping the watch into his vest pocket. "Yes, a good man, Miss Josephine. He wanted only the best for you. When Mr. Bilicke hired me to oversee his Tombstone business interests, he spoke well of you and your skills. 'Such a talent for management'... his exact words to me, Miss Josephine... 'such a talent'." Scott smoothed his right eyebrow and he nodded assurance.

Josephine was surprised. "I didn't know that, Mr. Scott. Albert never mentioned your business relationship with him."

"He knew how busy you were," said Scott as he folded his manicured fingers, placing his hands on the table before him. "The paperwork he needed me to review was merely an update of those first drawn and signed years ago when you two met in San Francisco, detailing your immediate ownership of The Josephine, and your eventual ownership of The Cosmopolitan Hotel... two inseparable real estate gems he insisted you have. It was fortunate I was able to complete the papers for his review and approval prior to his sailing." Scott shook his head sadly, bending forward to retrieve his brief satchel from the floor near his feet.

"Busy you were..." continued Scott as he withdrew a thick stack of legal papers, a bottle of India ink and a quill pen, "... busy you continue to be. I know how upset you must be at Albert's untimely death. So, let us quickly update your complete ownership of both the Hotel and The Josephine. I must file these papers in the Capital no later than tomorrow afternoon, now that we have news of Mr. Bilicke's passing."

"You do understand, Mr. Scott, that I bought The Josephine from Albert Bilicke several years ago and paid him in full. I only manage The Cosmopolitan."

Without batting an eye Scott responded, "Of course, Miss Josephine and that is the very reason I need these papers signed immediately. Albert told me that as the manager of his hotel property, you have the priority option to buy the hotel. You certainly don't want to jeopardize that advantageous opportunity when the Probate Court balances the assets and liabilities of Albert's estate."

Scott shuffled through the pages to find the pertinent one, dipped the quill, handed it to Josephine and pointed to a blank line. "Here please..."

Josephine paused. The volume of documents was sizeable. "The Marshal is away on business," she said. "I would like to have Kincade review these with me prior to my signing."

"Oh, no, that won't be necessary," Scott assured her. "Mr. Bilicke was quite specific in commending you, and happy with his decision that The Cosmopolitan and The Josephine should be yours. The Courts require the papers be filed immediately. I'll finalize the paperwork this afternoon and if I continue to work late into the night, I will still be able to leave on tomorrow's train to the Capital. While news of Mr. Bilicke's death is just now reaching Tombstone's newspaper, the estate's settlement concludes tomorrow afternoon. Once I file your ownership update at the Court, I will have the verification of your signing wired to you here in Tombstone. I will hand-deliver your originals upon my return to Tombstone this Monday."

"I really think..." Josephine began.

"I understand that the urgency of filing these documents is sudden, but neither you nor I nor Mr. Bilicke ever anticipated a day such as this," said Scott. "We must act, and act quickly. I would be happy to review the documents with you and Marshal Kincade upon his return. But his absence does not give us much choice, does it Miss Josephine?"

"I suppose..."

"Know that Mr. Bilicke was quite thorough in protecting you as these documents will attest." Scott dipped the quill in the ink a second time. "Please sign here." He placed the pen in Josephine's hand, and pointed to the blank on the document.

"Sign here please." She did. "And here..." She signed again.

Scott took the quill from her hand.

"Very good, and congratulations Miss Josephine." He withdrew the signed document, the ink and quill and returned them to his satchel, locking the clasp. "Forgive me for pushing business before you at this unfortunate time, but I have an obligation to Mr. Bilicke and his estate. I'm sure you understand. I must leave you now and complete the settlement of Mr. Bilicke's legal matters as he wished."

Scott pushed back from the table and stood. He smoothed his jacket. "Such a tragedy... Good day, Miss Josephine," he said as he reached the door, turning to her one final time. "Such a tragedy..." he muttered again.

Josephine watched Jeremiah Scott turn from the boardwalk to close the door behind him. Then she burst into tears and placed her head in her arms on the table. Had she watched him just a second longer she would have seen a broad smile cross the lawyer's face.

For several minutes her sobs could be heard all the way to the kitchen and Sam came to stand beside her. He didn't ask what was wrong but gently touched her shoulder. "Is there anything at all that I can do, Miss Josephine?"

Albert Bilicke dead! Josephine looked at Sam's sympathetic face and dabbled at her eyes with the napkin. With a deep sigh she patted his hand. "Yes, Sam. Would you please go to the livery and ask Curley to harness Clementine to the surrey and bring it here as soon as possible. Maybe a ride will clear my head..." She sniffed back another sob. "...and my heart." Sam nodded and Josephine went upstairs to change her clothes.

She stepped into the surrey, not knowing or even caring which way she would go, so she clucked her tongue and the mare trotted in its own direction.

"Oh, Kincade," she said to herself. "I need you. Please hold me. Comfort me. You wouldn't need to say a word. Come and let me look in your eyes."

But Kincade wasn't with her. She must overcome her grief alone until he returned. She began to recall all the goodness that Albert Bilicke had bestowed on her for so many years. He had given her sanction in Tombstone when Wil Logan had burned her Proud Cat Saloon in Benson and she had fled for her life. He had made it possible for her to refurbish and eventually own The Josephine Saloon. He had placed his confidence in her skills to assume management of The Cosmopolitan Hotel and perhaps now even arranged for her to buy it as well. Whenever she had gone to San Francisco, Albert and his wife, Juanita, had welcomed her into their home like a daughter. All these thoughts made Josephine's tears run down her cheeks like spring rivulets. And now she was riding in his latest gift, this precious little surrey with her own name engraved on the sides! "Oh, Albert, I have loved you like a father! I should have told you years ago. Now it is too late! You're gone from me for good..."

Then with a sigh of acceptance she slowed Clementine and made the turn back to Tombstone. "It is too little, too late," she acknowledged. "But it is all I can do for that dear, dear friend."

Josephine stopped in front of the Post Office. She wiped away her tears as she stepped down from the surrey. She moved onto the boardwalk and opened the door. "Miss Sadie," she said, "I need to send a telegram right away."

37

The soft dirt giving way beneath Gold Digger's hooves made the stallion's descent into Elfrida a whisper in the wind. No moon illuminated the dark figure on the palomino's back. The thrum in Kincade's head grew louder, clearing away any morals that might stand in the way of what the Other Voice had planned for the two men known to Kincade as Judge Simon Simpson and his henchman, Bowdrie.

Kincade pulled up behind a thicket of willows that lined the creek across from the livery corral. They would come. He would wait.

A lantern provided the only light in room four at the rooming house. But it was enough for the two men packing their valises. "Well, Billy, our court sessions have sewn up this backwater berg!" Simpson gloated over the contents of the saddlebags heavy with the spoils of their three days in Elfrida. "Today's penalties and fines could be one of our better hauls. These people are so busy pulling silver out of the ground, they have no time to build a real town let alone comprehend what just happened to them in court."

"A tent town suits 'em, Merv," said Bowdrie. "They'll be movin' on when the placer finally plays out."

"Tonight, Billy, we bid the good people of Elfrida adieu." And the two laughed again.

"Good riddance, Merv," said Bowdrie. "This rooming house oughta be burned down."

"Now, we can't have that," said Simpson. "Your wrecking the suite in Tombstone was one thing. But you set this tent city on fire and our exit from this snake hole might be curtailed by our neighbors near the livery."

"Yeah, I'm movin' kinda slow with all this gold I'm packing!" Bowdrie smiled.

"Most especially with that," agreed Simpson.

"I'm just glad we don't have to split the Elfrida money like we had to with that shyster lawyer back in Tombstone," said Bowdrie.

"Now, Billy, be considerate of our old friend. Gerry's encouragement to the good people of Tombstone to air their grievances before the bench, rather than in back-alley brawls, tripled our take."

"Maybe," said Bowdrie. "But he's pretty stuck on himself... him and his law learnin'."

"Aren't you and I fortunate, Billy" said Simpson, "not to have wasted our time at Yuma Prison studying the law. Remember it was old Gerry who taught us. We've gone right to work, helping to relieve hundreds of frontier families and bent-over miners of their hard-earned money. He's even given us fancy forged documents to sell when needed in towns across the frontier."

"Still don't like him – never have. His braggin' 'bout all that smart stuff he's pulled – just a blown up bag 'a hot air."

"The court finds you guilty of contempt, Billy," pronounced

Simpson as he pantomimed the pounding of his gavel.

"Guilty as charged!" said Bowdrie.

"Then the Court orders you and me to leave the fair town of Elfrida, and be on our way to Benson. The night beckons!"

From across the creek, Kincade could make out the shapes of two men leaving the rooming house. Their faces were shadowed, but he knew who they were, and where they were going. Gold Digger remained still as the larger of the two opened the corral gate, where three horses waited. The larger man secured their money bags to the pack horse saddle. The weight was considerable, as it held the booty from both Tombstone and Elfrida. He roped their valises to the rumps of the other two animals. As Bowdrie worked, the other lit a rolled smoke. Kincade could see from the small flame that it was Simon Simpson.

Simpson moved to take the reins from his bailiff, and hoisted himself up. Bowdrie quickly mounted, and the three horses quietly exited the corral. Kincade watched as the men rode down the back street of Elfrida, and on to the rutted road that led to Benson. After several minutes, satisfied they were out of earshot, Kincade turned Gold Digger to parallel the road traveled by the Judge and his bailiff. He would ride his golden palomino far enough to their flank that he would pass them without either being aware of a third rider.

The Other Voice whispered inside Kincade's head, "I LOOKED AND BEHELD A PALE HORSE. AND HIS NAME WAS DEATH."

•

38

Gold Digger's massive chest heaved, his nostrils flared as Kincade put his spurs to the stallion. With each stride, with each thrust of the palomino's powerful hind legs, Kincade boiled with anger.

Something was happening deep within Kincade's gut. The Other Voice was no longer content with whispered suggestions. Kincade's headaches were now inundated with unequivocal commands, ever louder, ever more powerful, flooding his soul and body. Kincade felt he was being drowned from the inside out, unable to distinguish right from wrong, forced to follow the Other Voice, without question or conscience. It demanded fire be fought with fire. Evil must be punished with even greater evils. Kincade was evolving into its instrument of death.

Down into a gulch and into the groves of cottonwoods that lined the creek, Kincade jerked Digger to a quick stop and jumped off. He led the stallion to the base of a large tree and let the reins fall to the ground, knowing the horse wouldn't move without his master.

Kincade untied a fifty-foot riata which hung from the saddle, moved through the blackness and onto the road to await the arrival of Simpson and Bowdrie. A dry breeze ruffled the leaves above Kincade's head. "SHOW NO MERCY," commanded the

Other Voice.

Kincade could hear the footfall of the three horses and the soft talk between the men whom he knew only as Simpson and Bowdrie as they came over the ridge and down the road towards the creek. The moonless night cloaked Kincade, making him invisible to the approaching riders, even though they rode straight towards him.

Bowdrie's voice became clear. "Merv, you're quite the actor. The way you looked at that widow lady when you ordered that she'd have to give the court five hundred dollars! You pounded your gavel and said 'Your dead husband failed to pay the state's mineral extraction taxes when he closed his silver mine. His debt has become yours!'" Bowdrie laughed. "Why, you didn't even flinch when the widow cried, 'Oh Judge Jasper! Please help me! I ain't got no money.' Merv, I had to bite my cheeks to keep from laughin'!"

Simpson gloated. "Remember my verdict, Billy? 'Two bags of gold, deposited with my bailiff within the hour. Miss the court's deadline, and you're a guest in the Elfrida town jail!'"

"She started to cry and then pulled that gold wedding ring off her finger. 'Will this pay the fine?' she done asked you. Merv, you are one greedy bastard."

"Hell, Billy, that little gold band should bring us a few dollars at a pawn shop in the Capital. What's she gonna do with it?"

"By the way, Merv, I didn't know there was a tax on mineral extraction."

"There isn't!" And the two laughed loud and hard.

"My favorite was your peddling one of those forged documents we got from Gerry so's the saloon guy could sell both liquor and tobacco. You had your eye on his gold pocket watch from the moment we walked into his bar."

"Yeah, Billy. I'm brilliant. We'd better get this loot back to the hideout. I've gotta be Judge Nicholas Polland in Benson in just a few days."

"I've forgot, Merv. What's my name supposed to be this next time?"

Their horses felt Kincade's presence first, jerking their heads in fear of whatever blocked their path.

"Whoa, whoa!" said the man called Bowdrie, trying to still his mount. "Who goes there?" But it was too late. Kincade was upon them.

Kincade shot his hand forward to snatch the bridle and bit of Bowdrie's horse, causing the beast to rear up in surprise. Bowdrie tumbled over backwards, dropped the lead rope to their pack horse, and slammed into the ground. The Other Voice laughed.

"What the hell is..." Bowdrie began. Kincade's anger exploded into a boiling inferno of rage stoked by the commands of the Other Voice. "GO AHEAD!" Kincade yanked his left shooter and put a 45 caliber bullet into the right knee of Simpson's body guard, completely shattering the bone. Bowdrie screamed in pain.

At the same moment, Kincade reached up to grab the coat of Simon Simpson, yanking him out of his saddle. His horse bolted as Simpson tumbled off, putting its rear hoof into Simpson's chest breaking three of the ribs as he crashed into the dirt several yards away from Bowdrie.

Kincade spun back to the bodyguard, threw open Bowdrie's coat and snatched the 6-gun from his holster, spinning the shooter in his fist to hold the barrel and expose the grip. With tremendous force, Kincade brought the shooter's metal backstrap down on the bridge of the bailiff's nose, breaking the cartilage and releasing a torrent of blood.

Kincade grabbed the fifty-foot riata he had removed from Gold Digger's saddle, coiled a loop within seconds and threw it over Simpson's head. As it slipped over his neck, Kincade jerked back on the noose putting a choke on Simpson that barely allowed him to breathe.

Bowdrie and Simpson reeled, the men trying to comprehend what had happened over the last twenty seconds. Simpson shook his head, trying to clear his vision as he looked up at the black figure towering over him. "Muh... Marshal Kincade! Is that you?!"

Kincade answered, but the words Bowdrie and Simpson heard were deeper, darker... not what they remembered from their time in Tombstone. What they heard may have been Kincade's voice, but the words passing over his lips were those of the Other Voice.

"SPILL IT!"

Simpson hesitated. "I... uh... I don't know wh..."

Kincade yanked at the noose. Hard.

Simpson gasped for air. "All right! What is it you want to..."

Another yank, harder than the first.

"Don't please! I'll talk!"

Kincade loosened the pull on the noose by a hair.

"It was Jeremiah Scott!" began Simpson. "He came up with a way for me, Bowdrie and him to make money... a lot of money. Told us about the towns around Arizona Territory all rolling in silver, and that it was ours for the taking. Said we'd get rich, not by force, but by bending the law... making up the law when we had to!"

Kincade didn't move as the Other Voice fanned fires of rage burning throughout his body and soul.

"Said he'd set up a lawyer's office in Tombstone," continued Simpson who knew that if he didn't talk, and talk fast, Kincade would drag him to the cottonwood at his back and lynch him. "As Bowdrie and I worked our way through countless towns, Scott got ahold of Tombstone mining deeds, titles to property, promising to review and update the documents. But he was tricking people into signing their ownership over to him. They couldn't catch him at it because he told them he needed to keep the papers in his office safe."

With each revelation spewed by Simpson, Kincade burned hotter, the urge to immediately kill held in check by the Other Voice. "NOT YET," it warned.

Simpson went on. "It worked too. Before long, he had enough property that he invited wealthy investors from back east to visit Tombstone, buy whatever they wanted. Scott even paid some old lady named Wappler $500 for her dead husband's played-out mine property. Then he forged assay documents and maps to show a cartel of businessmen from Chicago that rich ore was still in the mine and they could purchase the claim for only $5000. It worked! They paid Scott in cash!"

Kincade's grip on the rope tightened, increasing Simpson's fear of imminent death.

"Wait! Don't! There's more!" Simpson swallowed. "Scott got wind of some lady who ran the post office... Miss Sadie something... that she wanted to retire, sell her house, move to Denver. Scott was the agent she hired. He forged a deed to her house and sold it to some farmer named Jethro Wilcox in Julesburg for the full price. Scott kept the money and told the woman he couldn't find a buyer. She left for Denver without any money. When this Wilcox family shows up in Tombstone, their money will be gone and they won't own that house either."

The rage inside Kincade reached a level he had known only once before, when Sky's life was threatened. "NOW!' commanded the Other Voice.

Kincade dropped the rope, yanked both of his Colts, knelt to place both barrels into Simpson's eyes, and discharged two 45 caliber bullets through his brain, exploding out the back of his skull and into the bloodied ground where Simpson gasped his last breath.

"NOW BOWDRIE!" it hissed. "DO IT JUST LIKE I TOLD YOU!"

Kincade removed the rope from Simpson's neck, walked to Bowdrie's crumpled body, grabbed his right arm and began to drag him to the cottonwood where Gold Digger waited. Bowdrie was delirious.

Removing the Bowie knife from the sheath at his back, Kincade cut the riata into two pieces. He hoisted Bowdrie who screamed from the pain radiating from his shattered knee. Kincade pulled him up from the ground just high enough to tie Bowdrie's right leg and right arm to the tree's lower trunk.

"Digger!" said Kincade, and the palomino stepped forward while Kincade returned the knife to its sheath. Kincade took the remaining length of rope, tied each of the ends to Bowdrie's left leg and left arm, ran the rope's center back to the horn of Gold Digger's saddle, looped it three times to hold it fast, stepped into the tapaderos and swung up. With a slight nudge of his spurs, Digger moved forward to tighten the rope's span between the horn and

Bowdrie.

As the leather creaked, Bowdrie snapped fully alert, realizing he was starting be to torn in half.

Kincade's lips moved, but it was the Other Voice who asked, "YOU GOT ANYTHING TO TELL ME?"

Bowdrie panicked. "Oh god, no, please!..."

Kincade nudged Digger another three inches from the tree.

"Please!" pleaded Bowdrie. "Let me go. There's more! Scott's not finished in Tombstone. His last prize... it's your Josephine!"

From the center of his very being, a shock wave hotter than the molten tides of hell struck Kincade.

Bowdrie was now shouting the words, hysterical. "Scott has some scheme to get the Cosmopolitan Hotel and The Josephine Saloon into his own hands. He's tricking Josephine into signing the papers. I don't know exactly how, but he's got the documents. Scott was just waiting for you to leave town!"

That was enough. Like a scorching blast of fire exploding between Kincade's lips, the Other Voice bellowed, "YOU REMEMBER WHAT YOU DID TO JOSEPHINE'S VASE?" Bowdrie recalled shattering it against the wall of the suite at the Cosmopolitan Hotel, breaking it apart.

"HOW'D YOU LIKE A LITTLE TASTE?"

Kincade dug his spurs into Gold Digger's belly hard enough to draw blood. The stallion sprang forward like a coiled rattler.

The tear in Bowdrie's flesh began at his groin, ripped up through his spine, splitting his body into two eviscerated halves. Within the next twenty feet, Kincade released the dallie on the saddle horn.

The rope fell to the ground. Kincade picked up the lead rope to the pack horse carrying the gold that belonged to the citizens of Elfrida and Tombstone.

That horse, the Other Voice, and Kincade on Gold Digger, rode hell-bent for Tombstone...

39

The black of night through which Kincade rode paled alongside the darkness crashing its way through his head. Kincade felt as if the Other Voice was ripping his soul apart, thrumming within his skull without pause, consuming his every thought, directing each decision as it saw fit. Marshal Kincade was losing control.

"HE'S HURT JOSEPHINE!" shouted the Other Voice. "YOU SHOULD HAVE KILLED SCOTT WHEN YOU HAD THE CHANCE!"

Perhaps it was the horror of what happened beneath the tree, the screams of men being killed, but Simpson's loot-laden pack horse ran step for step behind Gold Digger, its eyes wild with fear.

Nostrils flared as the horses hungrily gulped down air, but both were used to heavy loads and long distances. After hours of running hard and fast, the eastern sky began to lighten as the sun struggled to rise over the Dragoons. Sage, cactus, thorn bushes were blurs as Kincade raced towards Tombstone... back to Josephine. "Dear God, let her be okay," Kincade prayed to himself. "If he's so much as touched her..."

The horses ran faster.

By seven, waves of heat were rising up like transparent specters unchained from the desert floor. By eight, Kincade could make out the rise upon which Tombstone sat, and soon thereafter, the graveyard of Boot Hill. "Digger," said Kincade as he leaned over the saddle to put his hand on the lathered horse's neck, "Thank you, my old friend. Thank you for getting me back to her."

Down Toughnut, turning onto Allen Street, Kincade could see The Cosmopolitan Hotel. The pack horse had begun to falter from the weight of the gold it carried.

Livery owner, Curley Smith, was walking down the boardwalk outside The Josephine and saw them first. Kincade leapt off Gold Digger before the stallion came to a full stop. Startled at the condition of the two horses covered with foam and sweat, Curley ran forward to take the reins and remove the pack horse's lead rope from Kincade's saddle. "What's happened?" asked Smith. "What's wrong, Marshal?!"

"Josephine! Have you seen her this morning?" Kincade asked loudly.

"No," Smith quickly responded. "I guess she's upstairs in her room. Josie's pretty shook up over yesterday's newspaper. Bilicke dead! Who could have imagined somethin' like that happening?"

Kincade couldn't believe Curley's words. Albert Bilicke dead? "What about Scott? Have you seen Jeremiah Scott?"

"Did earlier," Smith replied. "He was taking some luggage over to the depot. Looks like he's leavin' town on the noon train."

Kincade jumped from the street and onto the boardwalk, turning to speak. "Curley, can you take the horses down to the livery. I've ridden them hard... too hard." Kincade felt terrible at the abuse he had put the horses through. "Walk them, water them, cool 'em down. Make sure the bags on the pack horse are put in a safe place. Can you do that for me, Curley?"

Smith didn't need to respond and Kincade didn't wait for an answer.

Opening the side door of The Josephine, Kincade ran across the saloon and took the stairs three at a time to Josephine's suite. "Josie!" Kincade placed his palms on the outside of her door. "Josie! Are you there?"

He heard the latch turn and the door opened. Josephine stood there. She dropped her hairbrush and flew into Kincade's arms. Through her kisses, she said "Oh, my Darling. I'm so thankful you're back!" Tears of joy fell from her blue eyes.

He melted into her arms, kissing away her tears, running his hands through her blond hair, holding her face so he could look at her. "I was afraid you'd been hurt," he said.

Kissing her forehead in relief, he held her a half arm's length. "Did Scott do anything to you? Did he force you to do anything while I was gone?"

"Yes," she replied, almost ashamed, nearly weak in his arms. "How did you know?"

"Tell me what happened." He led her inside, closing the door behind them. They sat close together, hand in hand, on the edge of Josephine's bed. "What did he do? Did Scott hurt you?"

She kissed him in reassurance. "No, he didn't hurt me. But..." Josephine paused. Kincade could sense a deep concern, almost a fear in her eyes.

The Other Voice began to uncoil inside Kincade's brain. "Tell me," said Kincade. "Tell me what he did."

"Yesterday, Scott came into The Josephine. He had a copy of the Epitaph. There was a front page story. It said Albert Bilicke had drowned. Here, I'll get it." She released Kincade's hands, moved to her secretary where she sorted through several papers and returned to sit at his side.

Kincade read the article while she continued talking. "I was at breakfast and hadn't even opened the paper when Jeremiah Scott showed up and read me the article. He said that Albert had hired him to handle his Tombstone affairs."

"Had you heard about any such arrangement?"

"No, and I told him that. But... Oh Kincade!... the man talks so fast and is so convincing that I believed him."

"You aren't the first or only one." He held her trembling hands, moving his powerful fingers over hers. "Go on. Then what happened?"

"He convinced me to sign some papers to secure my position as owner of The Josephine and also to have the first option to buy the Cosmopolitan."

"Did he let you read these papers?"

Her regret was clear to Kincade. Josephine had always been a very smart businesswoman. She knew now that Scott had tricked her. "No, I didn't." Her pain and disappointment in herself was clear. "He pushed so hard....and I was so upset with the bad news...."

He cradled her in his arms while his head began pounding even harder than during his ride back to Tombstone. "Shusssh, my darling. You did nothing wrong. Your belief in others is one of the reasons I love you so much. Josie, you did nothing wrong. The Other Voice began to fill Kincade. "I'LL GET THOSE

PAPERS BACK!"

The Other Voice grew in power, telling Kincade, "YOU'LL HAVE TO KILL HIM TO DO IT."

Josephine sat back, squeezed Kincade's rough hands, and looked at him without blinking. "But that isn't all..." she continued.

She went back to the secretary and picked up two telegrams. "Albert meant so much to me. I felt I had to do something... as his friend, and as manager of the Cosmopolitan. I sent a telegram to the Executor of the Albert Bilicke Estate to express my sympathy and to see how I could help."

She handed Kincade a copy of her telegram and he read it quickly. "Am grieved to learn of Albert Bilicke's death by drowning STOP Will gladly lend assistance in settling Tombstone interests STOP I respected, admired, and adored Mister Bilicke as a dear friend STOP Josephine, Manager Cosmopolitan Hotel Tombstone"

"Within an hour, I received this response." She handed Kincade the second yellow sheet. He read: "You have been misinformed STOP Am well and happy in San Francisco STOP Personal sentiments returned STOP Albert Bilicke."

Kincade reeled. Scott had tricked her twice!

"I no sooner read this than I rushed to the Epitaph office and confronted David Cook. 'You published false information!' I yelled at him. I was so upset, mostly at myself for believing Scott at all. I gave Cook Albert's telegram. He was as shocked as I. 'Lawyer Scott brought me a similar telegram with the information I printed.' 'Then print a retraction! Right away!' He said he would. It will be in tomorrow's paper. David was so sorry... and more than a little mad at Jeremiah Scott!

"Oh, Kincade! If Scott files those papers in the Capital, The Josephine and the Hotel will be his!"

Suddenly Kincade's head was filled with nothing but the Other Voice – no ache, no throb, no pounding nor thrumming – only the powerful Other Voice, swelling to completely take command of Kincade's body and soul. It ordered Kincade to drop Josephine's hand, to stand, turn, leave. Josephine was startled by his abrupt change. Compassion was gone. It was like a window candle had been extinguished by a sudden gust. There one moment. Gone an instant later. Josie looked up into Kincade's eyes. They were dark. As dark as Josephine remembered the eyes of Kincade's twin brother, Wil Logan...

40

Kincade backed up to the door of Josephine's suite. It was almost like he was being pulled away from her, unable to speak or resist the power of the Other Voice coursing through his veins.

"Kincade..." said Josephine. "Where are you going? Don't leave me..."

No response - just his reaching back to the door's knob, his opening it, stepping through the threshold and into the hall, his dark eyes looking into hers. A pause in his step, then a grimace that lined his brow so deeply it was like the true Kincade had been incinerated from within.

As Kincade backed out of Josephine's suite, he tried to reach out to her, but the Other Voice would have none of it. "KILL SCOTT NOW!"

Kincade suddenly felt Wil Logan's Bowie knife, the metal hot, its blade sharp enough to easily slice through the leather sheath that held the weapon securely at the base of his spine.

The Other Voice commanded, "WHAT I DID TO YOUR NECK..." Kincade ran his fingers along the old scar hidden beneath the wild rag. "...YOU DO TO SCOTT!"

He turned, bolting down the staircase.

"Kincade!" Josephine quickly rose and ran to the open door. He was gone. She could hear the door to The Josephine slam. She began a rush to the head of the staircase, stopping when she realized she was still barefoot and in her dressing gown. She spun and ran back to her suite, grabbed the blouse and long skirt she'd laid out the previous evening. Disrobing, she quickly dressed as three, four minutes passed. She forewent her button and eye shoes. She would have to go barefoot. She had no time. She had to move now.

Out her suite, onto the landing, down the stairs. Josephine had never seen Kincade so wild with anger, even beyond the rage she saw in him the night Wil Logan had killed Jesse Keller. Kincade was going to kill Jeremiah Scott and she must stop him! She thought Scott would be at the train depot, headed to the Capital to complete his theft of The Cosmopolitan Hotel and The Josephine.

*   *   *   *

Kincade hit the street like a bolt of lightning. A boy who ran errands for the merchants and kept the boardwalk swept tried to jump out of Kincade's way, but the Marshal grabbed him by the shoulders. "Have you seen Jeremiah Scott?"

The boy was so startled when he looked up at Kincade's enraged face, he couldn't answer.

"SPEAK!" yelled the Other Voice.

"He's in his office!" Kincade thrust him aside and the boy backed up in fear.

Kincade bolted south down the boardwalk, crossed 3rd Street, down another half block, reached to grab the outdoor stair railing leading up to Jeremiah Scott's law office, and sprang up the wooden treads. Within seconds, he was at the top landing. Without stopping, he smashed his shoulder into Scott's closed door, shattering the wood from its hinges, and exploded into the office behind it.

Lawyer Jeremiah Scott snapped backwards from his open safe, his hands full of bundles of money. At his feet were two large satchels filled with even more money and deeds of trust stolen from the gullible citizens of Tombstone. Near the wall, the iron door of the office pot-bellied stove stood open, the flames of burning documents hungrily licking the air.

At the sight of Kincade, Scott's jaw fell open. The Marshal's eyes were filled with revenge and the promise of an agonizing and torturous death. Scott jerked his hand down to the grip of a two-shot Derringer secreted in his vest pocket.

Kincade leapt forward, his big hands outstretched, reaching for Scott's neck.

*　　*　　*　　*　　*

In her haste to catch up with Kincade, Josephine overturned two chairs as she rushed to the front door of The Josephine. Fumbling with the latch, she finally pulled open the tall door and ran onto the boardwalk. The train depot was only two blocks away. If she ran with all her might, she could catch Kincade and stop him from possibly killing Scott for tricking her. During the gunfight years before inside The Josephine, she had seen what Kincade was capable of doing to another man when he felt she was in danger.

Josephine ran north for the depot. Friday's train had not yet arrived. Several passengers waited on the depot platform. A wooden cart was covered with carpet bags and leather cases and steamer trunks all readied for loading into the baggage car.

Out of breath, Josephine reached the station looking for Kincade and Scott. Neither was on the platform. She ran inside to the ticket office.

"Harold, have you seen the Marshal?"

"No, Miss Josie. Not today."

"And Jeremiah Scott?" she asked.

"He bought a one-way ticket to the Capital this morning," replied the station master. "That's his luggage outside. He must be planning to be gone awhile. He went back over to his office a half hour ago. Said he had to get a couple more things, close up, and return by 11:30. He'd better hurry. Noon train will be here in another 20 minutes."

Josephine spun, ran out, and looked again at the platform. "Oh no," whispered Josephine. She leapt down the four steps, back into the street, and began the run to Scott's office, nearly five blocks away.

41

Scott's hand grabbed, yanked and cocked the hammer of his over-and-under Derringer, getting off one shot. The bullet whizzed by Kincade's hip and slammed into the wall. He began to cock a second time, but never made it. Kincade was on him. With his right thumb and forefinger, Kincade grabbed Scott's throat just below the jaw.

"ONE MORE MOVE," said the Other Voice, "AND I WILL CRUSH YOUR WINDPIPE. YOU'LL SUFFOCATE WITHIN SECONDS!"

Kincade squeezed. Scott dropped the Derringer and it clattered on to the floor. More pressure on Scott's neck. He began to choke and instinctively grabbed Kincade's hand, now tightening on his neck.

"SCOTT," said the Other Voice. "PUT YOUR HANDS DOWN NOW, OR I SWEAR I WILL RIP OUT YOUR THROAT."

Scott stopped his struggle against Kincade. Any further resistance would insure his own death.

Kincade held Scott's windpipe just hard enough for his thumb and forefinger to wrap around the sides and towards the back of Scott's larynx. No muscle protected the tissue from collapse. It was as vulnerable as an eyeball, and they both knew it. Scott stilled. Ragged gasps for air croaked from his mouth.

Kincade looked at what must have been tens of thousands of dollars stuffed into the two large satchels at Scott's feet. More money sat stacked inside the open safe, alongside deeds that clearly identified Tombstone's most profitable silver mines, buildings and properties. On the floor, Scott had dropped the deed for Miss Sadie's home. Clipped on to it was a large wad of bills.

"YOU DROPPED SOMETHING," said the Other Voice.

Scott's eyes were wide with fear.

"AND THAT MONEY," continued the Other Voice. "I'D WAGER JETHRO WILCOX SENT THAT TO YOU."

Scott choked again as Kincade tightened the lock on his throat.

"I WONDER WHY MISS SADIE NEVER GOT IT?" said the Other Voice. "YOU WOULDN'T BE TRYING TO STEAL THAT NOW, WOULD YOU, SCOTT?"

Kincade looked at the window to the street, half covered by a velvet drape held back by a heavy piece of fabric rope. The Marshal moved Scott towards the window, never releasing the pressure on his neck. With his free hand, Kincade grabbed the rope and tore it from the drape. He pushed Scott back to his office desk.

"BOTH HANDS TOGETHER, SCOTT, ON THE DESK, PALMS DOWN."

Scott hesitated. Kincade increased the pressure on his throat.

"All right, all right!" he gasped.

Just as Kincade had done with hundreds of cattle during his years as a cowboy, with a snap of his free hand, Scott's wrists were lashed together, his ten fingers fanned out across the desk's top.

Maintaining the death grip on Scott's throat with one hand, Kincade reached under his coat to the small of his back and withdrew Wil Logan's Bowie knife from its sheath. He snaked it out from its hiding place. Slowly, he held it in front of Scott's terrified face. The gleam of its razor sharp edge danced in the flames flicking up from the stove.

Kincade pivoted the knife blade slowly to the right, to center, then to the left, allowing Scott to get a good long look. Satisfied, Kincade moved the knife down to Scott's desktop, where several ink quills were scattered about. One by one, Kincade touched the shaft of each quill with the knife's edge, rocking it down to slice through the stem. The Marshal watched Scott's horrified eyes.

"I WONDER WHAT WOULD HAPPEN IF I TRIED THIS ON YOUR TEN FINGERS?" whispered the Other Voice into Scott's ear.

Through the shattered doorway, Josephine suddenly burst into the room.

42

She tried to take it all in, tried to understand what she saw inside the office of Jeremiah Scott.

The terror on Scott's face was so great, he must have been standing at Hell's gate. The fury radiating from within Kincade went beyond her comprehension. It was as though the flesh of the man she knew stood a few feet away, but the human being she loved was coming apart, disintegrating and rebuilding into someone who epitomized everything Kincade reviled. Something evil was waging a war inside Kincade's soul – a fight it was close to winning.

The Other Voice moved the Bowie knife to hover over Scott's outstretched fingers. It whispered, "DO IT!" Kincade pushed the wrist down while tightening his grip on Scott's throat where the fragile cartilage was giving way.

Josephine was frozen. "Kincade!"

The internal struggle waging inside Kincade was far greater than any battle he had ever fought. The wrongness of the Other Voice continued to strike at everything Kincade knew to be right. It pushed the blade downward as Kincade struggled to pull it back. With all his might, Kincade raised his face to look at Josephine.

"Put the knife down, Kincade!" she shouted. "Arrest him!"

"KILL HIM NOW!" commanded the Other Voice.

"Josie, help me..." The knife's blade quivered over Scott's fingers.

"NOW I SAID!"

"I hear this Other Voice. It wants me to kill him..."

"Listen to my voice... to your own voice," she said. "Which is stronger?... Kincade's fear of this Other Voice, or what Kincade knows to be right?"

Kincade's neck strained, he muscles ached. "I can't..." He struggled. "Too strong..."

"Kincade..." Josie begged. "Don't listen to it. Send it away."

The Other Voice inside Kincade's brain bellowed, "YOU'RE NOT JUST MY TWIN – ONE SEED, ONE WOMB, ONE BIRTH – YOU ARE ME!"

"Josie, I've turned into my brother!"

"Kincade listen to me." She looked into his eyes with every ounce of her being. "You have not been possessed by the ghost of Wil Logan. He was your opposite. Wil brutally attacked the innocent, the helpless. You only attacked the evil you saw."

Josephine's voice became softer. "There is a reason for all this. It is your Circle Of Life." She took a step towards him. "We all have a good and evil persona. Keeping them in balance is what allows us to fulfill our destiny. You have been listening to the evil side of yourself struggling to take over but your destiny is rooted in your good side."

As Kincade listened to the pleas of Josephine, something within him began to bend like a branch under heavy snow. Welling up from a deep place came a power which began to garrote The Other Voice.

Josephine took a second step.

"The evil in men you've had to deal with has drawn you towards them. The goodness within you fights to bring you back. You, I, we all will know the worst in life. If we don't dominate it, we will eventually become that evil, devoid of any ability to care for one another or for ourselves. The torture within you is testament to the goodness of your own soul. Kincade, you long for the best in life. You hope to be a better man with each day, with each breath."

The bending within Kincade's soul increased. "Josie, I'm afraid of the headaches. They warn me of what I am becoming..."

A third step. Josephine reached out to gently touch Kincade's face. "The headaches were the evil side of yourself struggling to take over. Your fear confirms your goodness and your power over all things evil. You are not the slave of some ghost. Your love for me, for life, and for the happiness of others is the greatest power of all. Sky knew it. I know it. Turn inside to the center of yourself. The true Kincade is there. You know it."

Josephine's unconditional love, her unbridled belief in Kincade, turned the bending into a break. It released a cool breeze, not harsh but caressing - a vanquishing swirl within Kincade, a clearing of smoke that revealed what had always been there: a simple and undeniable affirmation of a good man, and of the caring for others that he had held since birth.

Josephine lowered her hand.

Kincade dropped the knife. He released his grip on Scott's throat. "You're under arrest."

The Other Voice, had vanished.

The heavy door with its iron bars banged shut. Kincade twisted

the large key to throw the cell's bolt. He looked silently at Jeremiah Scott, who sat on a wooden bunk, head bent into both hands
as he stared at the floor. Scott knew the remainder of his life was
about to make its most dramatic change.

Kincade slowly turned to hang the jailer's ring. Josephine stood
in the cell block entryway, backing up as Kincade moved towards
her and into the Marshal's office. Kincade reached down to the
door latch, and closed it, leaving Scott to consider the harvest he
was about to reap.

She looked into his eyes, no longer dark, now the serene turquoise blue she had loved since they first met.

"Hello, Kincade..." she said softly.

He gently smiled with a sense of inner peace he had not felt in
an eternity. "Hello, Josephine." He looked at her dainty bare feet.

"You forgot your shoes," he said.

"You distracted me," she replied.

"You have pretty feet."

"I'm glad you like them."

"I do."

"I can see that."

And the two of them fell into a delicious, all consuming, silence.

In a few moments, she spoke. "I will be in my suite. When you finish securing Scott's office, I would enjoy your coming to call."

"Need help finding your shoes?" he asked, smiling just enough.

She nodded, ever so slowly. "Uh-huh..."

As Kincade left the jail, liveryman Curley Smith walked up to him. "Marshal, I wanted you to know that your horses are fine. Curried, brushed, watered, fed, and a big dose of nose-rubbin' thrown in to boot. I put 'em in your stable."

"Thank you, Curley," said Kincade. Another rush of relief, knowing he hadn't hurt the horses. "I'll take those saddle bags off your hands whenever it's convenient."

"I'm goin' back to the livery now. You want to come along?"

"All right." They walked down the street together. "How's that new grandson of yours?"

Curley beamed with pride, pleased to be asked. "Happy little fella! Clement and Blossom are so proud!"

Kincade nodded. "You're a lucky man, Curley."

"We both are, Marshal." They smiled together as they stepped into the livery office and Curley knelt at his safe.

"Appreciate your help, Curley," Kincade shook his hand and slung the heavy saddle bags over his broad shoulders. He then headed to Scott's upstairs office.

It took the entire afternoon for Kincade to gather Scott's papers. The money he and the team of Simpson and Bowdrie had stolen filled four large satchels. Among the deeds of trust, Kincade found the documents Scott had tricked Josephine into signing, assuring his ownership of both The Hotel Cosmopolitan and The Josephine. Kincade fed them into the stove's fire, feeling his heart soar as the burning paper turned into ash and wafted up the stove's pipe. Josephine was safe. What was hers remained hers.

Going downstairs into the barber shop, Kincade told the owner of the building that he had nailed the door to Scott's office shut, apologizing for the damage he had caused when he smashed in the door. "I'll pay for it," Kincade assured the owner. And two days later, he did.

The sun had set when Kincade stepped off the boardwalk in front of the U.S. Marshals Office. He took a deep cleansing breath. The weight of an entire world lifted off his shoulders. For some reason, he remembered when he and Sky had used Smoke's sensitive nose to identify the boy who had frolicked with Blossom Smith in the hay loft. Kincade smiled. Those were happy days. He relished the memory, the joy he'd felt back then, the even greater joy he felt now.

Kincade took another deep breath, exhaled slowly and looked up Allen Street to The Josephine. "I wonder if she's found her shoes?" He felt so happy.

"I'm a lucky man..." he said to himself as he began his evening walk – not to Lower Tombstone, but to Josephine's suite.

She opened her door.

44

Inside her suite, Kincade could see candles flickering here and there. Their softness cast an almost angelic glow on Josephine's beautiful face.

She had taken a bath. Dressed in a white silk gown that cascaded from her shoulders, over her curves to barely reach the floor, her still-damp hair glistened.

"May I come in?" he asked, removing his hat.

She nodded.

"Did you find your shoes?"

She shook her head, no.

Josephine stepped back to welcome him in, closed and latched the door. She took Kincade's hat, placing it on the brass stand to the right of the door. Standing behind Kincade, she slipped her hands over his shoulders, removed his frock coat, hanging it next to his hat.

Her room was so quiet. A gentle breeze flowed through the

open window's lace curtains, ruffling them ever so slightly. The candle flames swayed.

Josephine reached down to take Kincade's hand. She led him to a soft, red velvet, embroidered couch, its clawed feet carved from dark walnut. Extending her arm as an invitation, Kincade sat.

Josephine walked to a mirrored bureau. There sat a silvered tray and on it were two glasses. One was half-filled with golden tequila, the second held cooled beer. Josephine knew Kincade enjoyed both. She picked up the tray with its ornate silver handles, turned and walked back to Kincade. Extending her arms, Kincade accepted the glasses from the tray. A sip of the mescal, a chase of beer, and the liquid gently warmed Kincade. Josephine placed the silvered tray on an end table. She took the two glasses from Kincade's hands and placed them on the tray.

Josephine smiled. She unloosened Kincade's band collar and the top button of his shirt. He relaxed. She walked to her dressing table and studied her lotions, selected one, and returned to the couch.

Josephine knelt before Kincade. Removing the glass stopper from the petite bottle, she poured a dollop and gently spread the lotion over the palms of her hands. She replaced the stopper, and then placed the bottle on the silvered platter.

Looking up at Kincade for just a moment, her eyes then traveled to his left hand. She took it into her palms, and began to massage the rough flesh. One finger at a time beginning at the bottom, and moving slowly to the tip, then down again. The next finger, followed by another. Turning Kincade's hand palm up, Josephine rubbed the flesh below the thumb, and the thumb itself. Then, she took both her hands and caressed his entire hand, moving hers in circles over his.

She rested his left hand on his leg. She looked up into his eyes, smiling just the slightest bit.

She took the bottle of lotion a second time, and repeated the entire massage with Kincade's right hand, never in a hurry, thoroughly immersed in every motion, her every caress.

She stood from her kneeling. With both hands, she grasped the handles of the silvered tray, offering Kincade the refreshments. He accepted, taking another sip of each before she replaced the tray on the end table.

She smiled and once again looked lovingly into Kincade's blue eyes. She then returned the bottle of lotion to her dressing table and selected a second. Kincade watched the silk of Josephine's gown travel over her figure like gentle waves moving over a gossamer shore.

She stood before Kincade. With her right hand, she removed a crystal stopper from the new bottle and poured a small amount of lotion into her hand. She moved to the back of the couch, stopping to stand behind Kincade. She leaned over Kincade's right shoulder to leave the lotion bottle on the tray. Kincade caught the fleeting and inviting scent of her jasmine perfume. Strands of her silken blond hair cascaded over his shoulder, only to take wing as she stood.

Like butterflies, her open hands drifted and came to rest on his brow. Gently, almost imperceptibly, Josephine's fingers closed Kincade's eyes. For several minutes, Josephine hands remained there, without moving, her index and middle fingers on his eyebrows, the ring and tip of her last finger covering his lashes and upper cheek bones.

Her hands then moved to his temples, where they circled ever so slowly. Her littlest fingers would trace the edges of Kincade's ears so lightly that their touch might be mistaken for the gentle breeze floating through her suite.

The power emanating from her hands, and from her heart, seemed to draw every worry, every regret, and every remaining shred of fear from his body. Every part of him calmed, each muscle unwound, relaxed, every breath slowed.

Every worry but one.

"Josie..." he said.

She let her hands rest on his broad shoulders.

Kincade took her right hand, encouraging her to come around so he could look at her. She did.

Seated before her, Kincade looked up into her eyes. It was as if he were stepping into the heavens, cradled by countless stars. She looked back into his, her glorious eyes filled with unbridled compassion, understanding and unconditional love.

"Josie..." he began. "My greatest fear wasn't becoming my brother." He swallowed, and tried to moisten his lips. He took a deep breath and said, "It was the possibility of losing you..." Kincade's eyes turned to the floor.

She knelt before him. She reached forward to touch his lowered chin, raising up his face. Their eyes met. Josephine's tender smile swept away any shame or fear he may have harbored. An enormous burden lifted.

Josephine moved her soft fingertips to Kincade's lips. She traced the edges so gently, so completely, so very slowly. Nothing was spoken. Everything was said.

Josephine leaned forward to place her head on Kincade's chest. Her hands unhurriedly caressed his strong arms, then moved up into his hair, her fingers circling within the soft waves. She could hear the calm beating of his heart... the heart of a good man who had come home.

Warmth spread through Kincade unlike any he could ever remember experiencing.

His eyelids grew heavy as her fingers circled within his hair. Her perfume soothed him. Her gentleness brought a tranquility he had searched for his entire life. Josephine remained before Kincade, feeling the rise and fall of his chest. Sleep overtook him.

As the candles consumed themselves, Josephine stood and looked at Kincade. She had never loved, had never been loved, like this. Ever.

She walked to the side table next to her bed. She silently and carefully slid open a drawer. It was still there, just as she had left it. She picked up Kincade's medicine bag.

She walked back to sit next to him. Without disturbing his sleep, Josephine slipped the worn strip of latigo over his head, allowing the medicine bag and its beaded Circle of Life to rest on his heart.

She drew her legs under her, nestled her head on his shoulder, and closed her eyes.

45

David Cook came into the General Store and immediately caught the owner's attention. "Excuse me, Mr. Perkins, but I'm in a bit of a rush. Have to get back to the Grange, you know."

"You've been doing a fine job of covering the trial, Mr. Cook. How may I help you?"

"Do you happen to carry any of those large books with blank pages? I believe they're called scrapbooks."

"Scrapbook is correct. They're especially popular with children and ladies for items they've made or collected - scraps of this and that which are pasted inside. You'd like to see my stock?"

"If you would please." Cook followed Mr. Perkins to a section of books, large and small. "I'm going to make a portfolio of my articles covering the trial of Jeremiah Scott. Should I ever apply for a position with another newspaper, it would show the work I have done here in Tombstone."

"Fine idea. I understand your articles are being syndicated throughout the Territory."

David smiled without much modesty. "Well, it's an important

case…"

"…and a dramatic one," Mr. Perkins interrupted as he pulled scrapbooks from behind a counter. "I have three styles. The largest is this one with the dark green cover. This one has a simulated wooden cover and this type has satin covers in white or blue which the ladies usually choose."

"The green will be fine. And I'll also take two jars of white paste, please."

"Certainly. Shall I wrap them?"

"Please do. Will this amount cover the cost?" David held out a dollar bill.

"Yes, with change. Good luck, Mr. Cook, with your career. This trial could catapult you to the top of your profession."

In his small apartment, David Cook cut out the first article with his byline and spaced it carefully on the page before applying paste. Many were to follow.

- - - - - - - - - - -

MARSHAL KINCADE ARRESTS PROMINENT CITIZEN

Tombstone was stunned yesterday with the spectacular arrest of Jeremiah Scott who has been acting as an attorney in our fair city. Marshal Kincade told this reporter that the charges are fraud, extortion, and theft. There will be no release on bail because when the Marshal apprehended Scott he was apparently getting ready to skip town with a large amount of money and a valise of official-looking papers. Marshal Kincade has sealed the home and office of Jeremiah Scott until all evidence which might be found there has been gathered.

Marshal Kincade has wired Governor John Jay Gosper to send a judge and prosecuting attorney from the Capital to conduct the trial which will be held here in Tombstone. Since Governor Gosper appointed Kincade to the position of Marshal, the request will undoubtedly be granted. Scott says he will act in his own defense.

- - - - - - - - - - -

JUDGE AND ASSISTANT DISTRICT ATTORNEY ARRIVE IN TOMBSTONE

Judge Ostis O. Moore from the Territorial Superior Court and Assistant District Attorney Anthony Hershey have arrived from the Capital to conduct the trial of Jeremiah Scott. They are staying at the Cosmopolitan Hotel as guests of Miss Josephine. The selection of a jury will begin tomorrow at the Grange which is the only building large enough to hold the expected crowd. Those who wish to present evidence when the trial commences are to register at Marshal Kincade's office before 5 p.m. today.

- - - - - - - - - - -

OPENING DAY OF JEREMIAH SCOTT TRIAL DRAWS LARGE CROWD

A spectacular crowd assembled yesterday at the Grange for the first day of the trial against Jeremiah Scott. The defendant allowed the photograph, seen on the front page of this Tombstone Epitaph issue, to be taken of himself seated at the defense table. The proceedings began with the selection of a jury. However, there may be difficulty in finding twelve impartial men, and none were selected on this day.

- - - - - - - - - - -

TRIAL OF SCOTT IS PROCEEDING

After ten days of jury selection, the trial of Jeremiah Scott has gone into action. When asked how he pleaded, his response was oratorical. "Not Guilty." His voice could be heard outside the Grange.

Marshal Kincade and District Attorney Hershey have been sorting through the evidence found in Scott's office located above the Tombstone barber shop. When questioned on the stand, the Marshal said, "There was a considerable amount of money and valuable papers. I decline to give the total."

Scott admitted that as Trustee for several clients, he was planning to deposit their money in the Capital in accounts under their names. When asked why he didn't use the Tombstone bank, he responded that large birds do not build nests on small branches.

Marshal Kincade also found valuable jewelry in a leather saddle bag, including a cameo locket with pictures of a young soldier, a gold wedding ring with the initials LN TO MC engraved inside the band, a man's gold pocket watch with filigree fob, and earrings with two rubies and several small diamonds. Scott denied knowledge of any of these items.

By order of Judge Ostis O. Moore, the money is being held in escrow at the Tombstone bank and personal items are secured in the safe at the Cosmopolitan Hotel.

- - - - - - - - -

TOMBSTONE FILLING WITH
WITNESSES FOR SCOTT TRIAL

The article and photograph of Jeremiah Scott which The Epitaph printed two weeks ago and which was syndicated throughout the west has prompted an influx of interested parties from communities as far away as Colorado. The hotels and rooming houses in Tombstone are filled to capacity and a few tents have been erected outside the city limits. This reporter has learned from interviewing the strangers that the man we have known as Jeremiah Scott practiced bogus law under different names in several communities before coming to Tombstone.

One person whom we all recognize is Miss Sadie Shamrock who was our former post mistress and telegrapher. She has come to testify against Scott as the agent whom she hired to sell her house. Also coming from far away is the Jethro Wilcox family of Julesburg, Colorado who claim to have bought Miss Sadie's house and been given a forged deed by Scott.

Testimony from so many people has prompted Judge Moore to wire Governor Gosper to send a legal secretary to record the proceedings.

- - - - - - - - -

CITIZENS OF ELFRIDA STARTLE THOSE ATTENDING SCOTT TRIAL

A contingent of citizens from Elfrida headed by Sheriff Myron Sutton appeared before Judge Ostis O. Moore yesterday requesting that their personal items found in Jeremiah Scott's office be returned to them, as well as a great deal of money which was fraudulently obtained by cohorts of Jeremiah Scott. A bizarre story emerged. Two men claiming to be a Circuit Judge and his bailiff held what appeared to be a legal court in Elfrida for three days, imposing many fines and accepting valuables when a defendant could not pay cash. The description of these men exactly fits Judge Simon Simpson and his body guard Bowdrie who were in Tombstone only a few days before. Sheriff Sutton said these two, who were known in Elfrida as Judge Jasper Peterson and Cowdrie, were robbed and barbarically murdered as they left town in the dark of night.

The Sheriff continued, "Now that the personal items which were surrendered in Elfrida have been found in Scott's office, I strongly suspect that Jeremiah Scott hired an assassin to kill the two imposters who quite possibly had cheated him. The killer may have been paid from the Elfrida money but Scott kept the jewelry for himself."

Scott came to his feet to deny this accusation. Bedlam broke loose in the Grange. One spectator jumped up and declared he had seen Scott drinking with Simpson and Bowdrie in his office late at night. Another man rose and confirmed that a conversation he'd heard in an alley among the three had seemed more conspiratorial than professional.

A third spectator stood. "Your Honor, I bet that the assassin was Jake Jacobsen who just got out of Yuma prison. He's been seen in some of Lower Tombstone's bars braggin' that he had important connections in town. I myself heard him call his important connection 'Gerry'. I'll bet my last dollar that a deal was made with Scott 'cause I ain't seen Jake since Simpson and Bowdrie left here." The shouting continued with more sightings and suspicions.

Over the noise Jeremiah Scott tried to explain to the judge that he had only dealt with Simpson and Bowdrie on a strictly professional level and never suspected their masquerade. He also shouted that he had never heard of Jake Jacobsen. The crowd became so angry with his responses that Judge Moore at last pounded his gavel and ordered Marshal Kincade to take the defendant back to jail, and secure him from a possible lynching.

This reporter is only telling you the actions at yesterday's trial. I do not presume to be supporting any accusations yet to be substantiated.

- - - - - - - - - - -

WARDEN FROM YUMA PRISON AT SCOTT TRIAL

Warden Tom Doroff of the infamous Yuma prison arrived yesterday and conferred with Judge Moore, District Attorney Hershey, Marshal Kincade and Elfrida Sheriff Myron Sutton for some time before the opening session of the Jeremiah Scott trial. He also visited the jail to personally take a look at Jeremiah Scott.

The trial opened with the Warden taking the stand and being given the oath. His testimony was most unexpected. This reporter quotes Warden Doroff to the best of his ability:

"This trial has been given wide publicity which I have followed in every detail through the articles of David Cook. Several weeks ago a picture of the defendant, Jeremiah Scott, was published. He looked familiar but at first I didn't recognize the man to be Gerard Swart who had been incarcerated at the Yuma prison. He was serving a life sentence for forgery of government documents which amounted to treason.

"During his first few years at Yuma, Mr. Swart diligently studied all the law books in our library. He began giving legal advice to inmates as if he were a licensed attorney. I considered him a model inmate until I realized he was swindling the prisoners whom he counseled. His life was threatened so he took up with two other prisoners who acted as his body guards. These two prisoners were Mervin Smith and Billy Day.

"Swart, Smith and Day escaped the Yuma prison approximately ten years ago. They killed two of my guards and a price was placed on their heads.

"I'd not had any word of these three and had given up hope of their capture. Then I saw the picture of Jeremiah Scott in the Tombstone trial. He is older, heavier, more fashionable, but I definitely recognized him to be Gerard Swart. This was followed by the story of two swindlers who possibly could have been Smith and Day.

"I have come to Tombstone to see the man on trial and verify to my complete satisfaction that he is, in truth, Gerard Swart who escaped from Yuma prison. I have also brought the prison mug shots of Mervin Smith and Billy Day and Sheriff Sutton assures me they were the two who posed as a judge and bailiff in Elfrida.

"I have requested Judge Moore to release the man tried here as Jeremiah Scott into my custody, first as an escaped life-timer, and second as the murderer of my two guards. I do not know who actually fired the shots, but the complicity of the three is unquestionable."

It is thus that the trial of one Jeremiah Scott has ended in Tombstone. Warden Doroff has wired for the Black Maria to arrive as soon as possible for the transport of the defendant back to his cell in the Yuma prison. Marshal Kincade will be accompanying it as guard.

Attorney Anthony Hershey and the legal secretary will be staying in Tombstone for as long as necessary to make financial adjustments to those who have proof of fraud by Jeremiah Scott, Simon Simpson, and Bowdrie.

- - - - - - - - -

MARSHAL KINCADE RESIGNING HIS POST

Upon returning from Yuma, Marshal Kincade told this reporter that he has resigned as U.S. Marshal of Tombstone. He will be continuing his regular duties until a replacement arrives. When asked his reason he replied it was strictly personal and that the $5,000 reward the Territorial Governor insisted be given to Marshal Kincade for the apprehension of the escaped convict, Gerard Swart, had nothing to do with his decision.

46

The silver spoon circled within Josephine's porcelain cup of tea as she absentmindedly stirred the just-squeezed lemon. A freshly baked breakfast roll and dish of jam sat nearby. It had been nearly a month since Jeremiah Scott.... Gerard Swart... had been returned to serve out his life sentence inside the Yuma Prison. There was justice on the frontier.

Lazily turning to the next page of the morning edition of the Tombstone Epitaph, Josephine became aware that a man stood motionless next to the chair across from her.

"Will you permit me to sit with you, Miss Josephine?"

She looked up. He was tall and dressed in a black frock coat and trousers, a white shirt, and black string tie. Placed straight on his head was a black buckaroo hat. Well-spoken, well-dressed and most respectful.

At first she didn't recognize him. Not until his very familiar smile crept across his face. Josie dropped the spoon. "Sky?... Is it really you?!"

"You know any other Indian who would dress like this?"

She jumped to her feet and nearly flew into his arms. "I... we thought we'd never see you again!"

He wrapped his arms around her. She was even more beautiful than he remembered, like a desert rose in full bloom.

Releasing him, Josie looked down and behind him, her eyes darting around the floor. "Where's Smoke?" She remembered that the wolf was always steps away from Sky's feet.

Sky paused. With a bittersweet smile he answered, "Smoke has gone on to a happy hunting ground. I, on the other hand, am here in the flesh!"

She held Sky at arm's length. "You're so handsome, Sky! So grown up..." She moved her hands across the fabric of his coat. "...and elegant!" He beamed with pride.

She was beside herself with happiness. "Forgive me, Sky. Where are my manners? Please... sit."

"My dear Josephine first..." and Sky held Josie's seat out for her before seating himself.

"Have you eaten?"

"No, Miss Josephine."

Josephine called toward the door behind the bar. "One of the usual!" Sky chuckled with the memory of their breakfasts together long ago.

"Where's Marshal Kincade?" Sky asked. "I thought I'd find him at his office but it was locked. I knocked on his house door – no answer. Gold Digger is in the stable. Then I remembered that by this time he would be eating his morning breakfast with you. Is the Marshal out of town?"

"The Marshal goes riding every morning now, sometimes on Kinhuste. He frequently goes to where you and he trained Smoke to be a Law Dog. Afterwards, he visits Jesse's grave. He says it helps his head, and heart, to stay clear."

Sky was silent for a moment. "Does he still get throbbing to the right of his eye?"

"No, Sky... those days are gone."

"That's good to hear. I'm glad he still has Kinhuste."

"He's always said it was your horse."

Sky smiled. "Mitasunke - my horse."

She was so excited at seeing him. She sat forward in her chair, clasping her hands in front of her. "So dear, dear, Sky, what have you been up to since we last saw you? Must be something wonderful to be dressed in such a formal fashion."

"Not like the outfit you chose for me, Miss Josephine?"

"You were a boy then. You're obviously a man now."

His "usual" arrived and he dove into the eggs like always. She beamed at watching him. After the first few bites and a gulp of coffee, he took the linen napkin from his lap to wipe his mouth.

"Miss Josie," he began, "I need to apologize to the Marshal for the way I left. I idolized Kincade. I felt he was a god. No man could possibly live up to such expectations. Not him, not me, not anyone.

"I was a boy then. I felt betrayed when he killed those men at the Hanging Tree. Now, I understand that he was frightened for me, angry, trying to protect me. Since that day, I've thought long about Kincade and why he did what he did. I've thought about all that he taught me, how he cared about me, about the secrets of his medicine bag, and the true meaning of the Circle of Life. I now understand that we all have our opposite side, and that it's up to each of us to find balance."

Josephine listened. Both Sky and Kincade had been through so much since they last sat together at this very table. "He's had some hard moments. But Sky... he's happier and more in love with life than I've ever seen him." She paused to look at Sky with her beautifully compassionate eyes. "He's missed you."

He rested the fork on his plate. "I've missed you both. You changed my life forever. Marshal Kincade is lucky to have a woman like you."

Josephine was touched. "Sky... Kincade has resigned as Marshal."

He nodded. "I've heard. What are his plans?"

"He's not sure. He talks about studying law or perhaps going into politics with the possibility of eventually running for the legislature. He wants to have an impact on frontier justice. Right now he just needs time to sort out his future."

"Maybe that's why I'm here."

Josephine wondered what he meant. Sky smiled at her. "Tell me about you, Sky. A long time has passed."

He finished his coffee and leaned back in his chair. "After Smoke died, life was hard and terribly lonely. So I made my way back to the Mission School. The director of the school – you remember I chose to use his name – was impressed with the experiences I'd had in the white man's world. Someone had sent him several copies of the Epitaph and he'd read about my being a Deputy Marshal in Tombstone."

"Spectacular! I believe Mr. Cook called it." They both laughed.

"Anyhow, he asked me to stay on as a teacher. He also suggested that I apply for a position with the Bureau of Indian Affairs in Washington."

"They hire Native Americans?"

"Not usually. I guess I was just lucky."

"I bet the Mission School Director gave you a fantastic recommendation."

"That's possible." He looked embarrassed. "Anyhow, I was accepted. They decided to send me to a Law Enforcement Academy since I'd had Deputy experience here in Tombstone." He laughed. "I think they'd have kicked me out if they knew some of the law enforcement tricks that the Marshal and I used."

"Smoke too," she added without thinking, but he laughed even harder.

"Eventually, I'll be working in law enforcement on some Indian reservation as soon as they are better established."

"I'm so very glad you came to tell us this wonderful news. Kincade will be thrilled. He should be here for his breakfast before long."

"Please, Miss Josie, let me find him and tell him in my own way. Okay?"

"Of course. Where are you staying?"

"At the hotel – in a bed, with a dresser, a chair, a mirror, and wash basin with towels." They both laughed, and Josephine recalled how much fun life had been with Sky.

"Wash basin with towels.... Sky, do you ever forget anything?"

"How could I? I have loved you and Marshal Kincade since the first day we met. You are my chosen parents – hunkayapi."

"I refuse to look old enough to be your mother, Sky." She wrinkled up her nose and looked about twenty. Then she became serious. "Find Marshal Kincade whenever and wherever it feels right. I won't tell him you've been here."

Sky nodded. "Good. Thank you." He stood to go, then paused as if thinking. "Miss Josephine, did the Jethro Wilcox family ever move to Tombstone?"

"Yes, they came in time for the trial against a lawyer named Scott who had tried to cheat them. Jethro is our new Post Master."

"And the little girl Melissa?"

"Oh, she's quite the young lady now – a real beauty."

"I wonder if she'd remember me."

Josephine's only response was a smile.

The evening was early and the Silver Dollar was first on Kincade's nightly rounds. He surveyed the room. Although crowded, it seemed peaceful. He waved at the bar tender who nodded in his direction.

At one table near the rear, a disgustingly loathsome old man with long, dirty hair was making quick and easy friends. He waved a wad of bills, buying drinks for anyone who would listen. "No, I ain't one of them mountain men," he was saying. "My name's

Lobo, and proud of it."

Kincade listened without much interest. There was nothing illegal about an old coot acting loud and obnoxious.

"Never heard such a name. What's it mean?"

"Means wolf and I'm a wolver."

"Never heard of that neither."

"Well, I hunt down wolves."

"Why ya do that?"

"Buffalo and beaver is 'bout gone, so folks back east took a likin' to wolfskin coats. I get two dollars a pelt and I just brought in a bundle. And 'sides that, ranchers pay me even more for killin' critters that been attackin' their cattle." He flashed his roll. "I make a purty good livin'!'"

"Then buy us another bottle, Lobo."

Lobo wiped his nose on his sleeve. "Sure, pards. Go up there and get it." He loved the attention. "Say boys... you wanna know how to kill a wolf?"

Several nodded their heads and even Kincade listened closer.

"You can set a trap for 'um but that only gets one at a time. But if I stuff a dollar's worth of strychnine crystals inside a buffalo carcass, I can kill fifty wolves in a night! If I can't get a buffalo, most any critter'll do so long as it stinks real good."

"Sounds easier than trappin' beaver."

The wolver tipped the bottle and wiped the whiskey from his

tobacco-stained beard. "I like to put my bait 'bout sundown and go back ta check in the mornin'. Most of them wolves is dead by mornin' if they's et a lot. But if they's only nibbled around the edges takes 'um longer to die. I can wait. Ain't a pretty sight to watch. They's retchin' and jerkin'. If I don't get back for a day or two their fur's fell out and they wander around naked as ghosts, howlin' – like they's callin' me to put 'um out of their misery. But I don't never waste a bullet on 'um. They ain't got no pelts no more." His laughter was a high pitched cackle.

Several of his listeners had heard enough, and moved away to another table.

"Somethin' real funny happened couple years back. I went to gather up my night's catch and there was this Indian kid holdin' one of the dead wolves in his arms, rockin' and cryin' like a baby."

Kincade was startled. He was talking about Sky and Smoke.

"Both of 'um was skinny as rails as if they'd been starvin'."

Kincade moved closer, inadvertently putting himself to the ultimate test. Was he able to hear of life's injustice to those whom he had loved?

"I shot at the savage but he run away."

Kincade felt no pounding in his head – no Other Voice. He felt only sadness for what Sky must have felt, and a strange pity for the lonesome old man with stories to tell.

"What a terrible death for a wonderful animal," Kincade thought to himself. "I wonder what ever happened to Sky?" He turned to go, remembering how much fun it had been to be Marshal with his two Deputies.

As Kincade approached the door he saw a tall man in black

standing just a few feet away. The room was dark and smoky, but the figure looked familiar.

"Is my Intimidation as good as it used to be, Marshal?"

He blinked and shook his head. There was only one person who knew of The Intimidation. "Sky..., is that you?..."

"It's me all right." He came forward and put both his hands on the shoulders of his old friend.

"Look at you!" said Kincade, absolutely stunned to see the boy now grown into a man. "What are you doing?! Why are you here?" Kincade simply could not believe his eyes... Sky! "I want to hear everything! Town's quiet. Let's go over to The Josephine where we can talk. Josie will be speechless when she sees you're here!"

Just as they had so long ago, the two strode side by side along the boardwalks of Tombstone. They tipped their hats to passersby, offered well-wishes to citizens and strangers alike. Kincade walked with an enormous sense of pride. It felt like his son had finally come home.

As Kincade and Sky entered through the batwings of The Josephine, faces turned to welcome the Marshal. Many remembered Sky when Kincade introduced him. Josie stood back, watching with amusement. Kincade was like a proud rooster strutting around the yard. After a few moments, she came up to them both and expressed great surprise at seeing Sky, winking at him as Kincade continued to beam.

"Sky," said Kincade. "Let's go over there where we can talk."

Kincade kissed Josephine quickly on her cheek, and led Sky to a deserted corner. One of Josie's ladies came by and Sky ordered Kincade the tequila and beer chaser that he knew was his favorite.

"Water's fine for me, and thanks," said Sky.

The Marshal looked at Sky without blinking. He had wanted to say this for a very long time. "I'm not the man I was when you were here, Sky."

The words sank in. Sky thought, and then said "Well, I'm not either, Marshal."

"Yes. You've moved forward in your life. That's plain to see. Just look at you!" Kincade paused, carefully choosing his words. "I went backwards for a time. But that's over. Things are as good or better than they've ever been." Kincade looked over at Josie, who was in the midst of welcoming more guests into The Josephine. It was clear to Sky that their love for one another had grown in ways that no one but they could fully comprehend. He looked back to Sky and smiled. "I don't know exactly where I'm headed, but I'll know when I get there."

They both laughed as they had years past. Kincade took the shot glass, raised it to Sky, took a small sip and put it back on the table next to the beer.

"Marshal, I want you to remember a Sioux custom that I told you about a long, long time ago."

"All right." Kincade listened with great interest.

"A Sioux warrior will plant a stake in the ground. He will stand by it, defending himself against his enemy with only his hands, or a knife, or a spear. Do you remember the story?"

"Yes, yes I do. One of his tribe must come to his rescue on horse-back."

"Yes. He will pull up the stake and carry the standing-one away. There is bravery in the one who stands and bravery in the one who rescues."

"Why are you telling me this now, Sky?"

"Because you are the one who has been standing by the stake, fighting the evil enemies which you found on every side of the law. I am the one who will pull up that stake. You and I can now ride together for a more just world."

"He's everything I hoped he would become," Kincade thought. "Men like him will help make the world just, I'm confident of that." Kincade paused, and then spoke plainly. "Sky, you'll have to ride without me. I've resigned my position as Marshal. I'm just waiting for the Governor to name my replacement."

"I know. I'm it. I've been appointed the new Marshal of Tombstone."

Kincade leaned back speechless, his eyes wide as saucers.

"You, Sky? How is that possible?"

"It's a long story that I'll tell you when we ride Gold Digger and Kinhuste out to Smoke's training ground."

If Kincade appeared proud when strutting around The Josephine introducing Sky to the patrons, Josephine would now have to clear away the chairs and tables for the buttons bursting off Kincade's vest. "I simply cannot be any happier, Sky. I have new faith in our Governor! He couldn't have picked a better Marshal."

"I have just one problem. I'm going to need a Deputy. Would you consider the job? The pay isn't much but the stabling of a good horse is included and you can sleep on the floor in the tack room."

Kincade threw back his head and laughed out loud. "Marshal Red Sky, you now have yourself a Deputy!"

"I've also put in a request for one of those Law Dogs they were training at the Law Enforcement Academy."

"Spectacular, as David Cook would say! We'll call him Smoke Two!"

Josephine approached the two men in her life who were obviously having a grand time together. "Excuse me..." They both stood. "Sky, there is someone to see you. A lady. She's waiting in the lobby of the Cosmopolitan."

"For me?"

"Perhaps she knows you're our new Marshal and needs assistance." Josie's eyes sparkled. Kincade had seen this look before, and knew that something special was afoot.

Sky looked at Kincade, who shrugged his shoulders.

"Marshal... I mean 'Deputy', if you and Miss Josephine will excuse me..." They nodded, Sky turned for the door that joined the Hotel with The Josephine. Josie looked at Kincade, put her finger to her lips, and smiled as brightly as Kincade could ever remember.

Sky crossed into the stately lobby of The Cosmopolitan Hotel. There, facing away from him, waited the most spectacularly beautiful woman he had ever seen... Miss Josie excluded, of course. She wore a white lace dress topped with a form fitting bodice. The bustle just below her waist caught Sky's attention for more than a few moments. White gloves covered her hands and rose up to just above her elbows.

Her hair was golden... waterfalls and waves of curls reaching to below her waist.

Sky blinked, shook his head just enough to clear it, and reminded himself that he was now Tombstone's Marshal, and that this young woman might be here for help. "Ahemm..." he said.

The woman turned and looked into his eyes in a way he had never experienced. She waited there, looking into him. Sky swallowed.

"Miss Josephine said you wanted to see me?"

"Yes, please. I understand you are our new Marshal."

"Well, I guess I am. I mean, I am!" Sky thought his collar had suddenly become quite tight.

"Marshal..." she said. "I am here to report a theft."

"Oh," said Sky. "I'm sorry to hear of your loss. Did it just occur?" As Sky paused for her answer, Josie and Kincade quietly stepped in from The Josephine, and stood behind Sky, who was unaware of them. Kincade now knew that Josie definitely had something up her sequined sleeve.

She sighed. "No, Marshal. It happened quite some time ago."

"Do you know who stole from you?"

She nodded. "Yes... I do. A young boy. But he must be a man by now."

She looked at him. For a moment, Sky thought she was smiling at him in a coy sort of way.

She continued with a slight sad pout. "I'm afraid I'll never get it back."

"Well, I'll do my best. What was it this young man stole from you?"

She paused, and looked at him the way Josephine often looked at Kincade. An involuntary shiver coursed through Sky. He swallowed again. Then, it struck him. Could it really be her?

"I'm sorry Miss..." Sky approached her, stopping just as the tips of his boots barely touched the hem of the woman's dress. "What did you say your name is?"

Her eyes became lost in his. "Miss Wilcox," she said softly. "But you may call me Melissa."

Josephine looked up to Kincade, her eyes tearing with joy. She leaned her head onto his shoulder. Kincade reached down to take Josephine's hand in his. He kissed her hair.

"Josie... Josie...," he whispered. "You're such a romantic."

"Melissa said I couldn't tell," she protested.

"Mmm..." said Kincade. "I see."

Josephine and Kincade left Sky and Melissa in the lobby of the Hotel, and returned arm in arm to The Josephine. "Evenin' Miss Josie," said a local rancher who stood from his table to tip his hat to her. "Howdy Marshal."

Kincade reached out to accept the rancher's massive handshake. "Evenin' Hank. Good to see you. But it's 'Deputy' now." The rancher nodded. Kincade pointed his thumb back to the door that led to the Cosmopolitan. "If you're lookin' for the Marshal, he's in there."

"No trouble, I trust," said the rancher, reseating himself before another glass of beer to resume his card game.

"I hope not. Word is he stole a lady's heart..."

Josephine jabbed Kincade playfully in the ribs. "Kincade... Kincade...." she whispered. "You're such a romantic."

He smiled at her. "Josie, let's keep that between you and me. We don't wanna scare 'ol Hank."

Another jab to his side. "Darling," she began. "I never got to finish your massage. And I have all that lotion that mustn't go to waste."

"This dry climate may be a cure for consumption," he said, "but it can sure leave a fella with dry skin."

"Why don't we see if I can fix that after I close The Josephine tonight."

"I have a lot of skin..."

"I have a lot of lotion."

He nodded and reached over to lightly run his finger across her satin cheek. "I love you, Josie."

"I know..."

47

The honky-tonk piano player rocked back and forth on his three-legged stool as Josephine's guests laughed, gambled, drank and enjoyed one another's company. Offering "good-nights" to several, Kincade left The Josephine.

There was one more thing he had to do.

Through the front windows of The Cosmopolitan, Kincade could see Sky and Melissa seated together, utterly absorbed in what the other was saying. She held Sky's hand.

Kincade passed by the buildings, and through the memories of his time in Tombstone. Some were the brightest of his life. Others clutched his darkest hours.

Unlocking the door to the U.S. Marshal's office, Kincade stepped inside. There was no need to light a lantern. The moon was full and large.

He moved to his desk. There, arranged on the top just as he had placed them the day he first took the job, waited the Indian fetishes he'd gathered over the course of his life - the six directions and the Dream Catcher hoop with the tiny turquoise nugget.

Kincade opened the buttons on his shirt and withdrew his medicine bag. Opening the draw string, Kincade carefully picked up the little fetishes one by one and gently slid them down in the leather pouch, there to rejoin the very worn piece of leather beaded with K L on one side and W L on the other. Tightening the latigo strap, he replaced the medicine bag over his heart and buttoned his shirt.

He knelt down, removed the secret panel from the base of the desk and took out the item he'd left there.

Before leaving the office, Kincade removed his U.S. Marshal badge from his vest and placed it on his desk... Sky's desk. The front door clicked softly closed.

Down Allen Street, across to Toughnut, through Lower Tombstone he walked. Past the Silver Dollar, now nearly empty of its patrons, Kincade passed the old wolver, slumbering away from too much drink and far more loneliness.

Out of town, and up to the ramshackle front gate of the picket fence surrounding Boot Hill. Kincade walked through as he had done countless times since the burials of his two blood brothers.

"Hello Jess," he said softly to Jesse Keller's tombstone. "Nice night, my old friend."

Kincade turned and walked the several yards to the grave of his other blood brother, Wil Logan. Kneeling at the base of the headstone, Kincade gently scooped out a shallow hole. He placed Logan's Bowie knife in its final resting place, covering the metal and the memories with dirt.

He stood.

Returning to stand between the graves of Jesse Keller and Wil Logan, Kincade looked across the vast silence of the valley floor.

The moon floated behind his back, throwing his large shadow towards the open desert before him.

To one side, he felt the goodness of Jesse and the life he had chosen to live. To the other, he felt the pain and anguish of Wil, and the desperate paths he had walked.

Unafraid of what lay ahead in his life, Kincade stood balanced between the two. He took a deep and wonderful breath.

He was free.

THE END

A secret from the author...

If you visit the real Boot Hill in Tombstone Arizona, the curator will point out the graves of Billy Clanton, Tom and Frank McLaury, all killed during the gunfight behind the OK Corral in October of 1881.

Just a few feet away from those dead men, you'll see two graves laid side by side. Their tombstones say "Unknown."

But they are nothing of the sort. On the left rests Jesse Keller. On his right Wil Logan... the blood brothers of Kincade.

Michael,
I thought you'd like to see a
sketch of Kincade & Josephine.

Hiram